A FAULTY EVICTION

Daniel Adam Garwood

2QT (Publishing) Ltd

First Edition published 2021 by
2QT Limited (Publishing)
Settle, North Yorkshire BD24 9RH United Kingdom

Cover images: shutterstock.com

Printed in Great Britain by IngramSparks

A CIP catalogue record for this book is available
from the British Library

ISBN - 978-1-914083-07-5

What strange phenomena we find in a great city,
all we need do is stroll about with our eyes open.
Life swarms with innocent monsters.

Charles Baudelaire

CHAPTER ONE
Monday, 3rd June, 2019

THE body was covered for the sake of dignity in a lambswool throw featuring winsome pandas on a powder-blue background. Around the skull, the powder blue had morphed into an exquisite deep purple.

The high-pitched wail and yelp of sirens managed to cut through the random ascent of tobacco smoke emanating from the residents who circled the lifeless form. After two gut-churning deaths at Pendrick Court within the last twenty-four hours, only Edna had been expecting a third.

CHAPTER TWO
Monday, 20th May, two weeks earlier

WHEREVER Kevin went, silent applause rang in his ears feeding his already sated ego. The post office would be no exception. He strode in like a headmaster entering morning assembly, the toxic fusion of authority and anticipation exaggerating his usual strut.

His rapid breathing was due to the prolonged puffing out of his chest – a fruitless exercise, since his sheeny grey suit was far too shapeless to flatter his fifty-two-year-old carcass. He joined the queue and scanned the room with his laser-whitened teeth.

Not only did the British excel at queuing, but his compatriots were far too polite to reveal their instinctive interest in him.

Three other people joined the line while the same customer was being served. The speed of service – or lack of it – irritated Kevin. He scowled at Elizabeth, the only counter assistant actually serving who, apart from a convergent squint, was afflicted with an obsessive compulsion to pry. In his hands, he toyed with eight envelopes addressed to the occupants of each apartment at Pendrick Court.

He had bought Pendrick Court for a song in 2008 from a cash-strapped developer reeling from a crash in UK property prices. Eleven years later, it was time to remove the tenants and sell the property for a substantial profit. Kevin prickled with anticipation as he imagined the shock and subsequent disruption that the evictions would cause. Some of the tenants – including his own son – might not go quietly, but there would be no repercussions he couldn't handle. Electrified by his business acumen, he impatiently waited his turn to be served.

As the queue edged forward, still more customers joined its ranks. The only appreciable movement in the building stemmed from three flies performing aerial acrobatics above flower-filled plastic buckets. How Kevin wished he had been armed with an aerosol can of insecticide.

Eventually he reached the counter and pushed all the letters under the window to an expectant Elizabeth. 'I'd like a guaranteed delivery tomorrow and I'll need a signature from each recipient,' he said as he waited petulantly for Elizabeth to study the front of each envelope.

'We don't often see *you* in here, Mr Douglas,' said Elizabeth, looking up. 'You usually send one of your minions.' She raised her eyebrows in enquiry. 'I'll need to ask you what's inside ... for insurance purposes, you understand. Anything of value?'

'No,' Kevin snapped, avoiding eye contact. 'Just letters that need to be delivered and signed for tomorrow.'

'Oh, something of great importance then?'

Kevin ignored the question and thumped down his wallet on the counter. Elizabeth leaned in and lowered her voice.

'Edna Pembleton tells me the rents you charge are very reasonable.'

Kevin leaned in too and told Elizabeth through gritted teeth that he'd come to post letters not to discuss his business. Unperturbed, she asked whether the letters were informing his tenants of a rent increase. Kevin remained silent, seething at her audacity and supressing a bubbling urge to bark abuse. Elizabeth stopped talking and processed his mail.

Unbeknown to Kevin, Anah had joined the queue. Although she had recognised her landlord, his presence was of little significance to her. She stood unnaturally erect, eyes front, with both hands clutching a beige handbag that coordinated with her leather court shoes. Her floral-patterned, lilac-and-peach, round-necked top was her one concession to reckless frivolity.

Tightly pinching the receipt between finger and thumb, Kevin launched a dramatic exit from the post office. When he suddenly spotted Anah, he stopped abruptly. He offered her an exaggerated bow and said, 'Good morning, Mrs Agu.' Anah returned the greeting with a restrained nod of the head.

Kevin's departure was less dynamic than he had intended. Encountering Anah had distracted him. She had been a reliable and respectful tenant for eleven years, and he was slightly unnerved that she would become collateral damage in the impending battle. The rest of the ragtag community of weirdos and losers – his own son included – would be, he felt, deserving casualties.

Elizabeth waited at the counter, poised like a cornered cobra, to serve Anah. She sacrificed her customary probing of other customers to hasten the moment. 'Mrs Agu,' she began. 'What a bizarre coincidence that Mr Douglas should be here sending you a letter.'

Anah's mouth twitched, a signal Elizabeth read as surprise.

'He wants a signature and a guaranteed delivery before noon tomorrow,' she continued, drip-feeding information to a receptive Anah. 'It wasn't my place to ask the nature of the letters.'

Anah's brows drew together. '*Letters* ... more than one?'

'Yes, a letter for each apartment, 1 to 8. I happened to see you talking to Mr Douglas as he left. Didn't he mention them?'

'No, we didn't have a conversation. He just said hello and went.'

Elizabeth pursed her lips and gave a protracted blink. 'I thought as much. He's a devious one, that Kevin Douglas. Pompous as well. The way he behaves, you'd think he owned Walmart, not a handful of second-rate corner shops.'

'Perhaps he was in a hurry. I'm sure there's nothing to worry about. Anyway, on to business. Shall I pop the letter on the scales?'

'Yes, do. Nigeria again?'

'Yes, just my monthly letter to Oluchi.'

'You're a good sister to her, Mrs Agu, you really are. But I can't help thinking that your dear sister would be livid if she knew what underhand moves Kevin Douglas might be making.'

Elizabeth's boldness left Anah speechless.

'But I shall say no more about it,' the post-office assistant continued airily. 'Never let it be said that I interfere in other folk's affairs.'

CHAPTER THREE

THAT evening, Anah stepped carefully onto the decking of her second-floor balcony, slid the glass door closed behind her and balanced an ashtray on the wooden handrail. She lit a cigarette, holding it between the tips of her fingers, and rearranged the silvery Pashmina shawl about her shoulders. Outside was windless and warmer than she had anticipated. The starless, textureless sky had been washed in navy blue. Like a mother running fingers through a child's hair, the night soothed her.

She looked out onto the well-lit courtyard, which was empty except for a blue van whose signage read *Paul Stokes – Plumbing & Heating Engineer*. In the second-floor apartment opposite, the young couple were barely visible in the flickering blue light of the television. Beneath them, Anah could see the solitary, substantial frame of Alan at his kitchen table. It looked as though he were dealing out playing cards.

Anah reflected upon her experience at the post office. She had never before received correspondence from Mr

Douglas that required a signature. She took a long draw from her cigarette and pulled the smoke deeply into her lungs. Perhaps the long-awaited renovations were about to begin on the ground floor so Mr Douglas was informing the tenants about imminent building work. Or perhaps he was just adding even more conditions to the tenancy agreements. He was very keen on rules and procedures.

Anah heard the drone of an engine and looked down. To her right, Sean's white transit van entered through the large archway in the wall that formed the fourth side of Pendrick Court. Having opened the heavy wooden doors to the ground floor, he drove his van in and parked it for the night.

Anah drew on her cigarette again and wondered why Kevin Douglas, Sean's father, would need to send his son a letter.

Sean re-entered the courtyard, locked the doors behind him and looked around the building. Seeing Anah, he shot her a smile and waved. Anah waved and smiled back, her eyes transfixed by the tan, skinny chinos that barely restrained his muscular buttocks. Before Sean reached his apartment and turned on the lights, she had finished her cigarette.

❧ ❧ ❧

On the first floor, opposite Anah's apartment, Alan sat counting twenty-pound notes with his sausage fingers.

He looked up through his kitchen window and saw Anah leave her balcony and return to the confines of her apartment. He smiled.

He had enough notes to cram a thousand-pound's worth into one of the plastic coin bags. With an unnecessarily loud groan and an unexceptional release of wind, he got down on his knees to retrieve an orange plastic box that had once contained cheese biscuits. It was hidden behind part-used bottles of cleaning products in the cupboard under the sink. Reaching up, Alan placed the box on the draining board and, with great effort and a more impressive release of wind, he heaved himself up.

He waddled to the fridge, found the bottle of red wine that he hadn't finished the previous evening and poured a large, chilled glass of Cabernet Sauvignon. He added the bag of money to the others in the box, which he'd return to the cupboard once he'd caught his breath.

❖ ❖ ❖

Anah's short-haired black moggy, Toby, sat upright by the door and let out a wail, pleading with her to let him out. 'Sorry, young man, but it's bedtime. You're not going out again tonight.' Anah rubbed his head affectionately and made a mental note to discard her knickers. The elastic had perished and, for the third time that day, the waistband had found its way down to her crotch.

Toby admitted defeat and made for his food bowl.

Torn between going to bed and having one last cigarette, Anah submitted to her cravings. Hitching up her knickers, she stepped out onto her balcony again. Perhaps Mr Douglas was giving notice of a rise in the rent. To be fair, the rent he charged was modest. He did increase it every year, but he'd never seen the need to send notice by special delivery before. Maybe this year the increase would be considerable.

The evening was now stagnant. Stale, motionless air lingered in the red-brick court. As the temperature dropped, water-droplets clung to cobwebs. Calm had decomposed into lifelessness, and the sky into a deep, congealed midnight blue. Even the customary sound of sixties' rock coming from Paul Stokes' apartment was absent. A naked, wooden clothes rack stared into the night from Edna's balcony. The many retail units and offices that surrounded the former Pendrick's Brewery had been abandoned until morning.

Anah looked down towards Alan's apartment.

❖❖❖

Having finished the Cabernet Sauvignon, Alan was now wading through a bottle of Shiraz and eight awkwardly buttered crackers, each topped with a generous chunk of mature cheddar. Apart from the crunch of the crackers and the occasional slurp of the wine, his apartment was silent.

Oh God, how had he got into this mess?

He was seventy years old. His widowed mother had gone into the dementia unit of a private nursing home nine years ago, was still alive and still eating up his inheritance. She had given him and his sister power of attorney for her affairs. The nursing home was only eight miles from Pendrick Court, and his sister lived hours away in Scotland, so it made sense for *him* to do what was required, and he dutifully visited Mother every Monday afternoon.

Without his sister's knowledge, he had been amassing his mother's cash for more than a year. The orange plastic box now contained more than £40,000 in £20 notes.

❖❖❖

Anah extinguished the last of the day's cigarettes and decided to put off feeding the pots of petunias until the next day. She went back into her apartment and locked the patio doors. Toby was curled up on the sofa, instinctively protecting his doughy belly from errant foxes and eagles.

She tidied away the collection of remote controls and audio equipment, and took the mobile phone that never rang from her pocket to charge its battery overnight. Why hadn't Mr Douglas mentioned the letters when he'd spoken to her in the post office? Anah shrugged her shoulders. It was the end of the day. She'd find out in the morning.

CHAPTER FOUR
Tuesday, 21st May

THE next morning, there was no sign of life at Pendrick Court until twenty minutes past seven. In the two-bedroom apartment above Alan's, Megan waited for the bread to toast under the grill. Her cherry-blossom pink jogging suit was tastefully accessorised with hoop earrings, a metallic-pink hair scrunchie and a fresh love bite. While the bread was toasting, she finished off the sophisticated ensemble by applying brilliant rose-coloured lipstick and eyeshadow. A symphony in pink, and more than satisfied with her appearance, she called Jack a second time.

Jack was in the sitting room, frantically clicking away at his console to save the planet from a seemingly limitless volley of horrifying aliens. On Megan's third call, he paused his game and lurched into the kitchen. He was sporting a pair of white jogging bottoms but his skinny, pasty torso and abnormally large feet remained uncovered.

'Thought you were starting work at eight today,' Megan said.

'I am. I've got twenty minutes before I gotta leave.' Jack spread margarine and strawberry jam on two rounds of toast, put them on a plate and left the kitchen.

Megan followed him. 'You're not taking toast into the bathroom? That's so skanky.' Jack ignored her. She looked out onto the courtyard, just as Jessica from Apartment 4 headed purposefully towards the archway. 'Where's the fat ginger tart going at this time of the morning?' Megan shouted at the window, knowing full well that Jessica couldn't hear her, 'There's no need to hurry. McDonald's serves breakfast until eleven-thirty.'

A few minutes later, Jack came into the sitting room. He was pulling on a T-shirt. 'What? I couldn't hear what you were saying with the door closed.'

'I was talking about the ginger tart.'

'Not again. Why are you always hating on that girl?'

'Why are you always defending her? That's just typical of you, taking everybody's side but mine.'

Jack rolled his eyes and pulled on his white towelling socks. 'What time will you be home?'

'I don't know. The area manager's in today. I need to speak to him about a promotion. Do I look the part?'

'Yeah! Really ... pink.'

❖ ❖ ❖

Mornings didn't creep over Pendrick Court and leisurely stir into life, they launched themselves with a fanfare of whistles and warbles as boisterous starlings swooped onto Edna's balcony to feast upon chopped fruit. Today the birds arrived against a backdrop of muddy clouds that sagged in the sky. A cool May breeze refreshed the air in the courtyard. Cars and buses could be heard transporting passengers to their places of work. The day had begun.

Directly opposite Megan and Jack's apartment, Anah tightened the belt on the grey, full-length dressing gown she referred to as a 'housecoat'. Stepping onto the balcony in a dressing-gown would be undignified. She lit a cigarette, gripped the handrail and savoured the giddiness that came only from the first cigarette of the day.

More often than not, the blue van had left before Anah's early morning smoke. She glanced at her watch. It was still there, so Paul Stokes' first job of the day must be nearby.

❖❖❖

Jack lolloped down two flights of stairs with the ungainliness of a newborn giraffe. Anah watched as he dragged his pushbike into the courtyard. Before he set off on his twenty-minute ride to work, he stopped to roll a thread-like cigarette. Lighting it, he jumped on the bike and rode through the archway.

Megan didn't need to leave for another forty-five minutes. The store where she sold sport-inspired lifestyle products didn't open until eight-thirty and was only two minutes' walk away.

By the time Anah had fed Toby, eaten a bowl of fibre-rich Grape-Nuts and fresh blueberries, showered and dressed, Paul had left in his blue van, Megan was on her way to work and Sean was loading his van.

Alan clunked down the stairs, clutching the banister as firmly as his fleshy hand would permit. He noticed that the doors to the ground floor were open and walked over to them, humming a tune he'd just heard on the radio. 'Hello,' he bellowed.

A startled Sean appeared from behind a rack of canned drinks. 'Hi,' he said, walking towards Alan's outstretched paw. They shook hands.

Alan took a moment to survey the enormous quantity of goods stacked up in the room. 'Wow!' he exclaimed. 'Quite an Aladdin's cave.'

'Except there's nothing precious in here. It's just non-perishable food for my father's stores and pallets of tat he expects me to sell online,' Sean retorted.

Alan threw back his head and gave a loud guffaw. 'Well, they say anything will sell at the right price.'

'*They* must have been listening to my father.'

'A wise man is Mr Douglas, a very wise man. How many corner shops does he have now?'

Sean grinned and raised his thick, yellow-brown eyebrows. 'He wouldn't thank you for calling them "corner shops". He'd tell you he's the proprietor of six non-affiliated independent convenience stores. He'd probably throw in that he has a successful online retail operation too, selling high-quality consumer goods – that's the tat.'

'He's done very well for himself.'

'So he likes to remind us. Frequently.'

'Nothing wrong with being proud of your success,' said Alan, standing a little taller. 'I often reflect with a sense of awe upon my own achievements in life.' He paused to savour his words. 'It's a surprise to many that I haven't attained celebrity status, but I never courted fame for my accomplishments.' He closed his eyes and nodded, then resumed his monologue. 'Some say I was hindered by humility. I say I was graced with it.'

A small dimple appeared on Sean's right cheek as he tried to suppress a smile.

'However, young sir,' Alan wagged a chunky finger in Sean's direction, 'I didn't seek you out this morning to let you question me about my astonishing past. I came to request a favour.'

'If I can help...'

'I'd like to throw a party – not a street party, but a *court* party – and I need a trestle table.'

Sean stuttered his way through a sentence about the nature of the party.

'It is a long overdue gathering of the Pendrick Court tenants to help develop our community,' Alan replied grandly. 'So, Aladdin,' he beamed, 'are you able to rub your enchanted ring and grant my wish?'

'I thought Aladdin rubbed a lamp.'

'Let's not get bogged down with what was rubbed. Suffice to say, the story was suffused with gratuitous rubbing.'

Sean explained that he didn't have any trestle tables but he could offer Alan some plastic patio tables and chairs.

'As long as you have enough in the depths of your cave to seat all the residents, they would do splendidly. I think there are ten of us.'

'No problem. I'll give them a wipe over.'

'And if I were to approach your father, do you think he would allow us to hold the event on the roof patio?'

'I'm certain he wouldn't,' Sean said.

Alan took a step back; he looked as though he'd just discovered a skid mark on a hotel towel.

'He's very protective of his rooftop sanctuary,' Sean continued. 'Anyway, he never installed the safety-barrier things.'

'Balustrades!' exclaimed Alan. He reflected for a few seconds. 'Maybe a courtyard jamboree would be less perilous.'

'It would. When are you planning to hold the party?'

'Sometime in July when the weather is more predictable. You'll be the first to know, young sir.'

'I'll wait to hear from you.'

Alan left Sean and made his way very slowly to the nearest ATM with his mother's debit card.

CHAPTER FIVE

SMOKING only her second cigarette of the day, Anah watched Alan's sluggish exit from the court. She caught a whiff of fried onions coming from the apartment below, which revealed the presence of Susan and her peculiar little man.

The wooden doors to the ground floor were open so Sean was still about, but Anah noticed that Paul Stokes' van had gone. She wondered whether the sodden clouds above would drop their onerous load or just move on.

Minutes later, she carried Toby down two long flights of lino-covered stairs, opened the entrance door to Apartments 1 and 2 and put the impatient cat gently on the ground. 'There we are, young man. Time for your morning workout.' Toby bounded across the courtyard, stopping momentarily before climbing the wall to one of Alan's balconies on the first floor.

Above her, Anah heard the door open on the first floor. She waited, expecting Susan and perhaps her hostile sidekick to descend the staircase. She checked her watch; it was a quarter to nine. She waited long enough to convince herself that nobody was going to come down the stairs before she climbed them.

Outside the open door on the first floor stood an anxious Susan in a burgundy anorak. The two women exchanged greetings. With her eyes darting towards the open door, Susan said, 'I'm just waiting for Robert. We're on our way to ... oh, here he is.'

Robert appeared in the doorway. Anah smiled and greeted him. His lips, bordered by a white, neatly trimmed goatee, remained impassive.

'I was just letting Toby out. He likes to explore the court for a couple of hours after breakfast,' said Anah.

'We thought about getting a cat,' Robert said, sneering and puffing himself up to his full five feet one inch. 'If it weren't for the moulting and the apartment stinking of cat food and cat pee, we'd have had one by now.'

Anah frowned.

Susan expelled an involuntary snort. 'Well, you have a wonderful day, Anah,' she said, willing Robert to follow her immediately down the stairs.

'You too,' replied Anah, heading upwards to her own apartment.

Robert walked away with deliberately long steps, hoping any onlookers would overestimate the length of his stride. Susan scuttled along beside him. Their arrival at the archway coincided with that of Edna. 'We're all up bright and early today,' said Edna, 'I'm just off to the chemists.'

'We're going into the city too, Mrs Pembleton,' said Susan.

'Oh, how fortunate. I'll walk with you. And please, call me Edna.'

'We're going in the other direction,' interrupted Robert, grasping Susan's coat.

'I'll catch you later then,' said Edna as she trotted off.

Waiting until Edna had turned the corner, Robert turned to Susan and said with escalating fury, 'Why do you insist on engaging with these people? First Anah Agu, Dowager Duchess of Pendrick Court, craps on about her cat. Then I have to suffer the blather of the Pembleton crone.' Susan's nervous laughter kicked in but Robert ignored her and continued his rant. 'Let's get to the bank before another of them pounces and subjects us to a further onslaught of drivel.'

❖❖❖

Anah was on her balcony in time to see Edna leave the court. The poor postman wouldn't be getting many signatures today. She gazed above the two-bedroom apartment of the young couple opposite. At the edge of the flat roof, two ornamental concrete gargoyles, each impaled on a metal spike, glared unnervingly at her. Behind them, incandescent cloud peered around billowy, grey masses. Anah tutted as she watched Toby rub his body against one of the gruesome statues.

However did he get up there – and whatever had possessed Mr Douglas to instal such repulsive, radically out of place adornments?

Although Anah needed to pee, she was reluctant to do so. She knew that the moment she sat down, the postman would arrive with her letter and press the button on her intercom. If she didn't respond quickly enough, he'd leave a card telling her she could collect the letter the next day from the post office. She wouldn't wait another day so she stood motionless on the balcony with her legs crossed, waiting for the mail.

Two uncomfortable minutes later, Jessica from Apartment 4 sashayed through the archway of Pendrick Court, wearing tight, three-quarter length jeans and a stunning cobalt blouse with matching pointed shoes. Purple-framed glasses complemented her curly, strawberry blonde hair that she wore in a short bob, and her bejewelled hand clutched a large pizza box.

Anah glanced down and nodded. Jessica mouthed hello and returned the nod. She was so pleased that her spectacular entrance and pronounced hip movements had not gone unnoticed. Anah was impressed with, and perhaps a little envious of, Jessica's confidence, if not her garish dress sense.

There was no sign of movement in the apartment opposite. Anah had seen the young man leave on his bike and assumed his girlfriend had left too. Above their apartment, Toby was positioned, relaxed and upright, on the roof patio between the two gargoyles.

If Anah had been close enough, she was sure she would have heard him purr. Although he wouldn't be purring if Mr Douglas found him up there. Anah just hoped that Toby would get bored and return home before he arrived.

There was still no sign of the postman.

CHAPTER SIX

SEATED conveniently close to the fridge, Jessica feasted on peri-peri chicken pizza straight from the box. She read through friends' social media posts and replied, peppering her comments liberally with acronyms and emoticons. She helped eliminate cancer by sharing a post, and was about to start an online quiz titled *What South Korean Soap Character Are You?*, when her phone rang. It was her brother, Christopher. Swiftly emptying her mouth, she greeted him enthusiastically.

Christopher announced that he had been given a date for his ordination: on the 22nd August, he would be a deacon no more. Jessica took a small bite of pizza, gambling she'd have swallowed it by the time Christopher had finished talking. Her bite was mistimed so she swallowed the piece whole, congratulated him and promised to be at the ceremony. She enthused about her new job at Dino's Pizzeria, speculating that Dino had developed a crush on her. 'He used to give me the odd leftover pizza to take home. Now he cooks me a fresh one whenever I want. Best job ever!'

❖ ❖ ❖

By a quarter past ten, Sean had finished loading the van and was ready to deliver to his father's stores. Just as he was about to pull out of Pendrick Court, another truck pulled in. Sean cursed when he realised the quantity of goods he was going to have to unload from the truck. He still hadn't sold the first pallet of men's two-percent wool-blend duffle coats. How on earth did his father expect him to shift another?

❖ ❖ ❖

No more than a twenty-minute walk away, Sean's father sat at an immense barrel-shaped boardroom table that, with its chairs, was taking up every inch of his living room. Kevin had assembled this monstrous piece of furniture with a view to holding meetings around it with his staff and suppliers. The meetings never took place and the table had become a Petri dish for a growing culture of paperwork that now teetered in lofty, random piles.

Kevin exhaled fierce plumes of water vapour from his e-cigarette as he waited expectantly for his phone to ring. The letters could be delivered at any minute, and his whiney-arsed excuse for a son would be the first to call. Kevin wouldn't answer. No, he didn't have to explain himself – he didn't owe anything to anybody. He had never wanted to be a landlord. His only interest in Pendrick Court was the capital appreciation.

He picked up his phone before walking into the

kitchen to make a mug of instant coffee. As the noisy kettle popped and spat, Kevin boiled with delight. Tensing his body to contain his exhilaration, he imagined his first portfolio of blue-chip stocks. He'd spent years investing profits back into his business and now he was going to have some money just for himself.

❖ ❖ ❖

Had she not maintained her strict regime of pelvic floor exercises, Anah would have watered the petunias. Fortunately the postman rode into the court in the nick of time. She left her balcony and, with the deliberation of a drunkard crossing a pebbled beach, made her way downstairs. She reached the ground-floor entrance before the postman pressed the intercom a second time and signed for her letter.

'You'll find the young man from Apartment 6 through there,' she said, pointing to the open door to her left. 'I believe the young woman from Apartment 4 is here too, but everybody else is out.' The postman thanked her. Anah took a deep breath and headed hastily back to her apartment and the loo.

The postman dropped a 'something for you' card into the mailbox labelled, *Apartment 1 – Robert and Susan Page*. Next he approached Sean, who was still stacking boxes of the coming autumn/winter season's must-have fashion trend. 'Apartment 6 – Sean Douglas?' he asked. Sean signed for his letter and placed it unopened on a pallet of instant noodles.

Another card was thrust into the mailbox of Apartment 3 for Paul Stokes. Jessica hurried down two flights of stairs to collect her letter. Still more cards were left at Apartment 5 for Edna Pembleton, Apartment 7 for Alan Marshall, and Apartment 8 for Jack Green and Megan Davies.

❖❖❖

Peeing like a pressure washer, Anah opened her letter. She remained seated and started to read. By virtue of Section 21 of the Housing Act 1988, Kevin required possession of her home after the first of August 2019. No reason was given, just a request for an initial check on the property and an inventory on Saturday, the twentieth of July.

Anah's heart and breathing rate increased. Although she felt a mite giddy, she read the letter again more slowly. She had been given little over two months' notice of eviction. With no notice at all, her large intestine executed a somewhat merciless evacuation.

Clutching the letter and still a bit woozy, Anah switched to auto-pilot. She headed for the balcony and lit a cigarette, her vacant gaze into the bleak morning interrupted only when she saw Toby curled up against one of the gargoyles. The nicotine exacerbated her light headedness. Using the patio door frame for support, she stumbled back into the sitting room and flopped, limp as a post-coital penis, into her armchair.

❖ ❖ ❖

Having stacked the consignment of duffle coats, Sean tore open his envelope to reveal a completed form 6A eviction notice. It was clear enough: his father wanted possession of the apartment on the first of August. But it didn't make sense. Why would his father want him to leave the apartment, and where did he intend Sean to live? He called his father's phone, ending the call when it switched to voicemail.

Confused, Sean looked around and saw Jessica, red-faced and jumpy, standing in the entrance to the storeroom. This wasn't his usual self-assured, vibrant neighbour. 'Sorry to disturb you,' she said. 'I'm trying to reach your dad but there's no reply.'

Sean approached her. 'Has something happened?' he asked.

Jessica held up the same form that Sean had received. 'You've got one too!' he said, now even more mystified by his father's actions. 'I don't ... I mean ... I got one and I don't know why.'

'I thought I'd done something to upset him.' Jessica exhaled her words with relief.

'No. It's not you. I've tried to call him too but, like you say, he's not answering his phone.'

'Perhaps we've all been given eviction notices.'

'Well, yeah, maybe. I don't know what's going on.'

'Look, I saw the elderly lady on her balcony half an hour ago. Let's go ask if she got a notice.'

'Edna, who lives under me?'

'No, the lady who lives up there.' Jessica pointed in the direction of Anah's balcony.

'Oh, Anah. Yeah. Let's go see Anah.'

CHAPTER SEVEN

THE intercom's buzz jolted Anah from her motionless state. She sped to the door and pushed the access button.

'If the ceilings weren't so damned high, these staircases wouldn't be so damned long,' said Sean, resting for a few seconds on the first-floor landing. Jessica, who had been following, walked past him and led the way up to Anah's apartment.

Like a doorman sheltered by the awnings of a *grande dame* hotel, Anah held open the door and beckoned them into her palace. When they were inside, she smiled at Jessica and commented that they hadn't been introduced. Sean stepped up. 'Anah, may I introduce Jessica Perkins? Jessica, this is Anah Agu.'

Holding out her hand with the palm facing downward, Anah said, 'How do you do?'

Jessica reached out, waggled Anah's fingertips, cringed and instinctively performed a mini-curtsey. 'I'm doing well, thank you,' she said, cringing again.

'Pleased to meet you, Jessica.' Anah stretched out

her arm. 'Please go through to the drawing room and make yourselves comfortable.' She was most insistent that they take tea, coffee or a glass of blackcurrant cordial.

Sean and Jessica sat on the sofa while Anah prepared drinks in the kitchen. Wide-eyed, Jessica mouthed, 'Oh my God,' then whispered, 'Did she want me to kiss her hand?'

Stifling a laugh, Sean shook his head as Anah returned with a tray of cordial and a plate of chocolate and raspberry macaroons.

'Well, down to business,' she said, handing a glass to each of her guests. 'Am I correct in assuming you've both received an eviction notice too?'

'We have,' said Sean.

Despite a mild nut allergy, Jessica accepted a macaroon. She would take an antihistamine tablet when she got home. Somehow a rash, or even anaphylaxis, seemed preferable to disappointing Mrs Agu.

❖ ❖ ❖

Gripping its cellophane wrapper, Kevin chomped into a chicken pasty that was well past its use-by date. Flakes of pastry dappled his white shirt and glided to the kitchen floor. He studied his phone. As he'd predicted, Sean had tried to contact him – but he wasn't the first. There were several missed calls from an unfamiliar number.

The pie was moreish and there were another five that needed to be eaten, so Kevin took another from the fridge. Fortunately, an active lifestyle caused his metabolism to work faster than a prune soaked in castor oil.

Leaving his apartment wouldn't be a wise move; he didn't want to bump into Sean. He would stay put and occupy himself by part-paying some overdue invoices. If Sean came around to the apartment, he wouldn't answer the door. Kevin often left his car outside and walked through the city. The staff in the shop below didn't keep tabs on him. Sean would never know he was home.

❖❖❖

'He's still not answering his phone,' said Sean, perched on the edge of Anah's sofa. 'I spoke to him yesterday and he said nothing about evictions.'

Jessica refused a second macaroon; she was convinced that her lips were already tingling.

'It's all very peculiar,' said Anah. 'I've always found Mr Douglas to be extremely courteous.' A look of incredulity swept the face of her guests. 'I really would have expected an explanation before he sent these notices.'

Running his fingers through his hair, Sean hung his head and stared at his phone. Jessica peered into his face. 'Are you comfortable with hugs?' she asked.

Sean didn't reply immediately. 'It's not just my home I might be losing,' he said eventually. 'What about my job?'

Jessica played safe and gave him two gentle taps on the back. 'Your dad could just be trying to scare us,' she said, trying to reassure him. 'He probably thinks we'd pay a lot more rent to avoid the hassle of moving.'

'It is possible that the eviction notices are nothing more than leverage in a rent re-negotiation,' agreed Anah. 'But we'll make no headway with speculation.'

'You're right.' Sean stood up. 'I'm going to make my deliveries and find my dad. I'll fill you both in when I get back.'

Jessica stood with the intention of leaving at the same time, but the offer of oat biscuits and Roquefort persuaded her to stay a little longer.

❖ ❖ ❖

Sean pulled out into the courtyard and climbed out of his van to lock the stores behind him. An errant wind, unusually bitter for May, found its way through the archway and into Pendrick Court. The icy draught prompted him to reach into the van and grab a grey hooded sweatshirt. His azure-blue T-shirt – almost identical in colour to his eyes – offered little protection against the biting wind.

He looked up and slowly turned three hundred and sixty degrees. Among the thousands of now-grubby red bricks that had been used to build the towering brewery were two specks of life: Toby nuzzled up against the claws of a gargoyle, and the delicately folded buds of Anah's petunias which were yet to trumpet the arrival of summer.

Sean looked at his own balcony. It had been his for three years, the three happiest years of his life – the only happy years of his life. Contentment seeped from him and puddled the cold tarmac beneath him, to be replaced with uncertainty. He secured the stores and drove out through the archway.

❖ ❖ ❖

'Oh my God!' Jessica put her hand to her mouth. 'The Roquefort was delicious, but this ... oh my God!'

'I'm glad you like it,' said Anah.

'Jam and cheese!'

'A layer of amerena jam between the oat biscuit and a soft goat cheese.'

'Anah, you have magical powers. Honestly, you're up there with unicorns, mermaids and good witches.'

Anah laughed. She couldn't recall experiencing such a low and then such a high in the same day before. The young woman's vitality was infectious.

'If these eviction notices mean we really must leave, have you any idea where you'll go?' Jessica asked.

Anah sighed and shook her head. 'No, I haven't. When I retired at sixty-one and relocated here, it was to be my last move ... unless I needed residential care. I hoped I would only leave here in a body bag.'

Jessica shuddered.

'And what about you?' enquired Anah.

'No idea. It's going to be a nightmare.'

'Do you smoke tobacco?' asked Anah, as her thoughts turned to cigarettes.

'No. Smoking has never been one of my vices.'

'Do you mind if I retire to the balcony and have a cigarette?'

'Not at all. I'll just finish off the last of the biscuits, if it's okay with you.'

CHAPTER EIGHT

ANAH watched Edna emerge through the archway carrying two bulging white carrier bags, each displaying the green cross of a pharmacy.

Edna was a sprightly eighty-two, small in stature with rounded shoulders. Her scurry towards the entrance to Apartments 5 and 6 was reminiscent of a dung beetle scenting the bouquet of a fresh pile of doings. Very soon she would retrieve the card left by the postman from her mailbox. Tomorrow she would collect her eviction notice. Prewarning her might mitigate the shock.

Anah re-joined Jessica in the sitting room. 'Edna from Apartment 5 has just returned,' she said. 'I should go over and make her aware of the intended eviction.'

'You're very thoughtful.'

'Would you like to come with me?'

Jessica said she would and accompanied her new-found friend outside into the brisk breeze. Soon they were standing in the far corner of the courtyard at the entrance to Apartments 5 and 6. Anah pressed the intercom button and they heard Edna's voice. 'Hello?'

'It's Anah from Apartment 2. I wondered if you had a minute.'

'Hello,' repeated Edna. 'Is anybody there?'

Anah moved closer to the intercom. 'Yes, it's Anah from number 2.'

'I'm sorry, I can't hear you. I'll come down.' Edna raced down the stairs and opened the door. 'Oh, hello, dear. You need to speak into the box on the wall when you hear my voice.'

'I did.'

'Or you can press the trade button during the day and let yourself in. Anyway, if you've come about the noise, I can assure you that it's not coming from me. If it's pop music, it's the plumber at number 3; if it's whooping and hooting, it's coming from number 6 upstairs.'

'No, I haven't come about any noise—'

Edna turned to Jessica. 'I hope you don't think I'm responsible for the nightly bedlam. It's the boys—'

Anah took a deep breath and interrupted. 'Edna, we haven't come about the noise.'

'Please, call me Edna.'

'I did,' said Anah, trying to speak louder without shouting. 'We have some bad news for you.'

'Bad news! Who's gone and died now?'

'Nobody has died, Edna.'

'Thank the Lord.'

'Edna, we've come to tell you that all the tenants at Pendrick Court have received eviction notices. We are to leave by the first of August.'

With her left hand, Edna gripped the doorframe; with her right hand, she grabbed her left breast. As she swayed from side to side, Jessica and Anah instinctively lunged forward to support her.

'I'm going. I can feel myself going,' Edna whimpered. 'It's my heart. Please help me upstairs.'

❖❖❖

The route from Pendrick Court to Kevin's apartment wasn't an attractive one. Pre-war slums had been demolished and replaced in the sixties with pallid concrete offices, shops and a multi-storey car park. The red poles of the sideless bus shelters and the green, Victorian-style litter bins lent a much-needed fleck of warmth to an otherwise cheerless quarter of this great city.

Sean swung open the back doors of the transit van and clambered inside. Within seconds, the store manager arrived accompanied by two pimpled, adolescent youths both wielding a sack barrow. Without speaking, Sean started passing down cases of canned drinks. At the same time he threw surreptitious glances towards the entrance door to Kevin's apartment.

The store manager, Kelly, was ensuring the boys were splitting the load equally between their barrows. If they were filled at the same time, they'd have to be emptied at the same time and that would give her a few minutes alone with Sean. 'Did my cans of Mountain Dew come in, babe?' she asked, scrutinising Sean's skeletal muscles with the thoroughness of a medical student.

'Yep. They're on,' Sean replied without looking up.

'Oh, you do look after me. I was just admiring your physique. Do you work out?'

'No need to with this job.'

'You're amazingly buff,' Kelly exclaimed.

The boys nudged each other and smirked while Kelly hid her disappointment at Sean's disinclination to engage in flirtatious chat. Sean wondered whether she was about to display a swollen, pink, baboon-like backside and demand to be taken brusquely from behind. Mercifully for those present, she restrained herself.

The boys were sent off to unload their barrows. With a sensuous slink, Kelly drew closer to the van. Sean leapt down, passed a startled Kelly and hurried over to ring Kevin's doorbell. A minute later, he rang it again. He took a few steps back and looked up at the first-floor windows in the hope of seeing movement.

Kevin peered between two horizontal slats in the blind and sneered as he watched his son, head down, skulk back to the van to finish the delivery.

❖❖❖

Edna sat on a worn leather sofa between Anah and Jessica, interrupting her stupor only to take occasional sips from a glass of water.

Jessica's eyes traversed the room, examining the dozens of knick-knacks. Dusty figurines, wedged between grimy photo frames and cracked vases, gasped for air. Blister packs of tablets, bottles of medicine and tubes of cream all collaborated to conceal the water stains and scratches on the rustic coffee table. The room was a cross between a junk shop and a pharmacy. 'How's the heart now?' she asked.

'I've been spared on this occasion, dear,' Edna replied. 'The slightest shock and they could be firing up the burners at the crem.' She let Jessica pat her arm. 'Look!' She lifted up her feet and straightening her legs. 'Swollen ankles – a sure sign of a weak heart.'

Anah studied Enda's ankles. 'Forgive me, but it doesn't look like oedema.'

'Not eczema, dear. Swollen ankles.' With a self-satisfied smile, Edna circled both dainty ankles. 'The danger's passed so you can tell me more about these eviction notices.'

Anah took out her letter and read it out loudly. Edna's eyes and lips narrowed as she clenched her jaw. 'The son of a bitch!' she hissed, jumping to her feet. 'Who does he think he is? He's got another thing coming if he expects me to move.'

'Try not to get excited,' pleaded Jessica. 'You don't want to bring on another heart thingy.'

Edna gave her left breast a less than tender squeeze and sat down again. 'You're quite right. I won't be up to fighting if I'm full of embalming fluid.'

Anah suggested that Edna rest for the remainder of the day. 'Why don't you come over to my apartment in the morning when we've all had an opportunity to sleep on the matter?'

'I will. I'll come round when I get back from the pharmacy.'

Anah declined Jessica's offer to heat up some pizza. She had already organised her lunch and wanted to catch the other residents as they returned to Pendrick Court.

Jessica, defying an impulse to hug Anah, promised to see her the following day. She would come sooner if Sean returned with any game-changing news.

CHAPTER NINE

A mackerel, grapefruit and lentil salad later, Anah was back on her balcony. Her hooded eyes skimmed the court, a shawl about her shoulders shielding her from the wind. Grinding her cigarette butt into an ashtray, she caught sight of Alan entering the courtyard. He was walking tall and straight, advancing with small steps towards the entrance door to Apartments 7, 8 and the rooftop patio. A wide grin creased his face.

Clasping the railing with both hands, Anah called out but there was no break in Alan's momentum. She inhaled deeply and projected the words 'Mr Marshall' as her lungs emptied. This time, Alan froze. He looked up to the patio and scanned the balconies. It wasn't many seconds before he saw Anah waving, gesturing that she would come down.

They met at her ground-floor entrance. Unwilling to climb two flights of stairs unnecessarily, Alan turned down the offer of a cup of tea but happily stepped inside out of the afternoon's crisp clinch. Anah did battle with the spring-loaded hinges as she held open the door.

Before Alan had crossed the threshold, Sean's transit juddered into the courtyard. Sean saw Anah – now using a shoulder to defeat the spring – and walked towards her. Relieving her of her door-stop duties, Alan ushered her inside. 'Aladdin!' he boomed, displaying a rictus grin. Sean responded with a wan smile. Anticipating unwelcome news, Anah ran her fingers through her short zinc-grey afro.

'I'm sorry,' shrugged Sean, 'I still haven't got hold of my dad. We're none the wiser.'

Alan's eyes raced back and forth between Sean and Anah before settling on Sean's face. 'I'm deducing that something undesirable has taken place and that Anah was about to enlighten me when you arrived.'

'Yeah,' said Sean. 'Sorry. I thought you already knew. We all received eviction notices this morning. I've been trying to find out why.'

Alan gave a puzzled pout. 'Please come inside, young sir, before pushing against this door gives me a hernia.' Sean stepped inside and Alan thankfully let the door thump shut. 'Are you saying that your father is ejecting me from Pendrick Court?'

In a restrained, soothing voice, Anah related the contents of her eviction letter. Alan was conscious that he was sweating and that his heart beat was increasing. Neurons were exploding, causing one hideous notion after another, each more dire than the last, to assault his brain. Disguising his disquiet, he smiled and nodded at Anah.

'I've been thinking,' said Sean. 'We should get all the residents together. Tomorrow night, after work. We could meet on the ground floor.'

'That's a good idea,' Anah said. 'I'll make a point of letting everybody know. Would six-thirty suit you?'

'Six-thirty is good.' Sean opened the door. 'I'd bring a jacket – it can get cold in there.'

Alan shuffled across the courtyard like an emperor penguin returning to the sea as Sean drifted towards the white transit. Both were consumed by the magnitude of their situation; both were desperate to preserve the status quo, which had never before seemed quite so appealing.

❖ ❖ ❖

Adjusting her shawl, Anah stood at the entrance to Apartments 3 and 4. Through the intercom to Apartment 4, she reported Sean's lack of news to Jessica and passed on the arrangements for a meeting the following evening. She decided that it would be simpler to inform Edna when she called round in the morning. The prospect of re-scheduling her visit via the intercom provoked a deep sense of dread.

Steely-eyed, Toby padded across the courtyard towards Anah. Despite interrupting his progress every few steps to check over his shoulder, he soon caught up with her. She felt his warmth at her ankles and scooped him up into an adoring embrace.

Just as they were about to enter the building, Robert and Susan Page returned to Pendrick Court. Anah waylaid them at the ground floor entrance, much to Robert's poorly concealed annoyance. The particulars of the eviction and the intended meeting lit the blue touch paper within him. His testosterone level rose to that of a bull shark and erupted into a fusillade of spittle-soaked profanity that was focused, for the most part, on Kevin Douglas's failings.

Susan's eyes twinkled with tears, her bottom lip vibrated and a rush of air from the courtyard whipped her uncombed grey hair into her face. 'Let's get inside,' she said, following Anah and a puce-faced Robert into the lobby. 'Thank you so much for your help, Anah. I do apologise for our reaction to this news.'

Anah raised a hand as if to dismiss Robert's grisly tirade.

'And of course we'll join you all tomorrow evening,' Susan added.

Anah waited until the couple were in their apartment before carrying Toby up to her own home. She decided to brush him by the patio doors, in the hope of seeing Paul or either of the young couple from the apartment opposite arrive. Toby stayed within inches of Anah's feet while she collected his metal comb, brush and a rewarding catnip bite.

First to arrive home was Megan, looking like a genetically modified raspberry in a heavily padded, crimson puffa jacket. Anah hurried down the stairs. Her incredibly loud 'I say' from her ground-floor entrance caught Megan's attention. They met in the middle of the courtyard, where Anah revealed that Megan had missed delivery of a Section 21 eviction notice.

'I don't know anything about these twenty-one sections,' began a bewildered Megan. 'What's it about? What does it mean?'

'Well, it looks as though you – and everybody else at Pendrick Court – are being told to leave by the first of August.'

'What?' Megan shook her head in disbelief. 'Jack's gonna go apeshit.'

Anah pointed to the storeroom. 'It's been suggested that we all meet tomorrow evening at six-thirty on the ground floor to share our thoughts and decide what to do. You know – common goals, common action, that sort of thing.'

Megan nodded, thanked Anah and ran towards her apartment.

Paul Stokes didn't pull into Pendrick Court until nearly six o'clock. Anah had sufficient time to get downstairs and speak to him because he was gathering the contents of his van to store them securely in his apartment overnight. He listened in silence to her words, nodding to indicate that he understood. Anah was at a loss to know how he felt. He did, however, say he'd see her at six-thirty the next evening before thanking her for her trouble.

Anah returned to her apartment extremely pleased

that she wouldn't have to climb the stairs again that day. Too tired to stand on the balcony and smoke, she poured herself a small glass of sherry and sank into her armchair. Toby made himself comfortable on the sofa, ignoring his owner's repeated requests for a cuddle.

CHAPTER TEN
Wednesday, 22nd May

ANAH had already given up shouting into her intercom when the ferocious knocking started. She opened the door, worried that Edna would actually pound her way through it. 'I let myself in with the trade button, dear. Your intercom's not working.'

'I'll report it,' Anah replied. She sighed as she showed Edna through to the sitting room.

'Well, there's no point reporting it now. Kevin Douglas isn't going to worry about repairs if he's going to demolish the place.'

'Demolish the place?'

'Yes. They'll want to build a skyscraper, or a motorway through the city centre.'

'I don't think we've established why Mr Douglas wants us out.'

'It doesn't matter why. We've got to stop him. I'm not waiting for a thumping great wrecking ball to turn up.'

'And that's why all the residents are getting together this evening: to form a plan of action,' Anah said. 'I've already started to research our rights online, and I intend making a couple of phone calls.'

Edna's head bobbed excitedly. The excited bobbing slowed to a measured nod of approval as she made herself comfortable on the sofa.

❖ ❖ ❖

Kevin was inspecting the signatures on the Royal Mail's website. Satisfied that all the eviction notices had been received, he leaned back in his chair and laced his fingers behind his head. Dreams engulfed him like a cocoon of vicuna wool. He fantasised about the expeditious sale of Pendrick Court for a price far in excess of that envisaged by the estate agent, and imagined an investment portfolio bloated with the proceeds of the deal.

Without warning, he was wrenched from his wool-gathering. He always placed an order for beer and cider on a Wednesday and he had no idea what stock there was at Pendrick Court. He had two options: call Sean and ask him to check, or drive over and run into him. Sod it! He'd just have to call Sean. Cutting short a telephone conversation would be easier than terminating a face-to-face encounter.

❖ ❖ ❖

Alan was slumped at his kitchen table following a sleepless night and the collection of his letter from the post office. Despite the impression he tried to give, he'd be struggling to make ends meet if it were not for his mother's money. Fortuitously, in Mr Douglas he'd found a landlord who didn't use a letting agent, and the offer of six months' rent in advance had rendered the usual credit checks and references unnecessary. Prior to securing his apartment at Pendrick Court, Alan's reliance on housing benefit from the council and a benefit to top up his state pension had become a serious impediment to renting in the private sector. Do the final chapters of an otherwise riveting biography really need to be set in local authority housing, he asked himself.

He looked out of his kitchen window. The open door to the ground-floor storeroom offered a ray of hope. Word from Sean's father might just be the winch with which he could haul himself from the doldrums.

Alan mustered sufficient vigour to make the journey to the storeroom, where he hoped Sean would be the bearer of much-needed good news.

After the brief discussion with his father, Sean had called Ishaan immediately. The two of them were now huddled in a corner of the storeroom, absorbed in a spirited dialogue. Their exchange came to an abrupt end when Sean noticed Alan.

'Ah, Aladdin! And I see you have your genie,' Alan cried.

Ishaan threw Sean a bemused look.

'If only he could grant me three wishes,' Sean said. 'Alan, this is Ishaan. Ishaan, this is Alan.'

'I was just wondering if you'd discovered the rationale behind the evictions from your father,' said Alan.

'My father says he wants to sell the building and re-establish the ground-floor operation in a new location. Apparently, I need to stand on my own two feet. I'll still have my job but, like you guys, I need to find somewhere else to live.'

'Could we not rent from the new landlord?' asked Alan.

'He says a buyer will want to sell off the apartments individually, so he wants Pendrick Court empty. Dad really wasn't up for a debate.'

'Perhaps a spokesperson could persuade him otherwise? That's something we could discuss this evening. I shall bid you farewell. It was good to meet you, Imam.'

'Ishaan,' corrected Sean.

Alan set out in the direction of Apartment 7.

'What was all that shit about Aladdin and his genie?' asked Ishaan. 'Did he catch you rubbing your lamp?'

❖ ❖ ❖

In Apartment 3, Paul sat in front of his laptop with a cold bottle of Bud Light in his hand, availing himself of free video-chat services. Filling his screen was the face of Noi, his Thai girlfriend.

'Why is this big problem for you?' she asked, tossing her long, silky black hair.

Paul tried to convey the enormity of moving home and the added complication of his eviction date clashing with his visit to see her in Phuket. As Noi trivialised his concerns, his exasperation intensified. 'I do love you, but you don't understand what I'm trying to explain,' he said.

'I love you too, Paul,' said Noi, parting her full lips to reveal flawless, snow-white teeth.

Noi's screen wasn't filled quite so attractively. Although Paul had the tight, almost ripped body of a man much younger than his fifty-five years, his creased, dour face had the appearance of desiccated chamois leather. Together with his cropped white hair, he looked about seventy.

At six-thirty Paul ended the video session with a promise to call Noi the following evening. He pulled a Velvet Underground LP from his extensive vinyl collection and placed it on the turntable. He would listen to it over another beer after the meeting on the ground floor was over.

CHAPTER ELEVEN

LAST to arrive were Megan and Jack. They found a place to stand in the circle that had formed just inside the entrance to the storeroom and gaped with anticipation at Anah, who was inspecting those present approvingly.

'Thank you all for coming here this evening,' she began. 'As we don't all know each other, perhaps we could introduce ourselves. Shall we start with Apartment 1?'

'Yes. Hello. For those who don't already know us, I'm Susan and this is Robert.' Susan was smiling; other than a slight tic, Robert's face was immobile. 'We have the two-bedroom apartment on your left as you enter the court. We're on the first floor.'

'I'm Anah. I rent Apartment 2, directly above Susan and Robert.' Anah turned to Paul.

'Paul. Apartment 3.'

Jessica paused to ensure Paul had finished speaking then said, 'Hi everybody. Great to meet you all. My name is Jessica Perkins. I'm in Apartment 4 above

Paul.' She turned to Edna. 'Would you like to introduce yourself?'

'Mrs Pembleton, but please call me Edna.'

'Edna's on the first floor, Apartment 5,' Jessica explained.

'I'd never manage a second flight of stairs with my hips,' announced Edna. 'I'm a martyr to my rheumeoarthritis'

Robert snarled.

'Sean, Apartment 6. You probably know that Kevin Douglas is my father and that I work for him.'

Megan gave Jack a 'did-you-hear-that?' poke in the ribs.

'I want you all to know that I don't agree with what he's doing,' Sean continued. 'I've got to be careful, but I'll do what I can to support you. This is my mate, Ishaan. He doesn't live here.'

Alan stepped forward with open palms, as though he was about to face off in a presidential debate. 'I'm Alan Marshall, leaseholder of Apartment 7 under these good people.' He nodded towards Jack and Megan. 'This morning, I consulted with young Sean and I can confirm that it is Mr Douglas's intention to sell Pendrick Court with vacant possession. Although initially Pendrick Court was no more than a pied-à-terre, somewhere to rest my head when I visited Mother, I have grown attached to the place. I had hoped to while away my twilight years with you all. My plans—'

Anah interrupted Alan's oration. 'Could we just

finish the introductions first?' She smiled at Megan.

'Hi. I'm Megan and this is Jack. Yeah, and we live in Apartment 8.'

'Excellent! We all know each other now,' said Anah. She turned momentarily towards Robert and what she thought was a growl.

Turning back to the others, she explained that the tenancy agreements were in order; information about the tenancy deposit scheme, together with other necessary certificates and documents, had been provided. Kevin had also been careful to give the correct notice period and use the right forms. She concluded that the Section 21 notices were valid. 'We,' she said, 'are subject to a "NO-FAULT EVICTION", and it is perfectly legal.'

As the gathered tenants muttered Alan moved into the arena. 'It occurs to me,' he thundered, 'that since Kevin Douglas has yet to secure a buyer, he cannot know whether a new owner will sell on our apartments or rent them out.' Now certain of their full attention, he paced like a prodigiously proportioned lawyer addressing a jury. 'I put it to you that our first move should be to send a diplomatic envoy to try and coax Kevin Douglas into withdrawing the Section 21 notices.'

'If it takes a while to find a buyer, withdrawing the notices would benefit him. He'd continue to receive our rent,' said Susan.

'And if the buyer does want to rent out the apartments, he has a fabulous troupe of ready-made tenants,' said Jessica.

Megan looked at Jack and discreetly feigned a dry heave.

Alan clapped loudly. 'Now we're making progress. Unless anybody has a better suggestion, I propose we use Anah as an intermediary.' A murmur of agreement prompted Anah to say she would speak with Kevin as soon as possible.

'And if diplomacy fails?' asked Robert indignantly. 'He must have known for some time that he intended to force us out but he chose not to tell us. He's only given us two months' notice. Two months' notice might be legal but it's not moral. How do you appeal to the better nature of a reprobate?'

Jack was transfixed by Robert's ability to snarl, bare his teeth and speak all at the same time. Megan didn't know what a reprobate was but resolved to remember the word and put it to good use as soon as she could.

There was a brief lull before Paul's gravelly voice declared, 'If he doesn't agree to withdraw the notices, perhaps he could re-issue them with a longer notice period.'

'A *faulty* eviction! Diplomacy and longer notice periods!' cried Edna. 'What he needs is telling where to put his evacuation notices. If he wants to sell, he has to sell to a landlord and ... and—'

'And guarantee the security of our tenancies,' said Robert.

Edna raised her fist as a symbol of solidarity and

screeched, 'I'm with little Robin,' which raised Robert's hackles still further.

They all agreed that withdrawing the eviction notices would be the best option and, for the time being, should be their only goal. Sean declared that if anybody could influence his father it would be Anah; she was one of the few people Kevin ever referred to with respect.

Before the crowd separated, another meeting was scheduled for the following evening – same time, same place.

The wind had lost its muscle and the temperature had risen slightly. Muted, rusty daylight suffused the courtyard.

Jessica was touching up her eyeliner in readiness for an evening shift at Dino's Pizzeria. Paul was lost in the Velvet Underground. Anah was rehearsing a message, should Kevin's phone go to voice mail. Robert was on his knees, working through his rage by wiping down the skirting boards in the apartment. He wouldn't be wiping the ones in Susan's bedroom – she could wipe her own. Susan was taking refuge in a bathtub. Alan had tasked himself with cramming the entire contents of a packet of sliced corned beef into a baguette.

As dusk arrived, shadow dyed the entire courtyard indigo.

CHAPTER TWELVE

ALTHOUGH it was unlikely that she would catch a chill after her bath, Edna wore a full-length fleece dressing gown over her winceyette nightie just to be sure. With a mug of hot chocolate in her hands, she held her breath and stared suspiciously at the ceiling to better identify any noise from Sean and Ishaan above. There wasn't a sound, but that could have been her ears. The doctor called it age-related hearing loss but Edna knew her auditory nerves had been traumatised somehow — possibly with a cotton bud.

She hoped the Asian lad wouldn't be joining Sean tonight. Could she take another session of their incessant talking and laughter? What on earth did two boys find to do all night?

❖ ❖ ❖

'This is serious,' Megan shouted. 'I'm trying to talk to you and all you wanna do is play on that stupid game.'

Jack's fevered fingers continued unabated. 'What

do you want from me?' he asked from under his white baseball cap. 'I'm doing my best to look interested.'

'We could be homeless. There's no guarantee that my step-dad's gonna pay the rent on our next place.'

'He will. He's minted. He's not gonna risk you moving back in with him and your mum.'

'You know sweet FA,' spat Megan, hitting Jack with a scatter cushion. He didn't flinch. 'He's always making digs about paying our rent. He reckons he only agreed to pay it until we got on our feet. I keep telling him the deal was that I'd only move out if he paid the rent.'

'We'll be fine. I was in a house share—'

'With your parents.'

'No. For your information, I used to share a house on Cranwick Road.'

'No you didn't. Your druggie mates rented it and you used to doss there.'

'It was somewhere for us to do a bit of charlie after we'd been clubbing. Just up the nose. No needles.'

Megan convulsed with laughter. 'Well, at least you've cheered me up. A bit of charlie after you'd been clubbing? In your dreams. Those tossers wear electronic tags. I bet their curfew's eight o'clock.'

Jack's eyes narrowed with annoyance. 'That was yonks ago.'

'And the closest they ever get to snorting coke is popping a handful of Imodium. It gets them high, but they can't shit for a week.' Megan clutched the cushion as she cackled. 'You might have to start looking for a better-paid job. Your zero-hour contract at the supermarket won't pay the rent.'

Her goading was getting under Jack's skin. He attempted to wreak revenge by dropping a bombshell. 'Actually,' he said, looking into her eyes, 'I'm thinking of joining the Army.'

Megan jumped up, shrieking with laughter. 'You can't even push a supermarket trolley straight. Who's gonna let you loose with a machine gun?'

Jack threw down his console. As he stomped out of the room, he spun round and shouted, 'Twisted bitch!'

Megan replied with equal fervour. 'And you, Private Jack Green, are a *reprobate*!'

❖❖❖

Certain that there must be noise coming from upstairs, Edna opened the door to her apartment. Unable to hear anything and cursing her ears, she stepped onto the landing, She detected nothing other than the smell of chilli and garlic. She'd have to go up.

The hard, plastic soles of her slippers clattered on the wooden stairs that led to Sean's door. Before she'd climbed half the steps, the door above opened. Edna looked up. 'Did you call?' she asked brazenly.

'Did ... did I call?' replied a baffled Sean.

'Yes, dear. I thought you were calling for help. I'd never have forgiven myself if something had happened to you because I was too frightened to come to your rescue.'

'I didn't make a sound.'

'Thank goodness for that. Heaven knows what I could've done to help at eighty-two years of age.'

Edna turned and headed back down to her apartment.

'Well, thanks for checking on me anyway,' Sean said, still confused. 'Sleep well.'

Edna raised her hand.

❖ ❖ ❖

'What was all that about?' asked Ishaan.

Sean gave a broad grin. 'It was Edna giving her nose a ride. I think she was going to listen at the door.'

The combination kitchen, living and dining room enabled Sean and Ishaan to talk while one of them cooked. Ishaan was sitting barefoot and cross-legged on the sofa while rice simmered and Sean dropped a collection of ingredients into a wok.

'Have you thought about where you'll live if these evictions happen?' asked Ishaan.

'Thought of little else.'

'I know you don't like each other, but couldn't you live with your dad as a stopgap?'

'Not liking each other is a massive understatement. Three years ago, the week of my eighteenth birthday—'

'I know. You've told me. He treated you like shit and he threw you out. But that was three years ago.'

'The only relationship we have is one of employer

and employee. I work my nuts off and he knows it.'

'But you like working for him.'

'No. I *like* the job and he pays me surprisingly well. I give him the same rent for my apartment as Paul, Jessica and Edna. The others pay more because they have two bedrooms.'

'So, why not pay rent to another landlord on another place?'

'It's not going to be as convenient as this, but I guess I'm going to have to see what's available.'

'If you want any help...'

'I appreciate that. Really. Let's eat.'

❖ ❖ ❖

Edna reached for her well-thumbed medical encyclopaedia, lumped it on her lap and looked up insomnia. It recommended a warm bath and a milky drink, both of which she'd tried. She stuffed cotton wool into her ears and decided to have an early night. It had been a long day.

CHAPTER THIRTEEN
Thursday, 23rd May

ANAH was squinting at the screen on her phone while having her first cigarette of the day. According to the uplifting forecast, it was going to be fifteen degrees with sunny spells. She checked to see if Kevin had replied to her message. As yet there was no response, but she remained optimistic.

Susan and Robert were coming home from a brief trip into the city when they spotted Anah on her balcony. Anah gave an affable wave and a nod, which Susan returned.

'Would you just look at her?' said Robert. 'She thinks she's standing on the balcony at Buckingham Palace waving at the commoners and waiting for a bloody flypast. That woman really grips my shit.'

'Oh, Robert,' sighed Susan. 'Just when I thought the week had milked every last drop of your venom, you manage to hoick up another stream of vitriol.'

❖ ❖ ❖

Kevin was listening to Anah's message for the fifth time. Apparently there was an issue that she'd like to discuss as a matter of urgency. Surely if the issue was urgent she'd *need* to discuss it, not *like* to. Either the issue wasn't urgent or it was urgent only to her.

He surmised that the issue was that of the evictions. They had been executed by the book, so she couldn't be challenging his right to turf her out. If the message had been from any of the other tenants, it would have been easy to ignore, but Kevin was uncomfortable at the thought of being discourteous towards Anah. Perhaps he'd drive over to Pendrick Court at midday, enjoy an hour's fresh air on the rooftop patio and offer to meet her. Yes, he'd do that. He sent Anah a text message, offering to call in and see her at one o'clock.

Meanwhile he prepared for a series of disciplinary hearings to discuss spurious performance issues. It was expedient to dismiss all his staff, except for his store managers, before they'd worked for him for two years then they couldn't go to an employment tribunal. If other employers were fined for unfair or constructive dismissal, it was their own fault for allowing their employees to work for too long. Rules were there to protect the imbalance of power but employers had to stay on their toes.

❖ ❖ ❖

Just before eleven o'clock, Jessica went to see Anah on the pretext of wanting to know if she'd spoken to Kevin. In truth, she had enjoyed her time in Anah's apartment on Tuesday and wasn't working until the evening, so she hoped that Anah would once again invite her in.

Jessica was seated in the middle of three cushions on the sofa. She had sat there during her previous visit and this was now her seat. Anah was in her armchair with a bowl on each arm of the chair, one containing glossy-black Niçoise olives and the other olive pits. Despite Anah's assurance that the olives were superior to those on Dino's pizzas, Jessica had opted for dates stuffed with an assortment of nuts.

'Wouldn't it be fantastic if you got Kevin to withdraw the eviction notices,' she said.

'Of course, but we have no idea how amenable he'll be.' Anah removed a pit from her mouth. 'We may need to fall back on trying to negotiate a longer notice period. And if that fails—'

'We'll need a new plan.'

'We will.'

Jessica was staring at a collection of framed photographs on Anah's sideboard when she sensed an uneasiness in her new friend. 'I'm sorry,' she said. 'I shouldn't be so nosy.'

'You're not being nosy. If they were private, I wouldn't have them on display.'

'But they're personal and we barely know each other. Sorry.'

'Then we should get to know each other.' Anah went to the sideboard and picked up one of the photographs. Torment had etched the image onto her memory over thirty-eight long years, but she studied the subjects afresh before handing it to Jessica.

'This is you,' said Jessica. 'The others – your husband and son?'

'Yes,' replied Anah. 'My son is eight in the photo. He's forty-six now ... forty-seven on the eleventh of November.'

'And your husband? Were you widowed?'

'He did die, but after we were divorced.'

'Sorry to hear that. Sorry that he died, and sorry that you divorced ... if that wasn't what you wanted. The divorce, not the dying. Nobody would want the dying.'

Anah smiled and held out her hand to take back the photo. The image held her attention again. A card in 2004, announcing the birth of her granddaughter Madison Amber Agu, had given her renewed hope that she and her son Michael might be reconciled. It was a false hope. 'It's okay to have regrets. We all make mistakes – I just try not to let them consume me.'

❖❖❖

There was a padlocked iron gate several feet from Jack and Megan's apartment. Immediately behind it was a staircase leading to an unlocked door, which opened onto a large paved area on the roof. Kevin opened the padlock, put it in his jacket pocket and climbed the stairs.

In the middle of the patio stood a four-by-six-foot redwood garden shed. Kevin took out a traditional deckchair with red-and-white striped cotton canvas and positioned it to afford the best view of the city. Before settling down for an hour's rest under the sickly midday sun, he walked to the edge of the roof overlooking the courtyard. He turned both grotesque gargoyles slightly, changing the direction in which they were looking.

❖❖❖

Anah leaned forward in her armchair. 'And you? Would you like to share something about yourself, Jessica?'

'I'm twenty-two. Both my parents are dead but my older brother keeps an eye on me – and the trust fund my parents set up. And I'm single.'

'Were you orphaned?'

'Orphaned?'

'Did both of your parents die when you were a child?'

'No, Mum died when I was twelve and Dad when I was nineteen.'

'Gosh! I can't imagine—'

'Like I said, I've got Christopher, my brother. And I've had time to adjust.'

'I am pleased to hear that you have – *are* coping.'

'You already know I work at Dino's Pizzeria, and I like boys. Men.'

'You like men?' Anah asked.

'As opposed to women. I'm straight.'

'How delightfully modern that you don't assume heterosexuality to be the default orientation.'

'Sorry?'

'I'm *straight* too.'

CHAPTER FOURTEEN

JESSICA had left Anah's apartment before Kevin arrived at precisely one o'clock. She received him with the façade of politeness that she habitually employed both to endear herself to him and to ward off intimacy. She ushered him through to the sitting room. Kevin chose to sit in the middle of the sofa, resting his outstretched arms on the top of the back cushions and spreading his legs so wide as to risk a groin strain. Anah sat opposite him in her armchair, knees together, and kept her eyes above chest height.

With great aplomb, she started to extol the benefits of withdrawing the eviction notices: continued rental income during the possible lengthy period it might take to find a buyer and complete a sale; the appeal to a potential investor of a fully-tenanted property and, of course, the speed with which evictions could be carried out if all the tenants cooperated.

Kevin listened to her in silence. After she had presented her case, he didn't speak for a few seconds then waved the proposal away with his hand. Anah tensed like a kite string on a windy day and ran the tip of her tongue over her front teeth as she glared at Kevin's pock-marked face. His pitted complexion and badly-applied fake tan put Anah in mind of a fire-damaged traffic cone.

'There's no money in renting nowadays,' said Kevin. 'An overpriced property market, depressed rental yields, the stagnation of capital appreciation, increasing protection for tenants and costs for landlords ... I could go on. An investor will buy Pendrick Court, convert the ground floor into apartments and sell the units individually.' He moved to the edge of the sofa, as if he were about to get up and leave. 'All the political parties have policies to improve the private rental market for tenants and make it less attractive to landlords.'

Anah maintained eye contact as he spoke. 'I am following your observations with great interest, Mr Douglas. You are quite certain that Pendrick Court is not an attractive investment to a landlord?'

'I am.'

'Then, if you will not withdraw the eviction notices, could I ask that you contemplate reissuing them with a longer notice period?'

'You could ask. However, the eviction notices stand.' Kevin stood up. 'I respectfully suggest, Mrs Agu, that you look for alternative accommodation as soon as possible.'

'On a personal note,' Anah said slowly, 'I am disappointed that you did not inform me of your intention to send an eviction notice.' Kevin displayed both palms as a gesture of submission. 'I am also furious that you agreed to *me* refurbishing the apartment last year. You were aware of my intention to spend thousands of pounds – and I believe you were also aware of *your* intention to evict me in the near future.'

Kevin clenched his fists. 'Mrs Agu, please remember that you consented to a comprehensive background check when you asked to rent from me. We both know that your outlay on the refurbishment was well within your means.'

'My ability to fund—'

'The matter is now closed.' Kevin turned and walked briskly out of Anah's apartment.

Anah's face and neck flushed with indignation. For more than twenty years, she had trudged the corridors of Westminster as a senior executive officer in policy delivery for Her Majesty's Civil Service. Never in her professional life – and rarely in her private life – had she been spoken to in such a manner.

As an undeserved courtesy to Kevin, Anah had settled Toby in the bathroom before he arrived; her landlord had made known his antipathy to cats on several occasions previously. She marched to the bathroom to liberate her cherished moggy, still incensed by Kevin's conduct.

Toby, baffled that his captor was now his rescuer, darted past Anah the instant there was an escape route the width of his skull.

❖ ❖ ❖

As Kevin snatched open the door of his Audi, Sean careered across the courtyard from the storeroom. 'It had better not be about these sodding evictions,' his father shouted.

'Whoa! Where did that come from?' Sean asked.

'I've just had an earful from Anal Annie upstairs. I don't need the same from you.'

'Anal?'

'Uptight – I wasn't referring to any sexual predilection. Although a proficient sphincter-loosening might relieve some of her stress.'

'She's being turned out of her home. Of course she's stressed.'

'Perhaps you and the Paki could give her some tips on buggery.'

'I take it the meeting didn't go well. You still want us out by the first of August?'

Kevin ignored his question. 'You're not even discreet any more.'

'Two months is very little notice to find a new home and move in.'

'One of my staff said he saw you both at a bowling alley last week.'

'I don't suppose Edna and Alan are in good health. These are vulnerable people,' Sean persevered.

'Don't deny it. He said he'd spoken to you. You were eating cheeseburger and chips.'

'How long would it take you to print out new eviction notices that give us a bit more time?'

'Just the two of you,' Kevin fumed. 'Not a group of lads on a night out. No girls.'

'Delaying the sale for a couple of months isn't going to make any difference to you. It just means you'll get an extra couple of months' rent out of us.'

'You don't give a shit how your debauched lifestyle reflects on me.'

'These guys have been good tenants. Couldn't you just do it because it's the right thing to do ... the decent thing to do.'

'Lessons on probity from a sodomite!' Kevin shouted as he climbed into the Audi.

Sean sighed and walked back to the storeroom.

❖❖❖

Stunned by the conversation she had just overheard, Anah extinguished her cigarette and watched Kevin drive out of Pendrick Court. The contempt he had expressed for her, his son and Ishaan was sickening. How could such an astute, articulate man be so abhorrent?

A further shockwave pulsed through Anah's body when it hit her that she had failed. The evictions were going ahead.

CHAPTER FIFTEEN

TWO o'clock in the afternoon was no time to be drinking, Alan thought, as he took small mouthfuls of whiskey from a smoked-glass tumbler. He'd seen Kevin go through the entrance door to Apartments 1 and 2, and leave soon afterwards. Had Anah's argument been concise and compelling, or had Mr Douglas simply been unwilling to listen and unwavering in his intentions? A solitary lump of ice clinked against the glass as Alan drained the last dribble of liquor.

If Anah had been unsuccessful, he could ask someone to help him trawl the online classified advertisements for accommodation in the area. He'd be sure to find a landlord that didn't use an agency. He could avoid the usual credit checks again by paying six months' – no, a year's – rent in advance. A story about relocating back to the UK and waiting for the proceeds of a house sale in France would be feasible, particularly if he waved a year's rent under the landlord's nose.

Alan couldn't be bothered to replenish the ice, so he just sloshed another invigorating measure of Jameson

Irish Whiskey into his tumbler. The alcohol began to disperse the fog that had been blurring his deliberations. If Anah had been unsuccessful, it was just a hiccup, a stumble at the first hurdle. Edna was right: Mr Douglas had to sell to a landlord.

If subtlety didn't work, then pressure would have to be applied.

❖❖❖

Ishaan was sitting on a stack of empty pallets in the storeroom eating a second Snickers bar and watching Sean load his van. 'Your father is cruel and poisonous. You should just cut yourself free. I don't know why you put up with his abuse,' he said.

'I'm used to it,' replied Sean. 'It doesn't bother me any more – though I was angry when he referred to you as a "Paki".'

'Why didn't you put him right?'

'He doesn't care about your actual ethnicity. He was trying to be offensive.'

'He succeeded. Mr White British needs to look in a mirror. He's not white – he's the living image of my mother's tikka masala.'

Sean sniggered and stopped work for a moment. 'The staff are always taking the piss out of his face. I've heard him compared to buffalo wings, dried apricot and sweet-potato fries, but it's the first time I've heard tikka masala.'

'I am serious about you breaking away from him.'

'That's not going to happen. Not right now, anyway.'

Ishaan jumped off the pallets. 'Nothing's going to change. You're holding out for something that's never going to happen.'

'I know.'

❖ ❖ ❖

'Robert, why don't you sit down? You're working yourself up into a frenzy, marching up and down like this.'

Robert spun around on the carpet and jabbed an index finger in Susan's direction. 'Where are we going to find a place like this? We'd have to pack up everything and pay to have it moved.'

'I understand, Robert. You're right, of course.'

'And we'll have to fork out a deposit before we get ours back from Kevin Bloody Douglas. I am not moving.'

'I've read several articles in the newspaper about how rental deposits will be capped and letting fees banned from next month. That's got to be good for us.'

'It would be if we were moving, but we're not.'

'Anah might buy us some time, Robert. But we have to prepare ourselves—'

'For what?'

'For the possibility that Kevin doesn't sell to a landlord. And if that happens, well, we'll—'

'Then he needs to know that selling to a landlord is his only option.'

❖❖❖

Having spent the morning and much of the afternoon at the local council offices, Megan returned to Pendrick Court. She was bursting to discover whether Anah had succeeded in getting the evictions reversed and to share the information she'd obtained.

She decided to change into something more formal and pay Anah a visit. Opting for some nostalgic athleisure wear, she left Apartment 8 and headed for Apartment 2 in an ink-blue velour tracksuit.

She received a warm reception and was soon chewing on cranberry and pecan flapjacks in Anah's sitting room. They shared the news that Kevin would neither retract nor extend the notice period over mugs of hot chocolate. Megan was obviously disappointed and used a few expletives to describe Kevin's shortcomings, but she also showed genuine appreciation for Anah's endeavours.

Then Megan proudly produced a sheet of lined paper on which she'd written notes during her meeting with the housing options team at the council. 'They were really helpful. They said that if we don't leave on the first of August, Kevin will have to apply to the court for an accelerated possession order. If we don't challenge the application within two weeks, a judge will issue a possession order stating we must leave within a further two weeks.'

'Which would give us an extra month's grace,' Anah said, not a little surprised at Megan's resourcefulness.

'If we ignore the possession order,' Megan continued, 'Kevin has to go back to court and obtain a warrant of possession to arrange for a bailiff to evict us. Then we'd have to leave.'

'Well done, Megan. Sterling research.'

'They did say that Kevin would be entitled to deduct any court costs from our deposits. And we still have to pay rent until the day we leave.'

'But as a last resort, it could offer somebody a lifeline.'

'I did ask if they would house me and Jack if we're evicted but they said they wouldn't. The council will only house you if you're vulnerable and they don't think we are. They've got a list of what makes you vulnerable – you know, pregnant, really old, disabled, that sort of thing.'

'Again, that may be an option for one or two of us. I have to say, I find your ingenuity quite inspirational.'

Self-esteem oozed from Megan's pores.

CHAPTER SIXTEEN

SEAN was setting out a circle of plastic chairs in the storeroom when Jessica arrived. 'Sorry I'm a bit early. Am I okay to come in?' she asked.

'Yeah, of course. Thought I'd put some chairs out. Bit stupid standing around in a circle, when we could sit.'

'Have you heard from Anah?'

'No, but she didn't get anywhere with my dad.'

'Shit! Tonight's going to be fun.'

'Yeah, I'm worried Robert might literally explode.'

'I'll get my phone ready to record. An exploding pygmy could go viral.'

By six-thirty, the chairs were filled. Anah had been the final resident to arrive and wasted no time in apprising those assembled that Kevin would neither revoke the eviction notices nor extend the period of notice.

After no meagre exertion, Alan hoisted himself out of his chair and adopted an upright position in order to deliver his thoughts. 'Reasoned persuasion has failed. I now counsel coercion. Make no mistake,' he paused for dramatic effect, 'I am suggesting that we use threats and, if necessary, force to get the evictions quashed and Pendrick Court sold on to a landlord who is happy for us all to stay.'

An elated Robert jumped up. 'We're singing from the same hymn sheet,' he shouted enthusiastically. 'We've got to tell Douglas in no uncertain terms that he must make cancelling the evictions and the continuation of our tenancies a condition of sale.' Endorsement rumbled around the circle.

'He might just tell us to piss off,' said Jack.

'That's typical of you,' snapped Megan, glowering at him. 'You've always got to be negative.'

'The boy's got a point,' said Paul woefully. Jack winced at being referred to as a boy. 'What do we threaten him with?'

'We tell him he's got all of us furious and that if he doesn't write to us immediately cancelling the evictions, he's going to be sorry,' replied Megan.

All eyes turned to Anah as she stood. 'We've established that we have no legal recourse. If we deal with the matter outside the law, we have to be prepared for the consequences.' Her eyes moved around the circle, making eye contact with each resident in turn. 'Kevin Douglas is an odious, cold-hearted man who deserves no compassion from me.'

'So you're happy to operate outside the law?' asked Susan, quite staggered at Anah's attitude.

'I am,' stated Anah. 'However, I'd fully understand

if some of us were not. Anybody who is not should say so now.'

Edna raised a hand. 'I have nothing to lose, so I'm in. Those who are not can leave now with no hard feelings.'

Glances ricocheted amid the potential renegades, but each resident remained stoutly seated and loyal to the cause. There would be no deserters at Pendrick Court; the war cabinet was formed.

A frenzied brainstorming began, generating a whole raft of possible manoeuvres to act as a warning – or, if they were unheeded, retribution. Susan didn't contribute to the hysteria but cheerfully embraced the transformation of Robert's petrifying temper into passion. She was heartened by the fact that, amongst the destructive and brutal suggestions, semi-lawful proposals that might only constitute harassment were also being submitted.

'So, we're not threatening specific action,' said Paul. 'We're just telling Kevin he'll regret not meeting our demands. If he doesn't listen, we've got several options up our sleeve that will convince him.'

'I believe that's where we are,' said Anah. 'Now we need to decide who should deliver our message.'

Edna volunteered her services as spokesperson, asserting that she was not intimidated by Kevin and would relish the opportunity to give him 'a ruddy good carpeting'. Alan also offered, inferring that a combination of his physical presence and mental agility might prove intimidating. Not to be outdone in courage, stature or cunning, Robert put himself up for the assignment as well.

With trepidation, Susan rose from her chair. 'Whilst I think all three of you could accomplish the task – particularly you, Robert – I'd like to suggest an alternative strategy.' Seeing Robert's expression, she began to wring her hands. 'Sean can't make this threat but he could pass on a message from the rest of us.' She relaxed a little, as she noticed the spasm of pique lift from Robert's face.

Sean shrugged. 'That's fine by me.'

'Your dad won't know you're involved,' said Jessica. 'You can play dumb.'

'I'll tell him I have no idea what you're planning. But,' warned Sean, 'it's going to take some action, before he takes us seriously.'

'Then action he'll get,' shouted Robert, banging his fist onto the arm of his plastic chair. He banged again, hoping for a more resounding thwack that was not forthcoming. 'He'll soon find out what vengeance we can unleash.'

'Once we get started, he won't want to come to Pendrick Court and spend his afternoons on our roof,' Jessica said.

'If I could manage three flights of stairs,' added Edna, 'I'd get up there and toss him off.'

Luckily, they were distracted from that harrowing image by Sean's intervention. He would seek out his father in the morning and afterwards let them know if Kevin had refused to accept their ultimatum. If he hadn't, they would be free to dispense their justice.

It was Paul who suggested that each member of the group store the phone number of the others. Everybody except Edna had a mobile phone; she had sampled handsets from several manufacturers and tried all four mobile networks before yielding to her traumatised auditory nerves. Her refusal to persevere with a hearing aid had prompted her son to purchase an amplified corded phone for her apartment, which pretty much served its purpose.

Alan announced that while he didn't possess a smartphone, he'd learned how to receive and send messages on his antiquated dumbphone. Sean could text all the residents the next day, apart from Edna whom he would call or visit.

❖❖❖

Pendrick Court was built between 1889 and 1893 to house Pendrick's Brewery, which had ceased trading in 1975. For thirty years, left empty and unvalued, it had stood abandoned until work had begun to convert it into residences. Anah had been Kevin's first tenant back in 2008, the first person to call Pendrick Court home. Nine other residents now called it home too.

That evening, all ten of them left the storeroom optimistic that they would continue to do so.

CHAPTER SEVENTEEN
Friday, 24th May

KEVIN had transferred a heap of papers from the boardroom table to the floor to make space for a local wholesaler's brochure and his vast bowl of breakfast cereal. He was checking out the wholesaler's promotions and slurping his way through Honey Cheerios when he took a call from Sean.

Sean explained that he had been approached by a spokesperson for the residents of Pendrick Court, who had asked him to convey a message. The message was simple: cancel the eviction notices now and make the continuation of their tenancies a condition of sale, or suffer the consequences of their wrath.

Kevin flung his spoon into the bowl and milk splattered over the brochure. 'The cheeky bastards!' he shouted. 'What the hell makes them think they can scare me into jeopardising a lucrative business deal? Who do they think they are? There were less freaks in Barnum's circus than there are in Pendrick Court. The cheeky bastards!'

'I understand your annoyance, but I'm just delivering

the message.'

'Well, let me give you a message. If any one of those deluded misfits crosses me, I'll rip off their head and piss in their neck.'

'I'll be sure to pass that on.'

'Make sure that you do. And *you'd* better remember what side your bread is buttered on.' Kevin wished he'd spoken to Sean on the landline so he could have slammed down the phone.

His anger triggered the expansion of blood vessels in his face, transforming the orange tinge to an agreeable peach.

❖ ❖ ❖

It was only eight-thirty in the morning but Sean had already spent two hours in the storeroom before he had called his father, packaging and labelling goods that had been ordered online. He decided to have a breather before he took the packages to the parcel drop-off point at one of his father's stores, so he climbed the two flights of stairs to Apartment 6 and took a can of Dr Pepper Zero from the fridge.

Stepping onto his balcony, he placed his drink on the decking by his feet. He had just sent a text message to the other residents when he heard the patio door to his right slide open and Jessica appeared on her balcony. She acknowledged receipt of his text message and invited him over for a slice or two of pepperoni pizza.

Sean thanked her but said he wanted to visit Edna to give her the news.

❖ ❖ ❖

As Kevin mulled over the residents' message, he became more and more angry at their impudence. He hadn't planned on spending any time in his rooftop sanctuary that day but he rescheduled his diary to include an hour there. They needed to know that Kevin Douglas didn't run from anything.

❖ ❖ ❖

That afternoon, Jessica was back on her balcony, a slice of pizza in one hand and her phone in the other. She was catching up on her friends' social media posts, swiping the screen with a greasy finger, when Jack rode into the court after an emergency trip to buy cigarette papers. Jessica gave an involuntary yelp that caught his attention and he looked up at her expectantly.

She pointed to herself and then to him, indicating that she was coming down. As she ran down the stairs and across the courtyard, she realised she had absolutely no idea what she was going to say. 'Just wondered if I could scrounge a light,' she blurted out.

Jack rummaged in his sweatpants for a lighter, found it and held it out towards her.

'What an idiot I am,' Jessica said, her hands still

empty. 'I haven't got any cigarettes with me.'

'Do you want a rollie?' Jack asked.

'No thanks. I don't really smoke.'

'Trying to give up?'

'No. I've never actually smoked.'

Jack concentrated hard, hoping to make sense of their exchange.

'I think I was searching for a reason to speak to you,' Jessica continued, 'and I found a stupid one. I sound like a total numpty. Look, I've got an enormous box of pepperoni pizza. If you're at a loose end, would you like to share it?'

'Yeah, why not?'

❖ ❖ ❖

When Kevin arrived at Pendrick Court, the wooden doors to the ground floor were closed and locked. He parked his Audi saloon in front of them and swaggered across the courtyard and up to the roof. Custom dictated that he adjust the position of the gargoyles before making himself comfortable on the deckchair.

The day was no more than clement, but the muted sun petted his blemished skin. That, together with the hypnotic sounds of the city, soon induced sleep.

❖ ❖ ❖

'If we can't see him, he can't see us,' Jack said to Jessica. 'Maybe it's time for a warning shot.' He leaned over her balcony and looked down at Kevin's car.

'Oh my God,' Jessica said excitedly. 'You're going to let his tyres down.'

'I was actually thinking of taking a dump on his windscreen.'

Jessica subdued her laughter so as not to draw Kevin's attention. 'Let him know we mean business by doing our business on his car. I love it.'

'You think I should?'

'Who does your laundry?'

'Megan.'

'Go for it.'

Within minutes, Jack was climbing onto the bonnet of Kevin's Audi. He backed precariously towards the windscreen as he lowered his underwear and managed two vertical meaty stripes, of which he was justifiably proud.

As he headed towards his apartment to wipe his backside, Jessica came down and waited by the car. Ten minutes later, Kevin was staring at his windscreen in disbelief.

'That's absolutely disgusting,' Jessica said. 'This is all down to Edna.'

'Edna?' Kevin shouted.

'Yes. She puts out fruit for the starlings and we end up with bird shit everywhere.'

The war had begun.

CHAPTER EIGHTEEN
Saturday, 25th May

BONE-WHITE particles eddied in a shaft of light that probed Anah's kitchen and caressed a stainless-steel bowl from which Toby lapped water with a turbo-charged tongue. Anah was waiting for the promised call from a local newspaper and distracting herself by compiling a shopping list. His thirst quenched, Toby mooched out of the kitchen.

The indistinct voice of a young woman enquired through the intercom, 'Anah Agu?'

Anah pressed the entry button and invited her to the second floor. When she appeared, Anah was drawn first to a mass of tight, raisin-black, lustrous curls then to her face. Anah's eyes filled with tears and her nose prickled.

Without expression, the visitor said, 'You don't know me—'

'Of course I know you. I've been willing this moment for fifteen years. Are your parents with you?' Her breath constrained, Anah waited for a response.

'No.'

'Madison, please come in.' Anah beckoned towards the sitting room but Madison asked that they stand in the kitchen. Anah grabbed a tissue to wipe her nose. 'I'm so very pleased to see you ... to finally meet you.'

'Thank you.'

'When I retired, I moved here to be closer to you all. I've written many times asking to see you. I'd always hoped that one day—'

'Please!' interrupted Madison. 'I wanted to meet you too, but that's not the only reason I'm here.' Madison lowered her head. 'It was two days ago – Thursday.' She looked up. 'We lost Dad. He died.'

Anah tilted back her head, opened her mouth and a long, piercing screech filled the kitchen. After that, a lava-like suspension of pain and salt escaped from her eyes and nose in virtual silence. The shallow pant of her breath was the only sound. She placed a palm on each cheek then ran her splayed fingers through her hair.

Oblivious to the phone ringing on the worktop, Anah rocked. The caller was persistent, so Madison picked up the phone. 'I'm sorry, Mrs Agu isn't available right now. I'll have her call you back.' She turned it off and put it down on the work surface.

Toby cruised in out of curiosity or perhaps boredom. With feline poise, Madison crouched until her buttocks touched her heels. She rubbed Toby's chin and behind his ears and their bonding began. Toby's tail stood proud, like a vertical spar on a single-masted ship. He pushed his head into Madison's strokes, marking her with his scent until he tired of his new playmate and sailed into the sitting room.

Madison stood impassively, observing the harrowing display of Anah's reaction to Michael's death. Anah hadn't seen him since he was a teenager; where was this eruption of sorrow coming from? How was there loss after a thirty-year absence? Deny forever the loving embrace you've had every day of your life, and you've lost something – you have something to cry for. Were these simply tears of guilt? Madison's indignation prevented her from comforting Anah.

Anah cried not for her failings; those tears were exhausted long ago. She cried not for what she would miss but for what could have been, what should have been. She cried because fate had stolen the opportunity to put things right. She cried because she saw the smile on the perfect face of a child, running with outstretched arms calling 'Mummy'. She plucked a handful of tissues from the dispenser and started to clear the debris from her face.

She turned to Madison and looked at her through pink, puffy eyes. 'I'm so sorry you've lost your father. And I'm sorry for being so self-indulgent. The emotion of seeing my only grandchild for the first time was already bubbling up inside me when—'

'The shock of seeing me. The shock of Dad's death. I get it.'

'I've never met your mother. If there is anything

I can do to make this time for you and her any more bearable—'

'Mum divorced Dad years ago.'

'Sorry, I wasn't aware.'

'I know. Your Christmas card is always addressed to the three of us.'

'I got your mother's name and your address from the card announcing your birth. Does your mother live nearby?'

'No, she lives in Dorset. Dad's executor, Brian, is taking care of me until after the funeral.'

'When you'll move to Dorset?'

'Yes, unfortunately.'

'You don't like Dorset?'

'Nothing against Dorset. I don't get on well with Mum or her partner. I have a life here ... friends ... places I like to go.'

Anah persuaded Madison to go through into the sitting room and wait while she washed her face and made a pot of tea. Ten minutes passed.

Madison took a cup of tea from Anah. 'A Terry-Somebody called from the local newspaper. He said he was returning your call. I said you'd ring back.'

'Thank you. An hour ago that all seemed so important. I'll call him later.' Anah blew her nose again. She had a myriad of questions but knew that this was not the right time to ask them. They sat silently, while Anah contemplated Madison's predicament. Finally Anah said, 'It occurs to me that you have enough to bear with the death of your father. An unwelcome move to Dorset, away from your school and friends, will just add to your unhappiness.'

'That's a fair conclusion.'

'That's why – and I'm not expecting you to decide now – my home and I are at your disposal for as long as you want them.'

'You're suggesting I move in here?'

'I'm saying that if it would suit you and your mother approves, it's an option for you to consider.' Madison didn't respond. 'My tenancy here is coming to an end, but we could find somewhere suitable in the area ... if you decide to stay.'

No words, only telephone numbers, were exchanged over a second cup of tea. Before leaving, Madison agreed to think about her grandmother's offer and to speak to her mother if she decided to accept it.

CHAPTER NINETEEN

AS Alan crossed the court, a peal of laughter rang from the storeroom, drawing him in like a geek to a tech fair. 'Aladdin!' he shouted. 'And I see it's the delightful Princess Badroulbadour from the Principality of Apartment Four.'

'I've no idea what you're talking about, but I'll take it as a compliment,' giggled Jessica.

'It's good to hear you youngsters enjoying yourselves after the week we've had.'

'I was just telling Sean that Jack shat down Kevin's windscreen.'

Laughing heartily, Alan slapped a hand over his eyes and shook his head.

'I told Kevin it was the starlings,' Jessica continued. 'I do hope he used his windscreen wipers.'

'Is "shat" actually a word?' asked Sean, quaking with laughter.

'Grammatically speaking, the starlings could have "shit", "shitted" or "shat" down the windscreen,' replied Alan, relishing rather too much the opportunity for boorish discourse.

'It's hilarious.' Sean was still smiling. 'But pranks will just reinforce Dad's opinion of us. If we want his attention, we need to attack what he cares about.'

'What does he care about?' asked Jessica.

'His business and his image.'

'Well, Anah is contacting the local newspaper,' Jessica said enthusiastically. 'If she can persuade them to run a story about the evictions, it'll be on the paper's website. I'll share a link on all the social media sites.' With great tenacity and finesse, Jessica explained the concept of social media to Alan and how she might use it to share information about the evictions.

Alan was fascinated, if not a little dazed, by the possibilities. He began deliberating over ways he could damage Kevin's business using lower-tech methods. 'I propose that I reconnoitre one of his stores, perhaps the one below his apartment, to establish the areas outside the peripheral vision of the CCTV cameras.'

'Find the blind spots,' clarified Sean.

'Exactly! The blind spots where a dead rat could be planted. Kevin's selling food, so the Food Standards Agency would be interested. The local press—'

'If I can just interrupt.' said Jessica. 'Unless you happen to be a collector of dead rats, isn't there a flaw in your plan?'

Alan thundered, 'O ye of little faith! You don't live seventy extraordinary years without making a few shady connections, contacts who can procure the unusual without asking questions.' He tapped the side of his nose with his index finger.

Following a few seconds of stunned silence, Jessica said, 'Then we'll leave you to scout out the store and to your rat-planting. Let us know how you get on.'

Alan walked away, not nimbly but with at least enough vigour to make his movements look less painful than usual. Sean and Jessica were left speculating about the cost of dead rats in the criminal underworld and whether he would wear fatigues or a trench coat and beret for his reconnaissance mission.

❖❖❖

Surrendering to a burst of adrenaline, Edna tore down the flight of stairs and across the court with squirrel-like agility, determined to reach Megan before she made it into the building. She caught Megan by surprise, and with great fervour and no shortage of breath revealed her ruse to besmirch Kevin's name by making public the evictions. She wanted to enlist Megan's help.

Elizabeth from the post office had accepted an invitation to Edna's apartment for afternoon tea the following day. While Edna entertained and pretended to be interested in local gossip, Megan was to call around unexpectedly and mention the evictions. Edna would insist the news be kept secret, pretending to fear Kevin's retribution if he thought she had discussed his private affairs. Elizabeth would not be able to resist disseminating the information at every opportunity.

'What exactly do you want me to say?' asked Megan.

'Well, dear, you could be visiting me to find out how I was coping with impending homelessness.'

'Yeah, okay. What time should I come up?'

'Three-thirty on the dot. Press the intercom and I'll let you in.'

'I'll see you at three-thirty tomorrow.'

As Megan turned to leave, Edna said in hushed tones, 'I was going to ask your friend Jessica for help. But she comes across as a bit of a ... you know ... a bit of a giddy goat.'

'Jessica's most certainly not a friend of mine – though she does look a bit like a goat.'

'Oh, I am sorry, dear. When I saw Jessica and Jack laughing on her balcony, I assumed you were all the best of pals.'

'My Jack was in *her* apartment?' Megan demanded.

'Yes, dear. Yesterday afternoon, just before he sneaked down and pooped on Kevin's car. He's a sly one, that boy.'

'He certainly is, Edna. I'll be sure to tell him when he gets home from work.' Megan flounced up two flights of stairs and hurled her bags onto the sofa.

❖ ❖ ❖

Anah was on her balcony watering the petunias. The stress of a difficult week, along with the weight of the watering can, was making her hand tremble. How did Michael die? Would Madison object to her attending his funeral? If Madison moved to Dorset, would she ever see her again? If Madison moved in, would they get along?

But despite an angst-ridden spirit, she had managed to dam the torrent of questions long enough to focus on the evictions and return the local reporter's call. An eager Terry had been confident that he could create a scandalous human-interest story from the plight of the Pendrick Court residents. He had asked Anah if she could gather the more vulnerable residents for an interview on Monday morning. Anah had agreed and arranged for him to visit at her apartment at ten o'clock. She would speak to Alan and Edna the following day.

❖ ❖ ❖

Jack breezed into Apartment 8 to see Megan on the sofa with a glass of wine and a sober countenance. She calmly asked him to take a seat. 'Don't worry. I'm not angry,' she said. 'But I need to ask you something.'

Even with his limited intuition, Jack sensed that she was struggling to keep her annoyance in check.

'If you answer me honestly,' she went on, 'whatever your answer, the subject will be closed. And I'll pop out and get us some nice fish and chips.'

'I don't know what I'm supposed to have done, but—'

'Please let me finish, Jack. Yesterday, when you were in Jessica's apartment—' Jack's face reddened '—did any part of your body touch any part of hers?'

'I can't believe—'

'Yes or no?'

'One hundred percent no.'

'LIAR!' Megan jumped up and Jack recoiled. 'Lying! That's just typical of you! This conversation is not over.'

'But—'

'You can get your own dinner and you'd better make up a bed in the spare room. You're not sleeping with me tonight.' The kitchen door slammed shut behind her as she stormed out of the sitting room.

CHAPTER TWENTY
Sunday, 26th May

SUSAN gazed skywards, studying the thick sheet of cloud. Smudges of lustre were easing through the layer but with insufficient strength to cast shadows on the courtyard. She came in from the balcony. 'Are you writing a letter, Robert?' she asked.

'No.' He didn't look up. 'I'm formulating a plan.'

'You're very good at plans, Robert.'

'I know.'

'Are you planning something to upset Kevin Douglas?'

Robert raised his head. 'I can see I'll get no peace until I've told you what I'm organising.'

'I didn't mean to disturb you. I was only showing interest. I'll go and read in my bedroom.'

'No, I'll bring you up to speed. Now, try and keep up and don't interrupt.'

He stood in the middle of the sitting room using one hand to hold his notes and the other to gesticulate. He unveiled a plot to hold a demonstration outside their landlord's home, and therefore outside one of his shops. A small group of demonstrators would hold up signs calling for the abolition of Section 21. To all intents and purposes, they would not be protesting against Kevin Douglas but against the law that empowered his actions. The signs would not mention him by name – they did not want to be accused of harassment.

When Susan was allowed to interrupt, she asked if they needed to tell the police about the demonstration. Robert assured her that it wouldn't be necessary because the protest would be static rather than a march. The intention was simply to exercise their right to peaceful protest. He planned to inform the local paper, radio and television stations, and ask Jessica to circulate some photos on social media.

Prompted by a second question from Susan, Robert explained that he hoped Paul would make the signs; if Paul could install a central heating system, a few placards shouldn't pose much of a challenge. When the signs were ready, Robert would call the troops into action.

❖ ❖ ❖

By calling through the intercom to Apartment 7 and the doorway to Apartment 5, Anah had arranged for Alan and Edna to be at her apartment before Terry arrived the next day. She had declined both Alan and Edna's offers of tea; at that moment, talking about anything other than her family would have been disrespectful to Michael.

A dispirited Toby sat on the window sill above the

kitchen sink, lulled by the gentle murmur of rain on the glass. The kitchen window looked out not on his domain but the city. Beneath him, car tyres spritzed on a glistening road and pedestrians scurried about their business with their heads down. He should have been in the courtyard, running, climbing, safeguarding his kingdom alongside the gargoyles, but he was no fool. The rain might sound soothing but it would drench him without mercy if he ventured outside.

Anah was crying, not the throbbing wail of the previous day but a steady drone of resentment. She hoped it was his death and not Michael himself that had triggered her bitterness, but she could not be certain.

The phone rang. Anah blew her nose before answering. It was Madison. She had already discussed her wish to stay at her grandmother's apartment with her mother and Brian, and both had accepted her wishes. A surge of sentiment swamped Anah and incited further tears. Madison held the phone calmly until her grandmother composed herself.

Despite Anah's reluctance, Madison insisted that Brian call Anah to establish a suitable amount for her board and lodgings. Madison was keen to bring over her belongings and move in as quickly as possible. Brian had offered to transport her and her luggage after work the following day, but he had already done so much. If it was okay with Anah, Madison would take a taxi in the morning.

❖ ❖ ❖

'Come on up, dear,' Edna shouted into her intercom. 'It's the young woman from Apartment 8,' she explained to Elizabeth. 'I can't imagine what she wants.'

Elizabeth itched with delight. 'Health or financial problems, I shouldn't wonder. Or, if we're really lucky – I mean if *she's* really *unlucky* – relationship problems.'

'Well, if it's medical advice she needs, she's come to the right place.'

'Now, you mustn't let my presence put her off, Edna. You must encourage her to open up. Sharing can be quite therapeutic. Cathartic.'

Megan, mottled with raindrops and still preoccupied with Jack's betrayal, trudged up the single flight of stairs to Apartment 5. Edna opened the door with a flourish and a self-congratulatory smile. 'Come in, dear. This is an unexpected surprise. You'll have had no way of knowing, but I have a visitor.'

Megan looked at Elizabeth and took a step back. 'If this is a bad time, Edna, I'll come back.'

'Not at all. You come and sit down.' Edna introduced her guests to each other and poured Megan a cup of tea. 'So, what brought you here today?'

'Well... I think it can wait until another time. It not being common knowledge, and all that.'

Elizabeth shuddered and experienced a very small, unashamed orgasm.

'Elizabeth and I have no secrets, do we Elizabeth?' Edna asked.

Elizabeth shook her head briskly.

'Well,' began Megan, 'I just wanted to check you were okay. What with you being made homeless and all that.' She paused dramatically. 'To be thrown onto the street with only two months' notice at your age. And with poor health.'

'Edna!' said Elizabeth. 'Say it's not true.'

'I wish I could,' replied Edna, pressing the back of her hand to her forehead. 'My head is spinning and I feel quite nauseous.'

Elizabeth stood and offered to fetch a glass of water.

'That would be good of you, dear. And please, fetch me a couple of meclizine from the cupboard above the microwave.'

'I knew that Kevin Douglas was up to something,' Elizabeth called over her shoulder as she searched the cupboard. 'I said the same to Mrs Agu, the day he sent you all a letter. But don't worry. Not a word of this will pass my lips.'

CHAPTER TWENTY-ONE
Monday, 27th May

THE clicks and squeaks of starlings percolated through Alan's bathroom window as he splashed cold water on his face. He had planned to get up earlier to examine the CCTV cameras in Kevin's shop before the reporter arrived at Pendrick Court, but instead he was running late. Another disturbed night's sleep had left him drained and straining to concentrate. He was not looking forward to the looming rendezvous with the reporter, Anah and Edna, but he wouldn't disappoint his comrades. He needed to wake himself up and confront the louring day. By nightfall, he would be fit for nothing except the vain attempt to suspend consciousness for a few hours.

❖ ❖ ❖

Despite enjoying washing his van with his new toy, Sean switched off the cordless pressure washer and approached the taxi. 'Here, let me help you with those,' he said to Madison.

'Cheers. They're going up to Apartment 2.'

It hadn't occurred to Anah that Madison would turn up quite so early. However, her timing was fortuitous because if she'd arrived during the reporter's visit it might have been awkward. Anah pressed the entry button on her intercom and held open her front door.

Madison entered the apartment clutching a cardboard box. As she looked at Anah, her head moved slightly but her expression didn't change. Aware that Madison was mourning and that they barely knew each other, Anah hadn't expected a joyous reunion, but she would have welcomed a 'hello' or an attempt at a smile. A heavily-laden Sean followed Madison into the apartment.

The landing's light-grey carpet continued into what was to be Madison's bedroom. Behind a glossy white door, splashes of pale green enriched a pink colour scheme. A double bed between two chests of drawers and a cocktail chair in the corner were reflected in the mirrored doors of a built-in wardrobe.

'It's nice,' nodded Madison.

Anah felt a warm rush of relief. She didn't know which pleased her more: Madison's endorsement of the bedroom or the fact that she had spoken. 'And there's lots of floor space for you to drop your bags and boxes until you feel like sorting them out,' she smiled. 'Have you two introduced yourselves?'

'No,' said Sean.

'Madison, this is my friend and neighbour, Sean. Sean, this is Madison, my granddaughter. I hope she'll be staying with me for a good while.'

❖ ❖ ❖

One floor up from the dismal silence in Alan's apartment, Megan was drinking a mug of tea in deliberately loud gulps and looking daggers at Jack as he ate his breakfast at the kitchen table. 'So, she saw you in the courtyard and just came over to invite you to eat pizza in her apartment?' she quizzed.

'No. She asked me for a light first but then remembered that she didn't smoke – that she'd never smoked,' Jack replied, wiping crumbs of toast from his mouth with the back of his hand.

'Do you know how stupid you sound? If you're going to make stuff up, at least make it feasible.'

'I just fancied a slice of pizza and—'

'We both know you fancied a bit more than a slice of pizza. The question is, did you get it?'

'Nothing happened.'

'Then why were you laughing?'

'Laughing? I wasn't laughing.'

'Aha!' shouted Megan, slamming down her mug. 'Finally! Proof that you're lying.' Jack looked bewildered. 'Edna's already told me that you were laughing on the balcony.'

'Sorry! Maybe one of us said something funny. I don't remember. Maybe we were laughing about me taking a dump on Kevin's car.'

'Or maybe, you were flirting, enjoying each other's company. Maybe you were engaged in some erotic food play with that pizza.'

'What?!'

'Yes. I've hit the nail on the head – I can tell by the look on your face. She probably got you to smear pizza all over her bloated, naked body.'

'You really are—'

'I just hope the tomato sauce gives her a yeast infection.'

❖❖❖

Edna was lying on her bed, panting with exertion, legs parted and forced backwards until her toes touched the sheet above her head. She had moved her morning exercise routine from the floor many months previously to avoid bruising or tearing the paper-thin skin along her spine.

Trotting into the living area and collapsing onto the decrepit sofa, she used a tepid cup of coffee to facilitate the swallowing of an antihistamine tablet. Then, tilting back her head, she pulled out each lower eyelid in turn and gently squeezed a bottle of eyedrops until a pearl of liquid fell into each eye.

With blurred vision, she checked her watch. She needed to hurry because Anah was expecting her before ten o'clock. She unscrewed the top of a bottle of indigestion liquid, took a hearty swig, then massaged soft paraffin ointment onto each shin. That would have to do for now.

❖❖❖

The fridge door banged shut with a loud thud. Alan was disgusted with himself. It wasn't even ten o'clock in the morning and already he was reaching for the wine. Alcohol for breakfast wasn't a little pick-me-up to start the day, it was shameful. He squeezed his face. He was struggling to recognise himself – was this still him? He had to trust that there was enough of him left to get through the morning with his usual gusto. He practised smiling as he stomped down the stairs.

He had only taken a few steps into the courtyard, when Edna entered it. 'Wait up, Mr Marshall,' she called.

Alan turned and gave Edna a broad, well-rehearsed smile. 'Edna,' he bellowed, 'we must walk together. And we'll have none of that Mr Marshall nonsense. It's Alan, please.'

Edna simpered and slowed her pace so Alan could keep up with her.

CHAPTER TWENTY-TWO

TERRY, in his early twenties, swept into Anah's apartment wearing a close-fitting, best-in-its-price-range blue suit. He immediately started regaling the audience in the sitting room with the high points of his eighteen months in journalism. Not only was he a talented writer but, armed with his top-drawer Indonesian camera phone, he could match – or even surpass – the work of any paparazzo. It seemed that his lack of formal qualifications gave his work its distinctive edge; training and experience were no substitute for talent.

A chair was being scraped across the kitchen floor; Madison had evidently suspended her unpacking. Anah excused herself to Alan, Edna and Terry and promised to return with a tray of lemon muffins and a pot of coffee. Terry continued delivering a detailed breakdown of his envisaged career path while she went into the kitchen.

Seated at the kitchen table, Madison appeared ill at ease so Anah asked if she would lend a hand with the refreshments. She wanted so much to hug her granddaughter, to promise her that she would be happy again, but it was too soon. She would take every opportunity to connect with her and the right time would come.

Anah passed over a large, doily-covered serving plate and suggested Madison transfer the muffins from the cooling tray, while she ground some coffee beans for the cafetière and arranged cups, sugar, milk and spoons on a tray.

'We use ... *used* instant coffee,' said Madison. 'How long does this take to brew?'

'Only four minutes,' Anah replied. 'There are some very good instant coffees on the market. Grinding beans and using my French press is just a habit.'

'Seems like a lot of faffing about.'

'When you're retired, you have time to faff.' Anah smiled. 'But if there's a brand of coffee or anything else that you enjoy, please put it on my shopping list.'

'Thanks.'

'If you carry the muffins through to the sitting room, you can meet two more of our neighbours. But if you'd rather be alone, keep a couple of those muffins back for yourself and I'll pour you a coffee.'

After a short pause, Madison picked up the serving plate and stepped back so Anah could lead the way into the sitting room. Introductions were made and Madison accepted an invitation to sit through the meeting.

'So, let's get started guys,' said Terry, standing up. 'You're being evicted. It's legal but it's unfair. So we get a photo of Pendrick Court's vulnerable tenants, tell their heart-wrenching stories, and then we launch a campaign urging the government to end "no fault" evictions by repealing Section 21 of whatever the Housing Act is.'

'Housing Act 1988,' offered Anah.

'Made a note of that. Thanks,' Terry replied. 'Alan, can we start with you? I'm looking for public service, ill-health, personal tragedies ... anything that'll endear you to the readers. Let's start with your full name and age.'

'Then brace yourself, young sir,' said Alan, shuffling forward a little. 'It's Alan Marshall and I'm seventy years old. Two years compulsory National Service in Kenya – combat operations. They wanted to commission me as an officer but I turned them down. When I returned from Africa – are you getting all this down?'

'I'm recording it on my phone.'

'Now, I wouldn't say that I *founded* the Campaign for Nuclear Disarmament, but I was certainly a driving force. I also campaigned and got the death penalty abolished in the 1960s. In the seventies—'

'So, veteran and social campaigner. Any ill-health?'

'No, remarkably fit for a chap of my age. Probably carrying a bit too much weight, but a healthy appetite's not an illness.' Alan tapped his paunch. 'Being six foot four allows me to carry it well.'

'I take it you're retired?'

'Retired! Goodness, no. I'm still bombarded with requests for a humorous address at countless dinners.'

'After-dinner speeches?'

'They're the ones. Raconteur extraordinaire — that's me.'

'Still working into your seventies. Our readers are going to love it.' Fired up, Terry leapt towards Edna with his phone at the end of his extended arm. 'Edna, can I ask your full name and your age.'

Edna recoiled from the sudden thrust of Terry's phone then leaned forward to ensure it would capture her words. 'Edna Pembleton. Eighty-two. Retired.'

'What did you do for work, Edna?'

'Oh, everything hurts, dear. I'm afraid I don't enjoy Alan's good health.'

'Would you say you were disabled?'

'I would. Some days I can barely walk, and my heart could give out at any moment. On my last legs, so to speak. You can put that in your paper.'

'And what did you do for a job before you retired?'

'I was a dinner lady ... a cook in a primary school.'

'Excellent! Employed by the council to work in schools. Do you live alone?'

'Yes, dear. I moved here after the death of my husband.'

'Widowed ... that's marvellous.' Terry swung his phone in Anah's direction. 'And Anah, what's your story?'

'Anah Agu. I'm seventy-two and a retired civil

servant. I'm pleased to say that I have no health issues.'

'And you say Madison, your granddaughter, will be staying with you?'

Without a glint of emotion, Madison spoke. 'When her son died, Anah took in his child. She hasn't even buried him yet and she's having to deal with this eviction shit.'

Terry, Alan and Edna turned to Anah. After an awkward break in the dialogue, followed by a murmur of commiserations, Anah looked at Madison and said, 'There's no need to mention that in the newspaper.'

'You should,' replied Madison. 'The more sympathy you can drum up the better.'

Anah nodded and thanked Madison for her input.

'Any dogs?' asked Terry. 'According to our research, we've a whole demographic that cares more about dogs than people.'

'Anah has a cat,' chimed Edna.

'Perhaps Anah could cuddle the cat in a group photo,' mused Terry. 'I think we should take the photos in the courtyard with you all looking anxious or sad. Whatever you're most comfortable with.'

As Alan and Edna led the way, Anah put her hand on Terry's shoulder to hold him back. She spoke softly into his ear. 'I wouldn't mention Alan's National Service.'

'Why not?' asked Terry.

'Conscription ended in 1960. Alan's seventy. Do the maths.'

CHAPTER TWENTY-THREE

TERRY and Alan threw themselves into a protracted photoshoot, each feeding off the other's mania. An exasperating session climaxed when a doubled-up Edna stared into Anah's eyes, which glittered with tears of humiliation and fatigue. Astonishingly, Toby had cooperated throughout the entire pantomime. Terry left them with the promise that the story would run in this Wednesday's paper and with the assurance that the term 'money shot' was not exclusive to pornographic films.

Having been set down in the courtyard, Toby wasn't ready to go indoors just yet. A couple more hours' guard duty alongside the gargoyles would see his obligations discharged for the day.

Edna apologised for her lack of focus during the photoshoot; she had been distracted and disturbed by news of Anah and Madison's loss. Tenderly clasping Anah's forearm, she murmured, 'I don't know what to say except that I'm sorry.' Close to tears, she patted Anah's arm and sauntered back to Apartment 5.

'Whatever one says in these circumstances will sound trite,' decreed Alan. 'However, I'm of the opinion that it's better to say something clichéd than nothing at all.' Anah smiled. 'So I offer you and all those who loved your son, my sincerest condolences.'

Anah smiled again and looked up at Toby, who was rubbing his chin against the gargoyles. The cat, satisfied that he and not Kevin Douglas now owned them, resumed watch over the court while Alan took his leave.

❖❖❖

Paul used the button on his intercom to unlock the entrance to Apartments 3 and 4 and left his own front door ajar. As he heard Robert approach, he yelled for him to walk in. Wiping his hands on a cloth, he greeted his neighbour with a ferocious handshake.

'I saw your van pull up,' said Robert. 'Hope it's not a bad time.'

'Just had time between jobs to grab a bite. If you don't mind talking while I eat—'

'No, no. You carry on.'

Robert described the intended protest and asked if Paul could make some paperboard signs to display the slogans that he read aloud. Paul said he could; saving any emergency call-outs the following evening, he would drop the placards off to Robert on Wednesday morning. An overjoyed Robert effected a fist pump and a few upper-body movements before initiating a violent handshake.

❖ ❖ ❖

Quelling the impulse to pour a glass of wine, Alan filled the kettle and made a mug of tea. As the heat warmed his cupped hands, he looked out onto the court. Anah stood alone, adjusting a triangular shawl so the point went as far down her back as possible. Robert bounced back to his apartment from the direction of Jessica's and Paul's. Sean locked up the stores and left in his white van. Paul left soon afterwards in his blue one.

Alan was debating whether to go and keep Anah company when Madison appeared. Across a distance of several feet, a few words were exchanged. Anah nodded and followed Madison back into the building. The courtyard was now void of vehicles and life.

Alan supposed that Anah's son would have been about fifty. So much living yet to do. Such a gaping hole to leave in the lives of a mother and a young daughter. Alan's mother was in her nineties; she'd had her life. He decided to forgo her usual Monday afternoon visit – he'd got a dead rat to find.

❖ ❖ ❖

Robert pranced into Apartment 1 to be greeted by a beaming Susan. 'Can I assume that your impromptu meeting with Paul was a success?' she asked.

'You can assume that it was a *roaring* success.'

'That's fantastic, Robert. Well done! I've just—'

'Paul was extremely impressed with my plan and very keen to get involved.'

'Excellent! While you were—'

'Of course, he was content to handle the labour-intensive chores and leave the strategy to me.'

'You are an exceptional strategist, Robert.'

'I am.' Robert looked askance at Susan's broad grin and reddened complexion. 'And why are you so happy?'

'Chloe called me. She's being considered for a post in London and is very optimistic that she'll get it.'

Anger splashed across Robert's face and washed away his rosy-cheeked exuberance. 'A temporary or permanent post?'

'Well, she spoke of the whole family relocating from Baltimore.'

'That's all I bloody need. The buffer of an eight-and-a-half-hour flight between us suits me just fine.'

'I often wonder if you'd be quite so caustic about Chloe if you knew how much it hurt me.'

'Here we go again. Why is it always about you? This is about the impact *your* daughter has on *my* life. Why do you always have to play the victim?'

'I know you don't like her, but she's only ever been civil to you. She never runs you down in front of me.'

'I don't want any bloody favours from *her*.' As Robert turned to leave, he gave one last jab. 'I was in a first-rate mood when I returned from Paul's apartment. Would just a little encouragement have been too much to ask?'

❖ ❖ ❖

Alan had been racking his brain, trying to work out how he could get his hands on a dead rat. Resigned to the fact that he wasn't going to find one, or any other rodent for that matter, he contemplated the availability of other pests. In a flush of inventiveness, he lunged for his book of phone numbers.

He flicked through pages of scribbled names and numbers and when he got to the end, he started again at a more leisurely pace. Here it was: Ben Hammond – mole catcher.

Alan telephoned him and a brief conversation ensued, during which Ben agreed to deliver 'the biggest bugger' from the traps that day during the following evening.

It had been a demanding but fruitful few hours. The newspaper article was in the bag and a deceased, subterranean mammal had been promised. Tomorrow Alan would check out the CCTV cameras and he would plant the mole on Wednesday.

His day's industry should not go unrewarded. He uncorked a bottle of Châteauneuf-du-Pape, grabbed a glass and made his way into the sitting room.

CHAPTER TWENTY-FOUR

JESSICA, swaddled in a woollen, magenta-coloured trench coat, bumped into Ishaan as she exited and he entered the court. He was equally well-wrapped up in a long black quilted coat. Jessica was off to work at Dino's Pizzeria; Ishaan, now in his second year of foundation training at the city's teaching hospital, had finished his shift for the day and was heading to Sean's apartment for dinner.

'I've fries and BBQ ribs in the freezer and a bag of salad in the fridge,' Sean said, as he held open the door. 'If you don't want that, we can order a takeaway.'

'Ribs would be good. Cheers!' Still wearing his coat, Ishaan dropped onto the sofa. 'I'm knackered. You?'

'Nah. But then I didn't spend two years at college and another three at university sitting on my arse. You're out of condition.'

Ishaan laughed. 'It's not my physical state that's the problem, it's the lack of rest periods. You get more breaks than the waves on Blackpool Beach.'

Ishaan produced a brown padded envelope.

'Ah! The mystery parcel.' Sean drew closer to Ishaan, anticipating the big reveal.

Earlier that day, Ishaan had called Sean and asked if he could leave a package behind the counter in any of his father's shops without anybody noticing. Twice a week, Sean took cartons of cigarettes to each location and stacked them under the cigarette gantry; while the staff was serving, he could easily slip something onto a shelf under a till. The store on St Edmund's Street would be the easiest option.

The envelope had been stamped and post-marked. The address label had been removed with care and replaced with another that displayed Kevin's name and the full address of the store on St Edmund's Street.

'It'll look as though it had been delivered in the mail,' said Ishaan. 'I've left it open in the hope that when the staff discover it, they'll look inside.'

'What's in there? I hope it's not a turd.' Sean cautiously peered inside it.

'It'll look like he's ordered it. Word will spread amongst the staff like wildfire.'

'It's ... it's a butt plug!'

'Yep.' Ishaan grinned.

'If he knows – or even thinks – that the staff have seen... Where the hell did you get a butt plug from?'

'A couple of Christmases ago, I was rifling through the top of my parents' wardrobe, trying to find what they'd bought me for Christmas—'

'You are kidding.'

'I kid you not. The ultra-conservative Doctors Prasad and Mahiya Bakshi had a butt plug in their wardrobe.'

'Did you think it was your Christmas present?'

'I'll ignore that question. When I checked yesterday, it was still there. So I lifted it.'

'What if they notice it's gone?'

'I'll never know, because they sure as hell won't ever mention it to me.'

❖ ❖ ❖

Creedence Clearwater Revival, the warm, nostalgic crackle of vinyl and the smell of cooking sausages infused Paul's apartment. A crisp current of air was moving in through an open window to the combination kitchen, living and dining room; Paul always opened a window when he grilled sausages to avoid setting off the smoke alarm.

He'd found details of a couple of art supplies' shops in the city. The one on Corporation Street would be the most suitable as it offered thirty minutes free parking in front of the shop. He made a note to buy broad-tip marker pens in assorted colours as well as paperboard. It wouldn't take long to knock out the protest placards that Robert had requested the following evening.

Paul placed his dirty dishes by the sink, closed the window and opened a bottle of Bud Light. Making himself comfortable in an armchair, he chewed over his quandary. He was due to leave the country on the twenty-fifth of July and return on the ninth of August but he'd been told to leave Pendrick Court by the first of August. Should he delay his trip to Thailand until his housing situation was secure?

Paul's life had floundered for many years, but recently it had rallied and he really thought he'd turned a corner. He was settled in the apartment, work was plentiful and profitable, and he'd met Noi. Then Kevin Douglas had come along with a ruddy great spanner in the form of an eviction notice and chucked it into the works. Since that day, Paul had become restless and irascible. He fetched another beer from the fridge.

Looking around the clean but cluttered room, he couldn't decide who he blamed more for his current predicament: Kevin or his ex-wife. The legal costs of the divorce had taken a healthy chunk of what little equity they had in their property. She'd waltzed off with her share and moved into her lover's home, while he'd had little option but to rent privately. Karma was biding its time waiting to deliver the justice she deserved – but where Kevin was concerned, karma needed a little impetus.

A parsimonious Kevin had failed to install a single CCTV camera at Pendrick Court, so what was to stop Paul forcing entry to Kevin's treasured rooftop sanctuary and wrecking the contents of the shed? The cost of a broken padlock and some smashed-up garden furniture probably wouldn't even warrant an investigation by the police but the message to Kevin would be clear: we mean business.

You couldn't gain access to the building using the trade buttons between six at night and eight in the morning. He'd get the boy at number 8 to let him in. Perhaps he'd appreciate an invitation to join in the fun.

Paul put a visit to the rooftop patio on his 'to do soon' list.

CHAPTER TWENTY-FIVE
Tuesday, 28th May

ROBERT was marching purposefully across the court towards the store where Sean was industriously parcelling Internet orders. Anah, Paul and Jack, each on their own balcony, were inhaling the day's first cigarettes. On Edna's fruit-spotted balcony, the iridescent black plumage of starlings glimmered in cloud-filtered sunlight.

Sean gave Robert permission to use the store for a residents' meeting that evening. Apart from needing volunteers for his anti-Section 21 demonstration, Robert felt the action against Kevin had become uncoordinated. He would contact the residents and call for an urgent meeting at six-thirty – that he would chair.

❖ ❖ ❖

Wearing a fedora hat and a brown raincoat, Alan went into the shop beneath Kevin's apartment. Many minutes passed as he cruised the aisles and scrutinised the elaborate network of CCTV cameras on the ceiling. His behaviour didn't go unnoticed by Kelly, the store manager, who instructed the staff to keep an eye on him.

To Alan, the trip was a success. The toilet paper and paper towels' aisle was not covered by the cameras. It was the perfect place to plant a dead animal.

❖ ❖ ❖

Sean had arranged a circle of chairs for the six-thirty gathering. Jessica had sent her apologies; she had an evening shift at the pizzeria. Megan didn't hide her delight at Jessica's absence – nor Jack his relief. Anah formally introduced Madison to the group.

Without intending to offend him, Edna offered Robert a crate to stand on when he rose to speak. He forced himself to disregard this affront and expounded the concept behind, and the practical details of, his planned protest. Susan nodded agreement, complimented him and even applauded.

The demonstration would take place on Thursday afternoon. Susan, Anah, Madison, Edna and Alan immediately confirmed that they would attend. Paul said he had jobs booked all that day, and Jack and Megan couldn't guarantee being there because their working hours might change at the last-minute.

'The placards for the protest will be with Robert soon after the end of the meeting,' Paul went on. 'I'm planning to take my bolt cutters to the padlock on the access gate to the rooftop patio. When I'm on the roof, I intend to break into the shed and vandalise the contents.'

Everyone except Susan nodded their approval. Jack agreed to let Paul into the building and jumped at the chance to assist with the destruction of Kevin's property. 'Operation Rooftop' was pencilled in for Thursday night.

Alan, still wearing the raincoat, tipped his fedora at Anah. 'This morning,' he began, 'I did a recce of the shop beneath Kevin's apartment. I located a shelf which was outside the scrutiny of the security cameras. Tomorrow, I will return and plant a dead mole on that very shelf. I shall alert a member of staff—'

'Sorry,' interrupted Jessica, 'but how is the mole supposed to have gotten onto the shelf?'

'Now that's a question I had anticipated,' replied Alan. 'Let me assure you that not only do moles have the ability to enter a building but to jump onto a shelf. I take delivery of the mole tonight.'

Edna shuffled in her seat with excitement as she urged Anah to tell the group about the local newspaper.

'A reporter visited Pendrick Court on Monday,' said Anah. 'In tomorrow's paper, he's going to expose our unfair evictions and the law that makes them legal. He wanted to put a face on some of the victims, so Edna, Alan and I volunteered to be photographed.'

'Edna's been doing her bit,' announced Megan 'She

and I deliberately let slip to the lazy-eyed busybody from the post office—'

'Could we agree to call her Elizabeth?' pleaded Susan.

'Sorry,' continued Megan. '*Elizabeth* now knows that Kevin is chucking us out of our homes. She'll tell everybody she serves at the counter.'

Edna beamed when Alan referred to her actions as 'inspired'.

'Ishaan's been creative too,' added Sean.

Ishaan had chosen not to sit in the circle, but instead to perch on top of a stack of neighbouring pallets. He looked up from his phone and flicked a hand in acknowledgment when the eyes of the group veered in his direction.

'He's given me a padded envelope addressed to my dad which I'll be secretly dropping off at the St Edmund's Street store tomorrow. It's been left open so the staff can have a nose at what he's ordered. Inside is a butt plug.'

Edna's enquiry as to whether a butt plug was designed to control diarrhoea was responded to by Alan in far greater detail than anybody other than he was comfortable with.

Robert stood and proudly summarised the scheduled action. Then he continued: 'We should regroup on Saturday morning so young Jessica can attend.'

'Sorry, but Jack and I won't be able to come,' said Megan. 'We always get asked to work on Saturdays.'

'No problem,' said Robert. 'I'll take it upon myself to update anybody unable to attend a meeting, starting with Jessica. Anyway, I need to ask her if she'll be able to take part in Thursday's protest. We'll gather again on Saturday morning at nine-thirty.'

Sean locked up the store for the night and everybody except Robert trickled back to an apartment. Robert hung around in the courtyard, his smug expression fixed, his anticipation high. Under his leadership, the residents and the action against Kevin were coming together. He ought to buy himself a clipboard. Carrying a clipboard gave a man an air of authority.

A balmy blush from a window in each apartment leached into the courtyard. The feathery strings of daytime cloud had dissolved. Tonight, instead of a store and eight separate apartments, Pendrick Court was a red-brick monolith silhouetted against the city lights. Robert made his way to Apartment 1, hoping that Susan had mustered the good sense to put the kettle on.

Just as he entered the building, a van pulled into the courtyard with signage upon it reading: *Ben Hammond – Mole Catcher*.

CHAPTER TWENTY-SIX
Wednesday, 29th May

A copy of the day's local newspaper occupied the only available space on the barrel-shaped table. Kelly had been summoned from the shop below and instructed to read the story on pages one, two, and half of page three. As she did so, Kevin marched up and down the corridor with clenched fists.

Approached for comment prior to publication, Rosalind, the local Conservative MP, had given assurances of the government's commitment to abolishing 'no fault' evictions. The newspaper called for an urgent repeal of Section 21, using the devastating effect upon the residents of Pendrick Court to highlight the risk of any delay.

'I have to say,' said Kelly, looking up from the paper, 'they've laid it on a bit thick. Landlords abusing the law and all this imbalance of power stuff.'

'Never mind all the political nonsense. Look!' said Kevin, slapping the image on page one with the back of his hand. 'They've portrayed the residents of Pendrick Court as defenceless victims of an immoral landlord.' He scrunched up the paper and threw it across the room.

'But they've been careful not to mention *your* name,' said Kelly calmly.

'No, but how long will it take for my customers to realise that I'm the one making these bastard people homeless?'

'Well,' said Kelly sheepishly, 'quite a few of them already know.'

'What?'

'A woman behind the counter at the post office is friends with Edna, the disabled woman in the photo—'

'She's not disabled! There are firefighters that don't have her level of fitness. And that bastard old gossip from the post office—'

'Mr Douglas, our customers shop with us because we're cheap and convenient. They'll make a few snide comments, but they're not principled enough to shop anywhere else.'

'Those Pendrick Court bastards!' Kevin slammed his fist down on the table. 'Sell only the reserved copies of the paper. Clear the others from the shelves and stands. Tell the customers we've sold out.'

'But hundreds of customers—'

'I'll call the other store managers and get them to do the same. I won't keep you any longer. You've got work to do.'

'Before I go, there's something I need to tell you.'

'Well, spit it out.'

'The man in the photo. He was in the shop yesterday.

I think he was checking out the sprinkler system.'

Kevin's head jerked back. 'Smearing dog shit on my windscreen is one thing. Arson's a whole new ballgame.' He pulled out a chair and sat down. After a few seconds' reflection, he pointed at Kelly. 'I'm relying on you to spot the bastard as soon as he returns and to call me straight away.'

Kelly nodded and went back to the shop, confident that she would recognise the man the moment he dared to show his face.

❖❖❖

Alan entered the shop. Dressed like a 1940s' detective in his fedora and trench coat, he stuck out like a brunette at an albino orgy. Kelly immediately called Kevin, who insisted she follow Alan around the aisles with a fire extinguisher.

This was Kelly's moment to shine. Alan was hovering furtively by the paper towels – what better place to start a fire? She grabbed a fire extinguisher from just inside the entrance door and hurried towards him, pulling out the safety tag and then the safety pin. With one shaking hand on the handle and the other holding the discharge hose, she stopped ten feet away and watched him rummage inside his brown raincoat.

The moment Alan plucked something from inside his coat, Kelly opened fire. 'This is from Mr Douglas!' she shouted. A jet of ineptly aimed white liquid swiftly covered the mole in Alan's hand, and much of his raincoat, in foam.

Kelly put the extinguisher on the floor. Alan held the foam-covered mole aloft by its tail and stared at her. In return, she squinted at the mole.

'What – what's that?' she asked.

'This, young lady, *was* my hamster. I take him wherever I go. I was checking on his welfare when you engulfed the pair of us in foam.'

'Have I killed it?'

'Very much so. Death by drowning.' Alan placed the sopping mole in his pocket. 'I'm afraid there is only so much foam that a pair of hamster lungs can take.' He could see a crowd of shoppers and staff assembling behind Kelly, a few of whom were recording the spectacle with their camera phones. Playing to his impromptu audience, Alan spoke each word loudly and clearly. 'So, my soaking was from Mr Douglas?'

'I'm sorry,' spluttered Kelly. 'I got a bit carried away. Mr Douglas told me to follow you with a fire extinguisher.'

'Because he thought I was on fire? Or because I am a tenant he is trying to evict from Pendrick Court?'

'He didn't think you were on fire—'

'Exactly! The proprietor of this shop, my landlord Mr Douglas, is trying to intimidate me by assaulting and humiliating me in public!'

'He's not trying to intimidate—'

'Look at me,' said Alan, indicating his plastered

clothing. 'Not only have I been embarrassed in front of the customers and staff of this establishment, but I have to suffer the indignity of walking home like this.'

The shop was now vibrating with unsettled customers. Someone stepped forward to berate Kelly for her shameful conduct. Alan jumped to Kelly's defence, insisting she was only carrying out Mr Douglas's orders. Turning to the phone screens pointing in his direction, he implored the spectators not to share their videos on social media for fear of escalating the violence against him and the other residents of Pendrick Court.

With cameras still recording, he hobbled out of the shop with his head down, ignoring Kelly's repeated offers of an apology and a taxi ride home.

As Alan was returning to Pendrick Court and Kelly was explaining her exploits with the fire extinguisher to Kevin, Sean was on his hands and knees behind the counter at the St Edmund's Street store. While the staff was occupied serving customers, he broke off from stocking the cigarette gantry and sneaked the brown padded envelope onto a shelf between the two tills. He would bet his month's wages that somebody would find it and look inside it before lunchtime.

CHAPTER TWENTY-SEVEN

MOST people would have walked back to Pendrick Court in less than twenty minutes; it took Alan forty-five. He slouched into the court, coated in white powder and barely lifting his feet off the tarmac. He turned his head towards the sound of exuberant laughter and saw Jessica running towards him. She was flailing her arms and stretching open her mouth almost to the point of dislocating her jaw.

A few feet from Alan, Jessica's elation fled as concern swooped in. 'Oh my God. Don't move. You need to sit down.' She ran to the store and, seconds later, Sean came running out with a plastic chair.

'Thank you,' said Alan, slumping onto it. 'I'm not confident I'd have made it up the stairs without a rest.'

Jessica told Sean that Alan would be fine in her care then turned back to the old man. 'Well, you can rest your legs and get your breath back before you tackle the stairs,' she said.

'I do hope nobody turns up. I'm going to look like a complete nincompoop sitting on a chair in the middle of the courtyard.' Alan laughed as the ache drained from his legs and his oxygen levels restored. 'So, what was all the excitement about?'

'You!' smiled Jessica. 'The article in today's paper is on the paper's website, too. Somebody's sent in a video clip of you in the shop and it's been added to the story.'

Alan watched the clip twice on Jessica's phone. The recording didn't begin until after the drenching, but viewers were left in no doubt that Kevin Douglas was responsible for this humiliating assault on an elderly tenant he was trying to evict.

'And look!' said Jessica, scrolling down the page. 'The comments go on forever. Every one of them gives Kevin a roasting.' She read some of them aloud. Several argued that Alan's request not to post footage of the incident should have been respected because his life and that of the other residents might now be in jeopardy. Some advocated boycotting Kevin's shops; others suggested involving the police.

It had been an exhausting morning, but Alan was pleased that his efforts had paid off.

'Do you think you can manage the stairs now or would you like to sit a bit longer?' asked Jessica.

'I was running on empty but I've recovered now.' Alan stood up. 'I must be coming down with something. Ordinarily, a walk to the shop and back would be no challenge at all. I'm remarkably fit for a man of my age.'

'You are. And you're a hero for what you did today.'

'Yes,' said Alan, looking down at his clothing. 'I

certainly took one for the team.'

❖❖❖

Terry had spent the last twenty minutes with the paper's editor. The response to the story on the website had been unprecedented in terms of both speed and scale. The narrative was shifting from the urgent need to repeal Section 21 to the following day's headline: *The Battle of Pendrick Court*.

While the editor called her contacts at national newspapers and in television newsrooms, Terry was tasked with obtaining statements that related to the developing story and with writing the following day's front page.

His salary package didn't include a company car but he had a moped which enabled him to get around the city. His first port of call was the scene of the crime. Unfortunately Kelly wasn't available for comment; moments after the video was posted, she had agreed to take the rest of the day off as unpaid leave. Kevin, however, not only made himself available and invited Terry up to his apartment but even offered him a chicken pasty from his fridge.

Kevin was being very careful with his words but what he did say, he repeated several times. His message was explicit: 'The evictions at Pendrick Court are legal. There is no connection between the evictions and the incident earlier today involving Alan Marshall. That was a misunderstanding and at the time he was offered an apology and a taxi ride home. We will be contacting him to offer compensation for any damage our staff may have caused.'

Realising he wasn't going to get anything more out of Kevin, Terry left a message for Gary, the outgoing constituency Labour MP, and headed for Pendrick Court. His arrival coincided with Megan's. He introduced himself and asked if she would like to comment on the evictions and the attack upon Alan.

Megan hadn't seen the video so she watched it on her mobile. 'Well, that's just typical of Kevin Douglas. Thinks he can do whatever he likes.' She lit a cigarette. 'Sorry, but this has really shaken me up. Poor Alan. He's such a lovely man. I hope Kevin Douglas gets locked up for this.'

At that point, Gary returned the call. Terry thanked Megan for her time, turned his attention to his phone and invited the former Labour MP to comment on Section 21 and the evictions at Pendrick Court. The politician's thoughts were vague but sufficiently formed for Terry to create a quote and to call the Conservative MP, Rosalind, for a response to Gary's comment.

Terry didn't need to wait for a call back; his call was transferred immediately. Rosalind claimed she always read the local paper and thanked Terry for accurately reporting her government's commitment to abolishing 'no fault' evictions. Terry reported that Gary had referred to Section 21 of the 1988 Housing Act as 'shameful'.

Rosalind laughed. 'It makes you wonder,' she said. 'If it's so shameful, why couldn't the champagne socialists with their property portfolios find the time to repeal it during thirteen years of government. Is there a spokesperson at Pendrick Court? This would make an ideal photo opportunity for me.' Terry promised to pass on Rosalind's contact details.

Alan struggled to the intercom. Despite Terry's pleading, he was too tired to go through the details of the morning's episode.

'Could I just say that you're still in shock and unavailable for comment?' Terry asked impatiently.

Alan conceded.

Terry sent a text to Anah and hurried back to his moped. He had promised the editor he would finish the story by four o'clock.

CHAPTER TWENTY-EIGHT

ANAH read the message on her phone to her grand-daughter. 'Terry from the newspaper says Rosalind, the local MP, would like us to contact her. I think I'll give her details to Robert. He seems to have elected himself chairperson of our unofficial residents' committee.'

'Do you want me to pop downstairs and see Robert?' asked Madison. 'You're in the middle of cooking.'

As Anah handed over the phone, the intercom buzzed. 'It's Kevin Douglas,' came a distorted voice.

'What can I do for you?' asked Anah.

'I've come to sort out this nonsense in the newspaper,' he said brusquely.

'Then may I suggest that you contact the newspaper and tell them you're retracting the eviction notices? You'll probably make the front page.'

'I wouldn't advise testing my patience, Mrs Agu.'

'Are you threatening me, Mr Douglas?'

'No, but I would remind you that only tenants and people listed as occupants are allowed to live in these apartments. I read of your granddaughter's unauthorised residency—'

'Then you'll have read the dreadful circumstances around her need to move in. She's a child, for goodness' sake. I'm hardly subletting.'

'Children born or adopted while you're living here are automatically added to the tenancy,' Kevin argued. 'Any other person has to be authorised by me.'

Madison waved Anah's phone, pointed downwards and left the apartment. She didn't stop at the first floor and startled Kevin as she exited the building and brushed past him. She levelled a voltage-carrying glare at him and displayed her contempt by sucking her teeth.

Kevin stood back from the intercom and looked Madison up and down. She was only a teenager, yet she held herself with the confidence of any adult. 'You must be Anah's granddaughter. I've nothing to say to you. This is between me and my tenant.'

Madison took a step forward, brushed away the glossy curls that tumbled over her face and leaned in towards him. 'Well,' she said, with an edge that he found quite unnerving, 'I've got something to say to you.'

Kevin took a step back. 'I don't know who you think you are, but I suggest you mind your own business.'

'My grandmother *is* my business. If she's breaking the terms of her contract, then evict her.'

'She already has an eviction notice.'

'I know. So you can do jackshit about me living here.'

'I'm not going to be spoken to—'

'So, disappear before I call the police and tell them you're intimidating my grandmother.'

'I'm off.' Kevin pointed his finger in Madison's face. 'But go around speaking to people like this, and one day somebody will give you a good slap.'

Madison pointed her finger in his face. 'Maybe – but they'd need to be a damn sight bigger than you.'

Kevin thundered across the courtyard towards Alan's apartment as Madison climbed the stairs and knocked on Robert and Susan's door. Susan guided her into the sitting room, where Robert jumped up from his armchair.

'I've actually come to see you, Mr Page,' said Madison smiling.

Visibly pleased at her respectful tone, Robert shook her hand. He attempted a smile that manifested itself as an almost sinister grimace. 'Is it about our demonstration tomorrow?' he asked.

'No, Mr Page, it's not. Our MP would like one of us to contact her. My grandmother said that you were better qualified to manage an MP than she was.'

'That's very kind of your grandmother to say so. If you give me the number, I'll enter it straight into my phone.'

Madison gave him the number.

Red-faced, Susan spoke to Madison: 'Robert and I were very sorry to hear about your father's death. We will speak to Anah personally, of course, but please know we are thinking about you both.'

Madison reached out and shook Susan's hand and then Robert's. 'Your kind thoughts are very much appreciated.' Then, with a dignified, fluid movement, she said her goodbyes and left.

'What a gracious young lady,' said Robert. 'If your daughter had half her qualities, a great deal of unpleasantness could have been avoided.'

Susan ignored the comment, escaping yet another lecture on the subject of Chloe.

❖ ❖ ❖

'Robert seemed pleased you'd passed on the MP's details to him,' Madison said. 'How did you get on with Kevin?'

'It's odd,' Anah replied. 'He just stopped mid-sentence. I walked over to the patio doors and saw him walking across the courtyard. He must have decided to harangue somebody else.'

❖ ❖ ❖

Alan was savouring a pre-luncheon glass of wine when Kevin buzzed his intercom. Clambering out of his armchair, he staggered to the door. He hoped it wasn't Terry back to bother him.

'Alan, it's Kevin here. I've called round to apologise for this morning's debacle. Could I just pop up and speak to you man to man?'

'The time to pop up and speak to me man to man was before you posted the eviction notices. You didn't extend me any courtesy then, so I won't be extending any to you now.'

'Look, this is all getting out of hand. That bastard newspaper is doing its best to whip the locals into a frenzy of outrage.'

'Good! These evictions and your handling of them are outrageous.'

'I've followed both the letter and the spirit of the law.'

'Then, sir, the law is an ass!' Alan cried.

'Alan, the newspaper is running a story tomorrow about this morning's incident. This time I'm going to be named. My livelihood is in jeopardy!'

'My home is in jeopardy, Mr Douglas. That is of far greater concern to me than the profitability of your shops.'

'You could call the newspaper now, tell them that you've accepted my apology for the misunderstanding and I'm paying you generous compensation. I promise, the compensation *would* be generous.'

'The only compensation I'm interested in is you calling off the evictions. If that's not on the table, I shall bid you farewell.' With that, Alan finally took off his raincoat, postponed lunch and tottered into the bedroom for a cat nap.

CHAPTER TWENTY-NINE

'*SEAN!*' hollered Kevin from the threshold of the store.

'You're allowed to come in. It is your store,' Sean said as he approached.

'I'm not straying too far from my car. The last time I was here, some dirty bastard smeared dog shit on my windscreen.'

Sean was itching to see his father's face when he found out the excrement was in fact human, but telling him might have inferred complicity. Instead, he shook his head and mumbled, 'The dirty bastard.'

'Did you see the article in the paper about the evictions?' asked Kevin. 'They put the bastard thing online too.'

'Yeah, I read it. Tomorrow's fish-and-chip wrapper.'

'Except tomorrow they're planning a complete hatchet job on me.'

Sean concealed the long ripple of schadenfreude that was flowing through him. Although he thought the humiliation of a hatchet job in a local rag wouldn't begin to restore fairness for his father's past misdeeds, a rare smidgen of justice was enough to bring a degree of delight.

'The residents did say that you'd suffer the consequences of their wrath. Looks like they were serious.'

'And did you see the video of Alan online?'

'Yeah. The locals were getting a bit carried away with their comments.'

'If the locals were gainfully employed, they wouldn't have time to post all their bastard nonsense.'

'It'll all blow over.'

Kevin looked at Sean. This laid-back attitude of his son's had always disappointed – no, infuriated – him. As a centre midfielder for the school soccer team, Sean used to distribute the ball skilfully to the wingers but never had the mettle to go into the penalty area and take a shot himself. Even as a toddler, he would share his toys, giving them away with outstretched arms and a sanctimonious smile on his pathetic dimpled face. Nothing's changed, thought Kevin. He's as inadequate now as he was then.

'These no-hopers are doing their level best to harm my business ... your future.'

Sean looked confused.

'Well,' Kevin went on, 'I've nobody else to leave it all to when I finally check out. But believe me, if I find out that you're helping these bastards, I'll rewrite my will without a moment's hesitation... Do you hear me?'

'I hear you.'

'You're twenty-one years old. It's time you grew a pair of balls ...' The father–son bonding was interrupted by the vibration of Kevin's phone, alerting him to an incoming text message. 'It's St Edmund's Street. They've re-sealed a package for me marked "private and confidential". It was delivered opened. Nobody has looked inside.' Kevin sighed and shook his head despairingly. 'Why send me a text message about that? I'm surrounded by idiots.'

❖ ❖ ❖

His car door already open, Kevin glanced up at Jessica who returned his glower with a smirk. She was idly sipping on a can of Fanta, propping herself up against the balcony railing. For her, the association between daytime and boredom had intensified. Natural light callously reminded her that she was not only alone but failing to fill her days with anything meaningful.

Much as she adored her evenings at the pizzeria with Dino, taking the job had impacted negatively on her social life. When her friends were out enjoying the city's nightlife, she was busy. But neither she nor her friends worked seven days a week and there must be periods when their leisure time clashed. She promised herself that she would make contact and meet up.

The campaign against Kevin was a welcome distraction and it was bringing together all her neighbours. Awkward nods, grunts and waves were transforming into a community that was working towards a common goal. However, Jessica was aware that the crusade against Kevin was a diversion from the bleak reality of the inevitable evictions and the need to find somewhere to live. Kevin would ride whatever reprisals came his way and he wouldn't back down.

She knew that her brother Christopher would give her money from the discretionary trust fund to move home, but she didn't want to leave. What had seemed at first to be an austere edifice, ill at ease with its surroundings, had become a citadel into which she could withdraw and feel safe from the world. Pendrick Court was home.

Jessica brushed away a tear. 'You soppy sod!' she said out loud.

❖ ❖ ❖

'Robert,' pleaded Susan, 'let's talk about something other than Chloe. You've got tomorrow's protest to think about.'

'I'm just saying she's bad news,' asserted Robert, slicing the air with his palm.

'Are we all walking down to the shop together?' Susan asked.

'No. I want to avoid the appearance of a march. I'll carry the signs and we'll meet Anah, Madison, Alan, Edna and Jessica in front of the shop at two.'

'Oh, I'm glad Jessica can join us. The more the

merrier.'

'Merry? It's not a bloody Mardi Gras parade.'

'It's just an expression—'

'A poorly chosen one.'

'And do we know if Jack and Megan can come?'

'She texted to say she'd be working. Apparently, he won't know if he has to work until this evening.'

'So there'll be seven, maybe eight of us.'

'I spoke to the guy who wrote the article in today's paper. He said he'll come down and take some photos.' Robert was poring over the placards lying on the floor. 'He's done a good job, that Paul.' He turned to Susan. 'Jessica said she'll bombard the social media platforms with photos.'

'Do you think all this will do the trick?'

'Do I think Kevin will do a U-turn on the evictions? I bloody hope so.' Robert put on his glasses and picked up his phone. 'I'm going to try calling the television station again while you make a pot of tea.'

'That's a good idea ... a pot of tea.'

'And don't be filling the kettle right up. There's only two of us.'

CHAPTER THIRTY

MADISON and Toby were sharing the sofa. Toby was half-asleep, lying on his side with his legs stretched out in front of him, while Madison responded to a deluge of condolence messages that had flooded her phone. The aroma of baking cookies and the hum of a radio broadcast drifted in from the kitchen.

Anah switched off the radio, walked through to the sitting room and balanced herself on the edge of her armchair. 'Gosh,' she said. 'The last two days have been so hectic. I feel as if I haven't had time to come up for air.'

Madison could sense Anah's anxiety. She turned off her phone and placed it on the coffee table. 'Would you like to address the elephant in the room?'

'Is now the right time for you?'

'Ask away.'

'Well, I'd like to know what caused your father's death.'

'Pancreatic cancer.'

'How long did he have cancer for?'

'We don't know. By the time it was diagnosed fourteen months ago, it had spread.'

Anah nodded. On the cusp of tears, she took a moment to compose herself. 'Was the prognosis...? Did you expect him to die so quickly?'

'We knew it would happen sooner or later.' Madison answered her grandmother's questions solemnly, without revealing a trace of unease.

'Thank you.' Anah rose slowly from the armchair. The drawbridge was down, but now wasn't the time to storm the castle. 'I appreciate you sharing that with me. I'll let you get back to your phone and I'll see to the cookies. Thank you.'

❖ ❖ ❖

Ishaan entered the ground floor store waving a sandwich he'd bought from the hospital canteen. Sean grabbed two plastic chairs.

'This cardboard packaging is pathetic,' exclaimed Ishaan.

'It's eco-friendly,' Sean laughed. 'You can compost it.'

'Just another bandwagon for the hospital to jump on. This time it's the reduction of single-use plastics. Damp cardboard soaked with fat and salad dressing, and my sandwich tastes of paper.'

Sean smiled at Ishaan's irritation. 'Stop being so dramatic. If it's that bad, I'll eat it.'

'No, I'm hungry. I'll eat it under protest. Your dad received the butt plug yet?'

'No, but the staff found it and told him there's a confidential delivery for him.'

'I'd love to see his face when he opens it.'

'You should check out the video of Alan on the newspaper's website. One of Dad's managers set off a fire extinguisher. Covered him. Dad was here this morning, frothing at the mouth. The paper's gonna run another story about Pendrick Court tomorrow.'

'The protest outside your dad's apartment is tomorrow, too.'

'And tomorrow evening, Paul and Boy Wonder will be on the roof.' Sean stretched his legs, lifting the front two chair legs off the ground. 'Did you have a good morning?'

'Not bad. I had another patient ask me where I was from.'

'What did you say?'

'I politely said that ethnically I'm Asian Indian, but my nationality is British. That usually stops the questions.'

'Annoying. I'd wanna tell them it was none of their business.'

'I've had it ever since I started school. School was a safe place though – I just had to brush off the occasional Asian joke.'

'And outside school?'

'I've had plenty of racial abuse over the years.

Nowadays, I even get anti-Muslim shit thrown at me. Sometimes it's really scary. You never know if the insults are going to become physical.'

'There's no shortage of assholes.'

'They're not usually assholes on their own. It's when there's a group of them.'

'I had problems with bullying at primary school.'

'Really?'

'Yeah. I was proper skinny.'

'I can't imagine you skinny.'

'I used to hang out with the asthmatic kids until I was thirteen. Then I filled out and got into sport.'

Ishaan smiled. 'How many asthmatic kids were there in your school?'

'You only had to cough and the local GP would diagnose asthma. More kids in my school had a Ventolin inhaler than a Buzz Lightyear.'

Ishaan scrunched up the sandwich packaging and threw it into Sean's lap. 'I'm off. I really need to sleep. Perhaps you'll compost that for me.'

❖❖❖

Megan toyed with her hair as she looked through the patio windows onto the courtyard. The sun was trying to warm the afternoon. The hefty wooden store-room doors opened onto a barren carpet of grey tarmac that no longer shimmered black with moisture.

Just as she was about to turn towards Jack she saw

Edna, fresh from the hairdresser's, scampering across the court towards her apartment.

'Looks like Edna's had a perm,' Megan said to an unresponsive Jack. 'And have you noticed how fast she moves?'

Jack was engrossed in his video game. On the verge of reaching level thirty-eight, the next few seconds of play were far more important than anything Megan had to say.

'I might as well talk to myself. I *am* talking to myself.' Megan slouched into an armchair as Jack delivered a muted yap when he hit the next level. 'I sometimes wonder why I ever let you move in with me.'

Jack put down his console. 'You didn't *let* me move in; you *asked* me to move in.' He grinned. 'You *begged* me to move in.'

'I'm not taking the bait. You're just trying to wind me up.'

'But you did invite me. You said you didn't want to be on your own.'

'I might as well be on my own. All you ever do is play them stupid games.'

'Maybe you need a hobby, too.'

'What I need is for us to do things together as a couple.'

'Like what? What do you want us to do?'

'I don't know ... go for a walk or something.'

'Walk to where?'

'Just walk around and talk.'

'We don't need to walk to talk. What do you want to talk about?'

'Just forget it.'

'Well, if you think of something you want to talk about, I'm not leaving for work until nine-thirty tonight.'

'Even if they don't ask you to work tomorrow afternoon, I don't want you going to the protest.'

'By the time I've worked a night shift, I'll be ready for my bed. I doubt I'll be up in time to make work, let alone the protest.'

'Good. You should text Robert and let him know you won't be going,' Megan ordered.

'Is this about Jessica again?'

'Yes. I don't want you anywhere near the fat tart.'

'I don't know why you keep calling her fat. She's obviously not overweight.'

'That's just typical of you, sticking up for your bit on the side.'

'Texting Robert, as we speak.' Jack picked up his phone and sent a text confirming his attendance at the demonstration.

CHAPTER THIRTY-ONE

THE last time Paul had been in Phuket, he had proudly presented Noi with a prepaid debit card that he could load with Thai baht online in England. In return for Noi's undertaking not to work in a bar, he had offered to transfer money every month. The arrangement worked well, although occasionally he had to load more cash to cover the unexpected expenses for which Noi could not budget. That evening, Noi announced that her room-mate had disappeared the day before the rent was due, and that her mother had developed a chest infection so medicine was required.

Noi seemed genuinely embarrassed to ask for additional money, so Paul transferred the requested baht. She had offered to return to work on numerous occasions but bar work was all she knew. Paul was adamant that she was not going back to the bar; he'd seen the guys that preyed on Thai bargirls, and had never met one that wasn't old, ugly or damaged. He earned good money so his girlfriend would not be subjected to the attention of the oddballs who skulked around Phuket's unsavoury dives.

As dusk fell, Noi's face on Paul's laptop was the sole source of light in his apartment. An empty bottle of Bud Light, an open packet of cigarettes and a disposable lighter prompted him to take a break from the video chat. He promised to call back in fifteen minutes, fetched another beer from the fridge and went onto the balcony for a cigarette.

The subject of marriage hadn't arisen but Paul knew it would bubble to the surface before the night was out. Noi was keen to marry, register the marriage at the British Embassy in Bangkok and apply for a UK marriage visa. Paul wasn't so keen; he was certain that he loved Noi but was sceptical about marriage and a life together in England.

On countless evenings, he'd stood on the same balcony fantasising about a life with Noi at Pendrick Court. While he was out working, she would busy herself with domestic chores. There was an Asian food store within walking distance of the apartment where she could buy all the lemon grass, fiery chillies and curry paste she would need to produce her favourite dishes. After work, they would eat her creations, then make love until they fell, sweaty and exhausted, into each other's arms and coasted into peaceful sleep.

As he had honed the illusion over time, his qualms had distorted the dream. What if she couldn't cope with the British weather or being separated from her friends and family? Would the language and cultural differences overwhelm her? Were homemaking and cooking going to satisfy her? Where would she find new friends? With a thirty-year age difference, how would she feel about him in fifteen years when he was seventy and she was only forty? And, of course, how could his fantasy play out when it involved Pendrick Court? Kevin Douglas had put more than a spanner in the works: he had come armed with an angle grinder.

Paul returned to his laptop and called Noi.

❖ ❖ ❖

Edna was admiring herself in the full-length mirror that stood in a corner of her bedroom. Her recently permed hair would be the perfect complement to tomorrow's protest outfit. At Monday's photoshoot she'd dressed for sympathy; tomorrow, she intended to look glamorous. She'd bought a heavily discounted, sage-coloured woollen coat with fake-fur trim that she could partner with a pair of high-heeled, synthetic-leather brown boots she had purchased in the January sales. Nobody would see what she was wearing underneath the coat, so she'd opt for comfort.

Craning her neck to see herself from as many angles as possible, Edna thought that she looked like a Hollywood icon from the fifties. She shuffled to another corner of the bedroom, careful not to sprain an ankle, and sat down to remove her boots. Thankfully, she'd accepted an invitation to share a taxi with Alan to the protest site; walking there in heels, even at Alan's pace, wouldn't be wise. Alan had booked the taxi for ten minutes to two. Edna decided she'd put on her boots a couple of hours before it was due so she could break them in.

Suddenly, almost upended by a tremor of inspiration, Edna ran to the sideboard in the sitting room and foraged through its cupboards and drawers. Under a tobacco tin of used postage stamps lay a greasy pair of plastic sunglasses. They weren't corrected for her vision but, after a good wash, they could only enhance her protest attire.

Edna sat down. She felt full of vim and vigour tonight. The stress of the evictions had waned and peace prevailed; Paul wasn't playing his music and Ishaan wasn't spending the night upstairs. Most importantly, she was excited about the protest. Not only would she look stunning for the cameras, she would have a chance to humiliate Kevin Douglas.

Edna checked her watch. Her son could call from Melbourne at any time. He'd promised to telephone after breakfast on Thursday morning and that meant Wednesday night for Edna. She didn't want to be in the middle of changing her clothes when the phone rang, so she used the waiting time to select her make-up for the following day.

CHAPTER THIRTY-TWO
Thursday, 30th May

KELLY had the invidious task of taking the local newspaper up to Kevin's apartment and waiting while he read the article titled, *The Battle of Pendrick Court*.

The resentment in Kevin's voice increased with every excerpt he read aloud. '... *landlord harassment ... instructed staff to assault elderly tenant ... worried about further acts of violence ... constituency MP supports the residents ... If a crime is reported, a decision will be made in accordance with Home Office guidelines about whether we carry out an investigation ...*'

'I read it before I came up. I think the comment you gave them was excellent,' said Kelly.

'My comment is the only sane paragraph in the whole hysterical bastard piece. I'm absolutely seething. If it was legal, I'd drive over there now and throw each and every one of them onto the street, then light a bonfire of their possessions in the middle of the courtyard.'

'Are we going to sell the paper today, Mr Douglas?'

'Yes. Trying to contain this story will be like pissing into the wind. I need to clear my head. I'm off to St Edmund's Street to pick up a package.'

Kevin grabbed his car keys and followed Kelly out of

his apartment.

❖ ❖ ❖

'Ta-da!' sang Susan, as she pulled the newspaper from her shopping bag. Like a child presenting the day's artwork to a parent at the school gate, she handed it to Robert. He snatched it, ignored her and began reading.

Dispirited, Susan wandered into the kitchen where she combed the cupboards, fridge and freezer for something for Robert's lunch. From the sitting room, she heard the crackling of newspaper and the chortling of a man who would sit there until a meal was served and then comment that the vegetables were overcooked or that the plates weren't warm enough.

She found a packet of pudding rice and a plastic pot containing nutmegs. She'd make Robert a rice pudding – he'd like that. She'd invite him to grate the nutmeg because she was bound to use too much or too little.

Suddenly, a raucous 'Yes!' came from the sitting room followed by cacophonous laughter. 'Susan,' yelled Robert and she ran to the doorway. 'See this! They even have a statement from the bloody police. Kevin comes across like the villain in a Victorian melodrama with a curly moustache and a top hat.'

Susan smiled. 'Well, as long as he doesn't tie me to the railway track.'

'Don't be so bloody stupid. The heroine was always a blonde beauty – and young.'

'Yes, I suppose she was. Do you fancy a rice pudding?'

'As long as we've finished eating by one-thirty and you're not too heavy-handed with the nutmeg.'

Susan shrank back into the kitchen to peel some potatoes. Her thoughts turned to Chloe. Whenever they spoke of the weather, it was always warmer in Baltimore. Today, it was probably warm enough for the children to play outside in their T-shirts. If they moved to London, Susan could visit for a weekend and take her grandchildren to the park or to a zoo ... or wherever they wanted to go.

❖ ❖ ❖

'What are you going to wear for the protest?' asked Madison.

'Oh, goodness. I hadn't given it a thought.' Anah looked up from her mobile phone. 'But I'll put a pullover on. I'd rather be too hot than too cold.'

'Have you found the story yet?'

'Yes, it's called *The Battle of Pendrick Court*. It might be free to view online, but you certainly earn the privilege by wading through all the advertisements.'

Madison was emptying the dishwasher. Without looking at Anah, she stated, 'It was a week ago today.'

Anah carefully placed her phone on the table. 'It was. How do you feel? Sorry, that's such a foolish question—'

'It's not. Obviously, I don't feel happy, but I'm not

162

sad. I ought to be sad – I want to be sad. But I just feel nothing. It's like I've been drugged.'

'Are you saying you feel numb?'

'It's like the torture is over. I'd been living on a knife-edge for so long, wondering if today was the day he was going to die.' Madison was holding a wooden spoon, staring blankly at Anah. 'Maybe I'm experiencing relief.'

'You've been through so much. Perhaps your mind and body are just taking a well-deserved rest.'

'The dying was worse than the death.'

Anah's eyes pooled with tears. For the first time she could see through the façade that had been masking her granddaughter's private despair. She stood and held out her arms. Madison blushed and slowly shook her head. 'I don't ...'

Anah widened her arms but did not advance. With the spoon still in her hand, Madison stepped forward, put her arms around Anah's waist and her head against Anah's neck. There she stood, sobbing in her grandmother's arms until her tears ran dry and her head pulsed with pain.

❖ ❖ ❖

While Jack slept off his night shift in the apartment above, Alan was in his sitting room, showered and dressed. After a night of fragmented sleep, he had hoped that he would sleep on into the morning but that hadn't happened. He had been woken by the shrill bird song performed on Edna's balcony and hadn't been able to get back to sleep. Now he sat like a popped balloon in his armchair, shattered, mulling over his troubles.

Dragging his attention from the misappropriation of his mother's funds and the menace of homelessness, Alan considered the day ahead of him. He needed to eat before the taxi arrived. There would be something in the freezer that he could put in the oven. He could sit at the kitchen table and wait while it cooked. Yes, he would do that. By ten minutes to two, he would be a new man.

CHAPTER THIRTY-THREE

AT twenty-five minutes to two, Robert and Susan marched out of Apartment 1 armed with a collection of placards. Robert led the way, dressed for business in a grey-check three-piece suit. Susan was in less formal attire – her signature burgundy anorak.

Five minutes later, Anah and Madison emerged from Apartment 2. Anah was clothed in a black, formal outfit which contrasted starkly with Madison's white skinny jeans and parka. Madison's eyes were still a little bloodshot from crying. Anah gave her granddaughter's shoulder a gentle squeeze. Madison smiled.

At a quarter to two, Jessica burst into the courtyard in a bright-pink blazer and plum-coloured trousers. Jack had been watching the entrance to Paul's and Jessica's apartments and had hurtled down two flights of stairs when Jessica appeared. He caught up with her just as she reached the archway. 'Is it okay if I walk with you,' he asked.

'Of course,' she replied.

'You're looking smart. I made an effort myself. Brand

new Adidas trainers.'

At ten minutes to two, a taxi pulled into Pendrick Court. Edna struggled out of Apartment 5, impeded not only by the heels on her boots but by her oversized sunglasses. She could just about make out the taxi and assumed the shape moving towards her was Alan.

'Edna Pembleton,' boomed Alan. 'You're a sight for sore eyes! For a moment, I thought we were being visited by the ghost of Jackie Onassis.'

'Oh, get away with you,' said Edna, giggling. 'Would you help me to the taxi, please?'

'I'd be pleased to,' replied Alan, taking her arm. 'I think we've dressed for a red-carpet premiere rather than a demonstration. Do you consider my costume a little over the top?'

Edna squinted. 'Is it a cardigan?'

'No,' said Alan. 'I'm wearing a tuxedo.'

The taxi pulled out of Pendrick Court. Eight apparently well-dressed residents were on their way to protest.

CHAPTER THIRTY-FOUR

THEY assembled outside the shop; six of them, with their heads down, were packed around Robert waiting for his instructions. Outside the scrum Jessica was preoccupied with her phone, broadcasting news of the afternoon's rally to social media and the local newspaper's website.

'Don't block the pavement. Keep as close to the kerb as you can,' commanded Robert. 'If anybody asks, we're here to draw attention to legislation that allows landlords to evict exemplary tenants with only two months' notice.'

'What sort of tenants?' asked Edna.

'Exemplary tenants ... model tenants,' he clarified. 'Now, let's get this show on the road.'

'Righty-ho,' said Edna. '*Modern* tenants. But I don't think it's safe to move onto the road.'

'*Model* tenants,' snarled Robert, distributing the placards. 'And it's the *show* that needs to get on the road, not us.'

'Exactly!' beamed Edna, taking a sign reading

End Unfair Evictions. 'Trust me, we'll be safer on the pavement, Robin.'

'It's Robert. My name is Robert. ROBERT!'

Susan moved between the pair and placed a hand on Edna's heavy, sage-coloured coat to guide her as far away from Robert as was practical. She installed her on the kerb, her back to the road, facing the shop, at one end of the row of protesting residents. Next in line was Alan, towering above Edna in his penguin suit. Nestled next to him were Anah and Madison, then came Jessica, Jack, Susan and finally Robert.

Standing on tiptoes, Robert stretched up towards Susan's ear. 'What the bloody hell is Alan wearing?' he asked. 'If he's come as a prat, he's won first prize.' Susan paid no heed.

An amused Jack turned to Jessica and whispered, 'Did you hear that? Robert said Alan was dressed like a prat.'

'That's rich,' replied Jessica, 'coming from somebody who looks like a page boy.'

Jack laughed. 'What's a page boy?'

'The kid at a wedding who carries the rings on a cushion.'

'He reminds me of a leprechaun I saw in a movie, except the leprechaun had red hair—'

'And was taller.'

Edna was squirming to reposition her coat, worried that its weight would compact the vertebrae in her spine. She smiled at the featureless spectres she saw through inky lenses as they wafted past her on the pavement.

Breaking ranks, Jessica stepped forward and aimed her phone at the line-up. 'Could you all move closer together and make sure your sign is square with the camera, please?' She took a few snaps, chose the best and started circulating the image online.

❖❖❖

Kelly had been alerted to the demonstration outside. She hadn't spoken to Kevin since he had left for St Edmund's Street and was loathe to call him and be the bearer of bad tidings. He couldn't shoot the messenger over the phone, and she doubted that he actually possessed a gun, but she knew that somehow she would be held accountable for the protestors' actions if she notified him of their presence.

After the previous day's misadventure with the fire extinguisher, she thought that using her initiative to disband the assembly might redeem her in Mr Douglas's eyes. Seeking isolation in the staff washroom, Kelly reflected on what she might say to disperse the protestors.

Perhaps, she thought, it would be wise not to get involved. If her intervention went tits-up, she could find herself relegated to shelf filler, lose her manager's badge *and* the seventy pence an hour additional responsibility payment.

In the absence of any discernible option, she decided to call the police. She dialled 101 and expressed her concern about the throng of angry protestors besieging the shop. The contact centre advisor thanked Kelly for her call, promising to forward immediately the information to the local police.

❖ ❖ ❖

Outside, Robert was instructing passers-by to keep the pavement clear. Jack was holding his sign in one hand and Jessica's in the other, while she responded to comments on a host of websites. 'A few people have asked if they can come and join the protest,' she said. 'I said they could.'

'Shall we sing?' cheeped Susan.

'Let's bloody not,' snapped Robert.

Edna gave Alan a comradely jab with her elbow. 'Lots of people must have seen that video. They're shaking your hand and telling you how disgusted they were. You're quite the celebrity.'

'I'm told the video went viral,' said Alan.

'Right to buy!' shouted an enthusiastic bystander. 'That's the problem. More council houses are being sold than are being built. The waiting lists for a council house get longer and the stock of council houses gets smaller.'

'Thank you for your support,' replied Anah. 'Those in social housing properties enjoy greater protection from eviction than those of us in the private sector. And you're right, there's not enough social housing to go round.'

The bystander walked away, bobbing her head at the residents in a display of solidarity.

CHAPTER THIRTY-FIVE

SEVERAL car drivers had sounded their horn as they passed the protestors. Jessica had surrendered her *Ban No-fault Evictions* sign to a woman in her thirties with a mass of ineptly gathered bleached-blonde cornrows.

A grinning Christopher strolled towards the assembly wearing a grey blazer, black shirt and white clerical collar. Jessica ran over and threw her arms around his waist and he responded with a hug. She stepped back to study her brother's face. 'What's with the facial hair? Were you aiming for "vintage Wolverine"?'

'I thought it made me look more mature.' Christopher stroked his beard.

'If it's maturity you're after, you could lose the nineties' spiky hair. You've worn it like that since primary school.'

'Okay. Enough of the image appraisal. Is there room for another link in your human chain?'

'We're not holding hands. Here, come and stand next to me.' Jessica steered her brother between herself and Madison. 'Everybody, this is my brother Christopher.'

He exchanged greetings with the line of residents.

'Well, that's a relief,' said Robert to Susan. 'I thought she'd taken up with priest.'

'So,' enquired Christopher, 'is this young man your beau?'

'Beau! No, Jane Austen, he's not my *beau*. This is Jack, a friend from Pendrick Court.' Jack and Christopher shook hands.

Kelly's furtive glance at the crowd through the open door did nothing to ease her anxiety. The addition of twenty campaigners to the original line-up made for quite a conspicuous display and Terry was giving his Indonesian camera phone a workout. A handful of the website enthusiasts, lured by Jessica's posts, had turned up to take photographs, and a crew from a local TV channel was jostling for space on the pavement to film the event. When Kelly saw a van pulling up, emblazoned with the logo of a radio station, she ran back to the washroom to concentrate on her breathing.

Two Police Community Support Officers were meandering through the crowd, surveying the protestors in the hope of identifying their leader. Possession of a megaphone was a useful indicator, but nobody had one.

Robert solved their conundrum by waving and calling them over. 'This protest is a peaceful protest. It is perfectly legal and as such of no interest to the police,' he proclaimed.

'Sir,' replied a PCSO, 'our only interest is that of public safety. We're only checking that the public is safe and there's no likelihood of disorder or crime.'

'And are you satisfied that this is the case?' asked Robert.

'At the moment, it appears that your protest poses no risk to the public. Are you sure the protest will remain peaceful?'

'Absolutely!'

'And sure, for example, that nobody will interfere with the business of this shop or with access to this pavement?'

'We'll do our best to ensure that nobody does. As soon as the media have finished, we'll have the publicity we need and we'll be off.'

'Thank you, sir. We accept your assurances. We'll call back in about thirty minutes, if you're still here, to make sure everybody is cooperating with you.'

The PCSOs made a courtesy visit to an increasingly skittish Kelly to report that contact had been made with the protestors who were acting within the law. They promised to monitor the situation and gave Kelly the direct telephone number of the station where she could report any fresh concerns.

As the officers left the shop, Rosalind stretched out her hand over the sea of journalists, shoppers and curious onlookers. They parted, clearing the pavement so she could lead her entourage towards the protestors. 'I'm looking for Mr Page,' she called out.

'Over here,' shouted Robert.

'Ah! Mr Page. Please forgive the intrusion.' She

grasped Robert's hand, holding it tightly while she positioned him to make the taking of photographs easier.

'We weren't expecting—'

'Great to meet you in person, Mr Page. I won't keep you. I do need to find the gentleman from the video ... a Mr Marshall.'

'He's the chap in the dinner suit.'

'Excellent!' She grabbed a placard from one of her assistants and headed for Alan. 'Mr Marshall, I'm Rosalind, your constituency MP.' She tapped the blue oak tree logo on her sign. 'Conservative, of course.' The sign read *Standing Up for Pendrick Court* in bold, blue letters. 'I saw your video and read about your plight. I'm here to throw my support into the ring. If we could just get a few photographs of us together, that would be wonderful.'

Alan provoked a startled gasp from Rosalind when he pulled her in so close that she resembled a conjoined twin. She recovered immediately and they posed for the wall of lenses.

Edna dispensed a second shock to the MP by leaping in front of her, no mean feat considering the height of Edna's boot heels. 'I never miss a photo opportunity,' she cried, waving at the cameras.

Before she could answer any questions, Rosalind had returned her placard and was working her way through the crowd back to her parked car.

Moments later, a black Audi A4 saloon crawled

towards the shop and stopped at the kerb in front of the entrance to Kevin's apartment. The horn sounded three times.

'Well, that's illegal,' Jack stated confidently.

'What's illegal?' asked Jessica.

'It's illegal to honk your horn while stationary. I'm studying the Highway Code. I'm saving up to get some driving lessons.'

The protestors who were blocking the Audi's passage jumped out of its way. A steaming Kevin pulled into his parking space, clambered out of the car, slammed the door and glared at the signs outside his home. He muttered 'Bastards!' before entering the shop on the hunt for Kelly. A brown padded envelope swung at his side.

CHAPTER THIRTY-SIX

'KELLY. A word,' hollered Kevin, beckoning her to follow as he stamped into the storeroom. He shifted a couple of sack barrows and cast a pair of crisp boxes to the back of the store to create a little elbow room. 'Now, what the buggery bollocks is going on in front of my shop?'

Kelly thought about Kevin's enquiry. Obviously he had seen the demonstration, so pointing out that it was a protest would probably excite a sarcastic response. Perhaps it was a trick question; if so, a wrong answer would almost certainly lay the blame for the carry on at her feet. She needed to tell him what he wanted to hear.

'Well?' demanded Kevin.

'I called the police on them Pendrick Court bastards,' asserted Kelly. 'I said they were blocking the pavement outside, which was affecting our business. I said they chose this location to harass you—'

'Did they say how long it'd take to get here?'

'Well, I'm furious. They've come and gone. Two

PCSOs came and said the protesters weren't breaking the law.'

'They did nothing?'

'I told them you weren't going to be happy. I demanded a direct telephone number. Here.' Kelly handed it over. 'I thought you'd have something to say about it. I didn't think you'd want me to ignore the situation. You don't think I overreacted, do you?'

'No,' replied Kevin, looking at the telephone number. 'Not on this occasion. Before I go outside and deal with them, what do you make of this?' He pulled the butt plug from its packaging and displayed it on the palm of his hand. Kelly looked at it, then at Kevin, then at the butt plug again. 'It arrived in the mail yesterday.'

'I don't know what you want me to say,' she said, stupefied. 'It's ... very nice.'

'What do you mean it's very nice? What is it?'

Kelly lowered her voice. 'I'm pretty sure it's a sex toy.'

Kevin inched closer to Kelly. 'You mean a *dildo*?'

'Not quite. It's designed for your bum ... it plugs your bum ... it's a butt plug.'

Kevin was shaking, grinding his teeth, apoplectic with rage. He returned the toy to its padded envelope and concealed it in an inside pocket of his jacket. 'This,' he slapped it through his suit, 'is the work of the bastard tenants swarming outside my shop. Not content with trying to wreck my business, they want to strip away my dignity too. No doubt all the staff at St Edmund's

Street now think I'm a sexual deviant.' He wasn't too far off the mark; word had spread like head lice in a school playground. 'Unfortunately for them, they've met their match.'

He swept through the entrance door onto the pavement and gave the residents in the midst of the protestors a death stare. The line-up resembled the curtain call of a pantomime and yet these unassuming clowns were giving him quite a headache.

He stood in front of the ringleaders. Aware of the cameras aimed at him, he tried to remain composed. 'You are here today under the pretence of campaigning against legislation, but you chose this location with the sole purpose of intimidating me. I will not take this sitting down. I will be discussing this harassment with the police.'

'Your name doesn't appear on any of our signs,' Robert said. 'Access and egress have at all times been possible from your shop. We are simply exercising our right to peaceful protest.'

'And while I'm on the subject of harassment,' continued Kevin, 'your pathetic attempt to humiliate me by sending that depraved sex aid through the post—'

'I bet you won't be taking that sitting down,' chuckled Edna.

Kevin bounded towards Edna and pointed his finger inches from her chest. 'You disgusting—'

'Oi!' shrieked Edna, as she stepped backwards off

the kerb. Losing her balance, she stumbled and landed flat on the road. Jack leapt in front of her sprawled body and waved manically at an oncoming bus. The driver slammed on his brakes. Certain the bus wouldn't stop in time, Jack jumped back onto the pavement and tumbled into the crowd.

Camera lenses focused on Edna's motionless frame. The bus came to a standstill two feet from her head. The bus driver scrambled out of his cab and knelt beside the body.

Madison was already speaking to the ambulance service control room. 'A man tried to push her under a moving bus. The driver managed to stop but the woman hit the ground hard. The driver's with her now. I'll hand you over.' Madison passed her phone to the driver and turned to Kevin. 'For your sake, I hope she's alive.'

'I didn't touch her,' Kevin protested. 'I didn't touch her,' he repeated to the growing number of onlookers. 'She was goading me. I approached her and she moved away. She tripped in those ridiculous heels. Just look at them.'

'Save it for the judge,' spat Madison.

Edna's body lay, well dressed but limp, blocking a lane of traffic. Alerted by a CCTV operator from the city's control room, police officers were heading to the scene to manage the tailback. Crime scene investigators were on their way, having been contacted by the ambulance service operator. An ambulance, siren screaming and blue lights blazing, was racing from the opposite direction in which the bus had been travelling.

Kelly bustled through the rabble towards Kevin, who was surrounded by a pack of baying onlookers. She took him by the arm and led him to the entrance of his apartment. 'You'd best wait in here, Mr Douglas. If the police want to speak to you, they'll know where to find you.'

CHAPTER THIRTY-SEVEN

AFTER a routine examination, a breathing but un-responsive Edna was transferred by ambulance to hospital. Traffic resumed its usual flow. Police officers took statements, names and contact details from witnesses. Ensconced in his apartment, Kevin telephoned a criminal defence lawyer and endured a disheartening conversation.

After Anah had provided Edna's name and address to the paramedics, she took a taxi to the hospital in case she could be of use to the staff or to Edna. Outside Kevin's shop, there was much posting and sharing of sensational photos and videos and much speculation about the extent of her injuries – and Kevin's eventual sentence for attempted murder.

Terry was ecstatic. He'd been perfectly positioned to capture not only Kevin's arm thrusting towards Edna's chest, but also Edna in mid-flight. Tomorrow morning's story might not be enough to win him the Young Journalist of the Year award, but it had to be worth an upgrade from a moped to a company car.

Robert collected the placards, split them into two bundles and passed one to Susan. 'Right, we're done here. We can head home,' he said. 'Why don't you ask Madison if she'd like to walk back with us?'

'Can do,' replied Susan.

'You seem very gloomy. You should be delighted with the way this protest has turned out. Lots of support. Countless cameras – and another nail in Kevin's coffin.'

Susan hesitated. 'You organised the protest well, Robert, but Edna might be fighting for her life and Kevin might go to prison. Doesn't that cast a shadow over the afternoon?'

'By now Edna Pembleton will have self-diagnosed and be driving the emergency department staff crazy telling them exactly how they should be treating her.'

'I know you're being facetious, but I actually hope you're right.'

'And as for Kevin Douglas, I wouldn't lose a minute's sleep if he faced a firing squad.'

'Oh, Robert. This whole situation is spiralling out of control.'

'Don't be so bloody dramatic. Now go and see if Madison wants to join us.'

Madison thanked Susan for her offer but she'd already accepted a ride home with Alan in a taxi. A spry Robert and a fretful Susan set off for their apartment with the placards in their arms. Jessica said her goodbyes to Christopher before she and Jack left together.

Jack and Jessica walked side by side, he with a hand-rolled cigarette in his mouth, she with several peanut M&Ms in hers.

'Your brother seems nice,' said Jack. 'He's the first vicar I've seen without grey hair and wrinkles.'

Jessica smiled. 'Well, he'll probably have them one day. He's only twenty-nine.'

'I was a bit worried he was gonna talk about Jesus. Are you into all that church stuff?'

'I was baptised so I say I'm Church of England, but it doesn't mean anything to me.'

'You believe in God?'

'No. But I'm not going to argue about it. People can believe what they want to believe.'

'How long's he been a vicar?'

'He's actually a deacon – a vicar in training. He qualifies in August. After that, he's the real deal and can give out the wine and wafers.'

Jack stopped in his tracks then dug into his jogging bottoms and rooted around for his vibrating phone. Jessica waited while he read a text message.

'Paul wants me to let him in at nine-thirty tonight,' Jack told her.

'Ah. Operation Rooftop. I'm sure you'll enjoy it.'

When Jessica suggested that they stop at Dino's Pizzeria and collect a pizza to share, Jack checked the time on his phone to calculate whether he could eat and return to his apartment before Megan finished work. Deciding that he could, he accepted the offer. He and

Jessica negotiated toppings; the absence of anchovies was a must but, as a consequence of living with Megan, compromise and even capitulation came easily.

❖❖❖

Madison was unpacking the last of her possessions when Anah called from the emergency department with good news. To Edna's disappointment, she had only been winded. Although lumbar X-rays had been taken, they were more to appease her than to investigate damage. Anah said that as soon as the nurse had convinced Edna that organ failure was not imminent and she didn't need to be transferred to the intensive treatment unit, Anah would bring her home to Pendrick Court.

Madison agreed to tell the other residents about Edna's recovery and to feed Toby. Before filling his bowl, Madison treated him to a gentle neck massage. Then, keeping her distance, she knelt on the floor, fascinated to observe his pink tongue lick, lap and flick the claggy food into his mouth.

Rather than call or text, Madison thought she'd deliver the message to the residents in person. She pulled on her parka and skipped down the flight of stairs to the first floor.

CHAPTER THIRTY-EIGHT

'THANK you so much for sharing the news,' said Susan. 'You don't know how relieved I am to hear that Edna's fine.'

Robert grunted. 'There never was any good reason for her to go to hospital in the first place. Apart from wasting NHS resources, she took medical staff away from those who actually needed them. Entirely selfish if you ask me.'

With her back to Robert, Susan mouthed, 'Ignore him.'

Madison walked down to the courtyard. Paul's van wasn't there so she decided to text him after her visits in case he'd seen the afternoon's fracas online. She saw Sean's white van through the wide-open doors of the store.

'Sean!' she called. Sean came running. 'Did you hear about Edna's trip to the hospital?'

'Yeah,' he replied. 'Jessica sent me a link to a video clip. Is she okay and did Dad actually push her?'

'Edna's going to be fine. To be honest, I'm not sure

if your dad even made contact with her. I don't think anybody is. But nobody actually gave him the benefit of the doubt in a statement to the police.'

'At least she wasn't badly hurt ... or worse.'

'Manslaughter won't be on the charge sheet, but your father's not out of the woods yet.'

Sean thanked Madison for her visit before she left to buzz Jessica's intercom.

'Come on up,' shouted Jessica. She and Jack were sitting at a small table in the kitchen area. 'You can have my chair,' she continued. 'I'll stand.' She fetched an extra plate from a cupboard so Madison could share their pizza.

Jessica was unusually subdued. She supposed that Madison was Anah's messenger bringing an update from Edna's bedside, so she was preparing herself for the worst.

'I've just called round to let you know that Edna's on her way home,' said Madison.

'Thanks for bringing us the good news. I am a bit surprised though,' replied Jessica.

Madison was just as surprised to see Jack at Jessica's table. 'I must commend you on your heroic effort to stop the bus, Jack,' added Madison. 'You may have stopped Edna getting mashed on the road.'

Jack nodded and smiled, his mouth full of pizza. Madison gave the pizza a miss and walked across to Alan's apartment.

❖❖❖

Sean sat draped out of the rear of the van, his feet on the storeroom floor, looking out into the empty courtyard. His father might have been facing a prison sentence for pushing Edna in front of a bus, but all that concerned Sean was Edna's welfare and his father's business. He had rather liked the idea of running the business himself.

He reproached himself for his lack of compassion. He should have some remnants of affection for his father – they were blood. An intense surge of guilt studded his skin with goosebumps. If he hadn't made it so difficult for his father to love him, perhaps there'd be some semblance of a relationship today.

He was the one who had shunned his father; he had built the wall to keep his father out. He had been an angry nine-year-old, blaming his father for driving away his mother. By the time she had found the strength to leave, she was so screwed-up that she was in no fit state to take care of a child. Sean had been forced to stay with the man who had destroyed his family.

How could the family have remained intact? Surely the tumultuous rows after Sean's bedtime were a big enough clue. It takes two to argue, yet he had sided with his mother. He had judged without knowing the facts, and condemned his father.

In time, his mother was able to think clearly again. She divorced his father and fought for custody of their only child. Sean wanted to be with her permanently but the court felt that wasn't in his best interests. What had his father presented to the court that forced them to ignore Sean's wishes and refuse joint custody? His mother was granted limited access rights at specified times.

She travelled many miles to see her son, only to be told on many occasions that he was not well, had a friend's party to attend, didn't want to see her. The lies were endless, but persuasive enough to convince the court when his mother complained. This just reinforced the barrier between father and son.

His father repeatedly said that his ex-wife's instability worried him. Maybe she was neurotic. Was Kevin just trying to protect his son? Was Sean's revulsion towards his father unjustified?

After four years of patchy contact, his mother bought him a computer with a webcam for his thirteenth birthday. She set up a second email address for their correspondence because she suspected that Kevin would monitor their communication. She showed him how to use Skype and they agreed to abandon the regularly disrupted contact sessions in favour of technology until he was old enough to do as he pleased.

Kevin seemed delighted that the supervised contact had ended. Without his knowledge, Sean and his mother remained close via the Internet. Since moving into Pendrick Court, they had met several times – but the wall Sean had built twelve years ago between him and his father was too solid to tear down.

❖❖❖

Madison thought she'd try Alan's intercom one last time before resorting to a text message. She heard the buzz and familiar clunk of the door unlocking, entered the building and climbed the stairs.

As she approached the open door to Apartment 7, she saw Alan's tuxedo-adorned frame teetering towards the sitting room. She caught up with him just as he turned and was about to drop into an armchair. His flushed face and an open bottle of whiskey by his side suggested that he might well be inebriated.

CHAPTER THIRTY-NINE

THE twinkle from Alan's glassy eyes shimmered through the fragrance of musty clothes and burnt cooking oil which pervaded the air. He implored Madison to take a seat, waving his arm towards the sofa and suggesting she move the opened envelopes, letters and empty shoe box to free up some space.

Madison sat down and relayed her grandmother's message, for which Alan was extremely grateful. He proposed a cup of tea or coffee, adding that it was her age rather than his lack of hospitality that prevented him offering her a tot of Irish whiskey. Madison couldn't imagine Alan getting out of his chair and making a hot drink, so she said she'd had a coffee only minutes beforehand.

With a smile, she stood up and said she ought to be getting back to the apartment to wait for Anah. Alan insisted that she stay a few minutes longer so she resumed her seat while he refreshed his drink with a generous slug of Jameson.

'The circumstances,' Alan began, 'that brought you

to Pendrick Court are most lamentable and you have my sincerest condolences. But I have to say I'm pleased you are here. Everybody needs company, not least your grandmother.'

'I hope we'll be some comfort to each other,' Madison replied.

'I'm certain you will. The absence of a connection to other human beings takes its toll. In my younger days, I was pursued by many women. I sometimes wish I'd stopped running and let one of them catch me.'

Madison smiled again, not sure which was more amusing: the image of Alan sprinting from a lustful admirer or the slow, slurred speech of a man whose dignity was disappearing as fast as his whiskey.

'I nearly got hitched to an American woman,' Alan continued. 'It was the summer of sixty-nine ... New York. Ring any bells?'

'No.'

Alan raised both arms jubilantly. 'Woodstock!'

'You were at Woodstock?'

'Oh yes. And before Woodstock, the Newport Folk Festival and the Monterey Pop Festival. By the time I was back in Old Blighty at the Isle of Wight Festival, I was an old hand and a familiar face.' Alan poured another measure or two into his glass. 'It's a different world now. Sex, drugs and rock'n'roll have given way to food intolerances, veganism and Korean pop music. South Korean, that is.'

'K-pop.'

'K-pop *indeed*. Talking of festivals, you may have heard from Aladdin about the forthcoming party in the courtyard.'

'Aladdin?'

'Young Sean.'

'I always pictured Aladdin as Middle Eastern or Asian, not blond.'

'It's not his appearance. It's a long story. Anyway, Aladdin – *Sean* – is going to provide plastic tables and chairs so we tenants can gather for a party.' Alan's hand fumbled for the whiskey bottle.

'That sounds like an excellent idea. Have you fixed a date?'

'No, but you will be one of the first to know. I was hoping your grandmother might coordinate the food.'

'I'm sure she'll be pleased to help.'

As the ratio of alcohol to Alan's blood increased, he seemed oblivious to Madison's presence. He started a meandering soliloquy laced with literary references in which he considered his relationship with each of the tenants at Pendrick Court. Madison used the time to exchange texts with Paul.

When she'd finished, she made her excuses again and returned to Apartment 2, leaving a soused and maudlin Alan to slumber where he sat.

❖❖❖

With one hand on the wooden handrail and the other holding a can of Fanta, Jessica looked out onto the court. Soon after Jack had galloped back to Apartment 8, the blue van rolled in. She watched Paul unload tools and spare parts and carry them into the apartment below.

As she chewed over what she might wear that evening at the pizzeria, a black cab pulled in. Anah stepped out, paid the driver and helped Edna climb out.

'Can I take your arm, dear?' Edna asked. 'I won't make it to my apartment on my own. My extremities are tingling. It'll be the spinal injury.'

Anah extended her arm. 'You were X-rayed at the hospital, Edna. The doctor said there wasn't the slightest damage to your spine.'

'I told the doctor that I needed a magnetic resin scan. X-rays can only see the bones. You need the magnets to see if the spinal cord has snapped.'

'I'm sure your spinal cord is intact. You've just had a nasty shock.'

'Look at me, I'm all over the place. I can barely walk.'

'I don't think the boots are helping. Let's get you inside.'

❖ ❖ ❖

Like a barn owl listening for the rustle of leaves below, Robert perched on his first-floor balcony. He watched Edna reeling across the courtyard and wondered if he'd catch a glimpse of Paul heading for the entrance to

Apartments 7 and 8.

Susan came to the patio doors, holding up a mug of tea as she whispered his name. He took the mug from her and returned to his armchair.

'If no harm came to Edna,' said Susan, 'I don't suppose the police will take any further interest.'

'You can't go around pushing elderly women into moving traffic. That's got to be an offence and I hope the police pursue it.'

'Well, I don't. I think this has gone too far.'

Robert slapped his hand on the arm of his chair. 'I'm only just getting started. I want Douglas to suffer. I want him to tear up those bloody eviction notices and apologise.'

Susan slunk off to the kitchen muttering something about a Napoleon complex under her breath.

CHAPTER FORTY

AT exactly nine-thirty, training shoes and hoodie already on, Jack scrambled from the sofa to the door in response to the intercom's buzz. He hurriedly locked up the apartment and ran down the corridor to wait for his accomplice by the iron-grille gate.

Paul emerged carrying an unwieldy, canvas tool bag. He gave Jack a perfunctory nod; he seldom smiled – that was saved for those who had earned it. After all, if he smiled at everyone his smiles would have little value.

As his bag clattered to the floor, he stooped and took out a pair of bolt cutters. He positioned the padlock so as to get a clean cut through its brass body. 'When you're cutting, don't cut through the shackle or you'll bugger the jaw of your cutters.' Jack grunted to show how much he was impressed by the manoeuvre and grateful for the advice.

Paul swung open the gate on its screeching hinges and led the way up a steep staircase to an unlocked door. White light from the LED lamps in the courtyard, together with the yellowish-orange lustre from the street lights beyond, lit the paved flooring, the wooden shed and both gargoyles.

'I've never been up here,' said Jack. He walked towards the gargoyles and peered down onto the court. 'We're only on the third floor but that's a long way down.'

'It's because of the high ceilings.' Paul was inspecting the exterior of the shed. 'Keep away from the edge or Megan will be finding up next month's rent on her own.'

Jack moved over to join him. 'It's not even locked.' He opened the shed door and pulled out a deckchair and a plastic coffee table. 'There's a few cardboard boxes in here too.'

'I'm going to tear it down,' said Paul. 'It won't take many minutes to rip this apart. There's a blade in my bag for the deckchair. There's also a can of spray paint, if you wanna get creative.' He started work with a screwdriver and crowbar while Jack rifled through the boxes.

'The boxes are full of shit waiting to be smashed. Cups, an alarm clock, a flask. Just shit.' He started ripping through the red-and-white striped deckchair canvas with a Stanley knife. 'What do you think about throwing the gargoyles into the courtyard?'

'No. Keep the mess up here.'

'Okay.'

'You could turn the gargoyles inwards so they're facing the door. Be careful, though.' Paul had levered off the window and door frames and was about to start on the roof. 'I'll need a hand in a minute.'

Jack shattered some dirty coffee mugs and stamped on a plastic alarm clock, then tentatively moved one of the gargoyles on its metal spike. They moved easily and he soon had turned them both around. Next came the red spray paint. He experimented with different graffiti tags and writing any obscene words he could spell on the paving slabs.

Demolishing the shed was taking longer than Paul had predicted. He interrupted Jack's artistic efforts and, with much straining and cursing, they tore off the shed's roof and collapsed its walls. They sat on the floor for a few minutes to catch their breath and admire their work.

'I think we're done here,' said Paul. 'You can join me on my balcony for a cold beer and a cigarette, if you want.'

'Yeah. I don't wanna be around Megan right now. She's driving me crazy. She's loving the photos of me trying to stop a bus from running over Edna and she's posting comments everywhere, telling the world that she's my girlfriend. But she's savage that I went to the protest after she told me not to.'

Paul frowned. 'Why didn't she want you at the protest?'

'She didn't want me near Jessica.'

'Oh. A jealous lover. I think you've earned that beer.'

Jack grinned. He took a brand-new padlock and key

from his pocket and brandished them. 'I bought it. It's exactly the same make and size as the old one. We can lock up before we go – but Kevin's key won't fit it.'

'He'll have to cut it off. He'll be fuming even before he discovers the damage we've caused. You're full of surprises.'

Jack was more than pleased with himself. He walked a couple of paces behind Paul back to Apartment 3, careful not to say anything that might make him look stupid or uncool. Paul took two bottles of Bud Light from the fridge. As they stepped onto the balcony, he placed a glass ashtray on the railing then passed Jack a cigarette and lighter.

'Do you think Kevin's gonna cave in?' asked Jack.

'He's a funny bloke to work out. If I wanted to sell Pendrick Court, I'd sell it fully tenanted. It's not that big a deal to get rid of tenants.' Although uncertain as to exactly what he was acknowledging, Jack nodded and took a long drag from his cigarette. 'I don't know whether he's starting to break or we're just making the situation worse.'

'How could we make the situation worse if we're getting chucked out anyway?' Jack asked.

'He could delay the return of our deposits from the scheme that holds them. He only has to claim the deductions for damage are greater than our deposit.'

'Then we'd ask the scheme to sort it out.'

'Even if Kevin agreed to use the scheme's dispute resolution service, it would take weeks to get the money back. If he doesn't agree to use it, we'd have to take court action.'

'That's not fair.'

'Life rarely is. Justice is all smoke and mirrors, Jack. The system is designed to favour the interests of the rich – or at least of the well-educated with good jobs.'

'Then the system needs to change.'

'It can't because the system is maintained by six hundred and fifty of those it's designed to favour.'

'Six hundred and fifty?'

'MPs. Anyway,' said Paul, changing the subject, 'does Megan have cause to be jealous? Are you—?'

'No!' Jack shuffled sheepishly. 'It's not like that. We're just neighbours. Maybe friends.'

Paul smiled.

CHAPTER FORTY-ONE
Friday, 31st May

WHILE the starlings were devouring a plate of defrosted mixed berries on her balcony, Edna was enjoying the undivided attention of two policewomen who were sitting on her leather sofa. The overloaded coffee table had been moved into the kitchen area, clearing a space for Edna to re-enact the events of the previous afternoon. Questions were asked and information exchanged until the officers felt Edna's usefulness had been exhausted.

It was a glorious morning. Spears of sunlight from a molten-gold sun toasted the tarmac at Pendrick Court. The windows in all the apartments except Alan's were thrown wide to let in air from spring's last day.

Jessica hadn't seen the squad car arrive so she had no idea who the police were here to see. She was waiting patiently on her balcony to find out when the two policewomen left the ground-floor entrance to Edna's and Sean's apartments and returned to their vehicle.

Certain they must be visiting Edna, Jessica pulled on a pair of sandals and ran down two flights of stairs. Rather than speak to Edna through the intercom, she let herself into the building using the trade button, climbed the staircase to the first floor and knocked loudly.

'I thought I heard someone,' said Edna, opening her door. She seated Jessica on the dilapidated sofa, then started preparing a pot of tea. 'The police were here asking me about yesterday.'

Jessica shouted in the direction of the kitchen area, 'Really? I came to ask how you were but I'd be very interested to hear what the police had to say.'

Edna walked through with two mugs. 'I said, the police were here this morning. Asking me about Kevin, they were.'

'I actually came to ask how you were. But do tell me about the police.'

'Lovely girls, they were. I'll tell you all about it. But first I need to find some omeprazole.' Edna knelt and sifted through the pharmacy on the coffee table. 'They're in a packet not a bottle.'

Jessica took that as an instruction to help and started checking any packet she could see. 'What's it for?'

'You take omeprazole to reduce acid, dear. According to my medical encyclopaedia, I should really be taking antibiotics as well. I woke up this morning with a peptic ulcer.'

Jessica looked quite shocked. 'Oh, Edna. My father had a peptic ulcer before he died.'

'I'm sorry to hear you've lost your father, dear. You and poor Madison. What did he die of?'

'Sudden and serious gastro-intestinal bleeding. You really should speak to your GP.'

'Here they are,' beamed Edna, popping one tablet from the blister pack and swallowing it with a mouthful of tea. 'Now, about those girls.' She described how she had played out the scene for the officers, how they'd written down her comments and asked her to sign them.

'Did Kevin actually push you?'

'Well, I made it clear to the officers that I couldn't swear to that. He came for me and I thought he was going to hurt me.'

'You don't remember any pressure from Kevin's hand?'

'That bit of the story's a bit blurry.'

'So what are they going to do about Kevin?'

'They asked me what I thought should happen to him. I said he'd ordered Alan to be attacked and he'd attacked me. I'm not a vindicative woman, but society would be safer if he was behind bars. I said I'd be happy to sign their consent form if they needed to look at my medical records.'

'Were you injured when you fell?'

'The doctors didn't want to panic me so they told me I'd be fine, but I think my spinal cord is holding on by a thread. If I lose the use of my arms or legs, they'll have egg on their face.'

'Let's hope the doctors are right.'

'I was seen by a very nice Indian doctor. He knew where I was coming from. Then he went and I had some posh white doctor, proper la-di-da he was. I asked him if it was the plum in his mouth that made him talk out of his arse.'

'Oh, Edna, you didn't.'

'I did. He just wanted to get rid of me. For what? So some hypocadillac with a grazed knee could have my bed.'

Jessica started to laugh. 'Do you think the police'll arrest Kevin?'

'They didn't say. They did say it wasn't the police who decided whether to take somebody to court. But they can give somebody a caution. He wants more than a slap on the wrist, I said. He wants locking up.'

'He's certainly got a temper. The way he launched at you.'

'I'm expecting acute stress disorder to rear its ugly head any day now. According to the encyclopaedia, I'll be getting flashbacks. Those lovely girls offered me a telephone number for Victim Support.'

'That could be useful for you to talk through your feelings.'

'I don't believe in mollycoddling folk. It's all a bit self-indulgent for my liking. No. I shall struggle on alone. I'll cope.'

'We all need a bit of support now and again. Would you like a hug?'

'Would I like a hug? I'm eighty-two years old, not in nursery school. If you want to be helpful, you could go in line and find up some photos from yesterday on your phone.'

'Of course, there's plenty to see.'

CHAPTER FORTY-TWO

MEANWHILE, in Apartment 2, Anah was filling Toby's drinking bowl. She added a couple of ice cubes to keep the water cool and placed it on the kitchen floor.

Madison walked in holding up a lambswool throw. 'I've managed to find somewhere for all my bits, but this hasn't got a home yet.'

'Are they pandas?' asked Anah.

'Yes.' Madison smiled. 'They're a bit childish, but then it is from my childhood. It used to belong on my armchair at home. I was wondering if I could put it on the sofa where I sit.'

'Of course.'

'I know it doesn't go with the décor.'

'This is a home, not a show house. I think a personal throw is a wonderful way of marking your territory and it's far preferable to the way Toby used to mark his.'

'Thank you. I don't mind if you hide it away when visitors come.'

Toby stole into the kitchen, walked up to Anah, looked at her and let out a piercing yowl.

'He's telling me he wants to go outside. Come on, young man.' Anah scooped up Toby and carried him downstairs to the courtyard, while Madison adjusted the throw over the sofa. Her phone pinged and she read the text message. She was rereading it when Anah returned.

'I've had a message from Brian. We have a date for the cremation ... Monday, the tenth of June. It's going to be a secular funeral at the crematorium.'

'I haven't asked before. I didn't want to hear that Michael had left instructions that I wasn't to be invited. But how do you feel about me going to the funeral? I will totally understand—'

'If you want to come, then come. Dad said funerals are for the bereaved, not the deceased.'

'Thank you,' Anah said. 'That is such a relief. I wasn't sure it would be appropriate for the estranged mother to attend.'

'Dad never spoke about your estrangement – he just brushed it off as the past – but why *are* you the estranged mother? What could possibly have happened that would prevent a parent and their child from speaking for thirty years?'

Anah sighed and sat in her armchair, daylight drawing her gaze through the window. As the seconds passed, her contemplation trawled through scenes from her memory, trying to establish the starting point of her passage to purgatory. Mistrust over the authenticity of her recollections caught in her throat.

'When your grandfather decided to leave me, your father chose to go with him. They were always very close. Your grandfather had been the principal caregiver and he was very good at it.'

Madison was listening carefully, expectantly, perhaps even with some excitement.

'Their leaving crushed me. I did my best to hold myself together and continued with a very demanding job.'

'You still loved your husband?'

'Yes. He was just tired of playing second fiddle to my career and deserved so much more than I gave him.'

'It was your work that came between you and grandfather?'

'I thought so at the time but it wasn't the work that was at fault, it was me. I was always chasing the next promotion, wanting to make myself indispensable. I worked such long hours. I used to tell your grandfather that I was doing it for us – for him and Michael. But I was doing it for me.'

'Did you contact Dad?'

'Yes, I called him. He was fifteen at the time. He wasn't very talkative and I became self-conscious that I was asking the same questions every time we spoke. I felt guilty that I didn't know my own son. After a few months he made excuses not to take my calls.'

'Did you ever see him after they left?'

'Your grandfather tried to help. He was a good man. He arranged to bring Michael over at Christmas but

Michael refused to come. I kept myself busy and our relationship drifted into birthday and Christmas cards.'

'You stopped calling?'

'I took to writing him long letters, acknowledging that I hadn't given him enough time when he was growing up, telling him how much I loved him and that I wanted to see him.' Anah was becoming visibly upset. 'There was never a reply.'

'So there was no incident? Nothing happened?'

'It wasn't what happened that caused the problem, it's what didn't happen. I was the adult. When we were together my priorities were wrong. The moment they left I should have gone to Michael on bended knee if I had to. But I didn't. I didn't deserve the love of a husband or a child.'

'You did the best that you could at the time. We can change the future but never the past.'

'Sometimes it's too late to change the future.' Anah averted her eyes from the window and looked at Madison. 'I'll never get a chance to be reunited with Michael, to be a good mother. But I've been given a second chance with you. I'll be a good grandmother.'

'I have a feeling you will be, too. Did you ever remarry or meet somebody special?'

'No. A few men turned my head, but I just became more deeply involved with my job. I was very successful. But the day I retired, the machine carried on perfectly well without me.'

'Dad smiled a lot but he didn't say very much. He

put up with a lot from me. I got into trouble at school. It was difficult being a pupil in a school where he taught.'

'When your grandfather was alive, he kept me up to date with your dad's progress. I knew about his degree and teacher training. Didn't he teach French and German?'

'Yes. He was Head of Modern Foreign Languages at his high school. I moved to a different school a couple of years ago where it was better for me.'

'No more getting into trouble?'

'No broken bones, just a few chancers with hurt pride.'

'You're certainly a force to be reckoned with.'

'I like to give back more than I get ... whether it's kindness or malice.'

CHAPTER FORTY-THREE

JESSICA was squinting as she re-entered the courtyard. She shielded her eyes from the sun's brilliance with her hand and waited for Jack, who was rollicking towards her waving his phone. Megan had already left for work, so he invited her to his apartment for a drink.

Once inside Apartment 8, Jack hurled two giant beanbags onto the balcony, suggesting a cold drink in the fresh air. Within minutes, they were slouching in the sun, each holding a can dripping with condensation.

Jack relived the previous evening's escapade on the roof and referred to Paul as a 'top bloke'. He marvelled at Paul's prowess, exaggerating the size of the ruptured padlock and the speed at which the shed was levelled. He catalogued his own contribution to the shenanigans in detail, leaving Jessica surprised and inspired, particularly by his idea to replace the padlock.

She took out her phone. They looked at images of the protest and the comments on social media before accessing the article on the local newspaper's website. As their laughter echoed around Pendrick Court, Jack offered Jessica another drink.

When he returned to the balcony, Jack was clutching two cans in one hand and his smoking paraphernalia in the other. More notably, he had removed his T-shirt.

❖ ❖ ❖

Downstairs, Alan had been awake for some considerable time. He'd nailed about four hours of delirium-charged sleep before being roused by his bladder screaming to be emptied. He had remained inert in his bed through the sounds of Sean opening the doors to the store, Paul's van starting and a car pulling into and out of the court. Only the howling from the couple upstairs on their balcony prompted him to stir.

He sat on the edge of his bed, his head bowed, his brow furrowed. It was here that he usually planned the day's tedious itinerary. He wanted a copy of the local newspaper, so would have to go out, which called for a shave, a shower and a clean shirt. He decided to dress before he ate. There was always the risk that, following breakfast in his bathrobe, he might not move from the kitchen table until lunchtime.

❖ ❖ ❖

Kevin answered the door and waved Kelly through to the kitchen. She didn't need to be psychic to determine that his feathers had been ruffled – possibly even plucked out. As he poured hot water from the kettle onto the coffee granules in his mug, she mistakenly thought he might offer her a drink.

'Three hours,' he boomed. 'Three bastard hours. Five minutes for me to give an account of yesterday's farce and the rest of the time for their buggering about.'

'Very frustrating,' stammered Kelly. 'Did they arrest you?'

'Oh, they arrested me early this morning when they invited me to the station for a voluntary interview. I told them I'd come down when it suited me, and they arrested me for common assault.'

'Have they let you off?'

'No, I've been released under investigation. Apparently, you don't need to make physical contact with somebody to assault them.'

'That's ridiculous.'

'If the person fears immediate violence against them, it's assault. The fact that I didn't touch Edna Pembleton is not a defence.'

'Is she pressing charges?'

'They don't need the cretinous old witch's support to prosecute me.'

'The PCSOs were talking to the short bloke with the white beard. He was in charge. I bet he's behind all this nonsense.'

'That jumped-up sales assistant! He retired from selling insurance for a two-bit agency. Thinks he's smart, but I'll put him in his place.'

'You will be careful?'

'It's them that need to be careful. I'm about to up my game.'

'You really don't need any more trouble with the police.'

Kevin threw Kelly a look that let her know her counsel was unsolicited and unwelcome. He held out his hand to take the newspaper that he'd told her to bring up. 'I've been bracing myself to see what they've written about me.'

'You might want to read it alone. It's not good. Shall I leave you to it?'

'Yes. And if you've got a couple of packs of out-of-date sandwiches, send one of the boys up with them. I'm going to spend an hour or so at Pendrick Court. Those bastard residents need to know I won't be intimidated.'

'Any particular filling?'

'No. And send up a couple of pies or sausage rolls too – only if they're out of date, mind.'

❖ ❖ ❖

'What time does your shift start?' Jessica asked Jack.

'Two. I'll leave here about twenty-to. Do you want another can? We've finished the Coke, but we've got Sprite.'

'No thanks. I'm going to make tracks and fix myself something to eat.'

'No pizza today?'

'Nope. I've got a bag of salad and I'm having it with a tin of tuna. You're welcome to share it.'

'You got enough?'

'I'll open a tin of new potatoes. That'll stretch it out.'

'Excellent!' Jack looked down to roll a cigarette and asked, with the reticence of a pensioner driving on a motorway, 'Do you think you and I could... Could we be more than friends?'

Jessica stood with as much dignity as one could when rising from a sloppy beanbag. 'No, because you wouldn't want that. Any man that takes a friendship to the next level while he's in a relationship is a dickhead. And you're not a dickhead.'

Jack flushed and kept his eyes fixed on his rolling. 'You're right.'

'So, now we've established that we're good friends and not flirting, are you still up for that tuna salad?'

'Yeah, sure.'

CHAPTER FORTY-FOUR

SEAN had been instructed to leave his van in the courtyard so the Audi could be parked in the store. He had also been told to keep himself busy nearby as his father was not prepared to risk more filth being dumped on his windscreen. He was quite content to pick orders and assemble them on pallets next to the car.

Head held high and a paper bag of rations in his hand, Kevin strode to the entrance to Apartments 7 and 8 and the rooftop patio. Two flights of stairs later, he placed his lunch on the floor so he could manipulate the gate's padlock. Although his key slid into the lock, it wouldn't turn. He re-inserted it several times, each time using a different amount of pressure to try and turn it. Exasperated, he called Sean, and asked him to find some 3-in-1 oil.

Sean gave his father the oil and suggested that he call their usual shop fitter if it didn't do the trick. When it didn't work, Kevin called the fitter and asked him to come to Pendrick Court as a matter of great urgency. He decided to return to the store and eat his drying sandwiches and pies while he waited for the cavalry to arrive.

He froze at the store's entrance and glowered suspiciously at Ishaan, who was leaning against some shelving and talking to Sean. Good manners prevented Ishaan from ignoring Kevin, so he forced a nod of acknowledgement. Kevin wasn't so polite and brusquely asked Sean why he was entertaining guests at work. Sean smiled and said that he'd invited Ishaan to join him for lunch, that they had intended to eat upstairs in the apartment, but Ishaan had thought it wise to remain in the store to watch over the car.

Kevin grudgingly dropped his objection to Ishaan's presence and demanded a chair. Sean and Ishaan sat on a pallet, laughing and sharing a box of Krispy Kreme doughnuts.

Kevin sat just outside the store, waiting for the fitter and gulping down a turkey sandwich, a roast-beef sandwich and two barbecued-chicken pasties. At the bottom of the bag, he found a bar of Hershey's Cookies & Cream, which Kelly had sneaked in. The use-by date had expired, so he forgave her.

He hadn't once looked up and noticed that the gargoyles had their backs to the court.

Fifteen minutes had passed by the time the shop fitter drove in and got out of his car wielding a pair of bolt cutters. Kevin led him to the gate, where he promptly snapped through and removed the padlock.

Kevin tucked a note into the fitter's hand, explaining

that it was to cover his petrol; that was his way of saying that he wasn't expecting to be charged for the visit. As he opened the door to the roof, warmth and blinding light washed the staircase behind him. He stepped out onto the patio, his head sweeping back and forth like a gun turret on a tank. He was paralysed with disbelief. The dismantled shed lay in a heap; the contents of boxes were scattered and broken; the deckchair was slashed; paving slabs were defaced with red paint, and the gargoyles were staring at him mockingly.

What he saw thrust him into motion. He marched purposefully forward to study the debris and the words and markings. What impudent bastard had dared to violate his rooftop retreat? How had they got up here?

His hands trembling, he repositioned the gargoyles to face the court. He sensed eyes upon him from the windows of the apartments below. It was them: they had done this. They were more grotesque than the gargoyles. He stood at the edge of the roof and roared, 'Bastards! You're all bags of shit.' Then he gave a bellow of contrived laughter so those listening would know he wasn't fazed.

He had to act quickly. The residents needed to understand that this contemptible act was nothing more than a minor inconvenience to Kevin Douglas. He took a few deep breaths to subdue his fury and started formulating a plan as he headed down to the store.

Kevin's barking from the roof prompted Ishaan to leave Pendrick Court; the initial plan to witness Kevin's reaction to the havoc was abandoned for safety reasons.

Sean walked across the courtyard to meet his father.

'There's been a break-in on the roof,' announced Kevin, shrugging his shoulders. 'And some petty vandalism. I'm going to drive to the shop to collect three or four pairs of hands. While I'm gone, I need you to fill the tank on the portable pressure washer and take it to the roof.'

'What have they done?' asked Sean.

'You'll see for yourself when you get the pressure washer up there. When I get back, you'll need to supervise the cleaning of the paving slabs and load your van with all the rubbish to take to the tip.'

Sean played along with the charade of his father's placidity. 'No problem. I'll see you when you return.'

'I've been considering treating myself to one of those plastic storage sheds and a reclining chair for some time. This silliness on the roof has been the kick up the backside I needed. In fact, as soon as I drop the staff off, I'm going to look around a couple of garden centres.'

'Good idea,' encouraged Sean.

'I'll pick up a new padlock while I'm there.' Kevin clapped his hands once and rubbed his palms together. 'Yes. I'm confident that I'll be taking lunch on a new and improved roof patio tomorrow.'

He climbed into the Audi and squeezed the steering wheel as tightly as he would like to have gripped the throats of the Pendrick Court residents.

CHAPTER FORTY-FIVE

'WELL, we can safely assume that Kevin has discovered the aftermath of Operation Rooftop.' Robert moved proudly around the sitting room like a schoolboy who had just been nominated milk monitor.

'What was he shouting?' Susan asked.

'"Bastards"! And then something or other about shit. I hope that lummox of a boy didn't defecate up there. I specifically told him not to.'

'Do you think he'll call the police?'

'He might, but they won't be particularly interested. Did you fetch me the paper from the shop?'

'You can see I did.' Susan passed it to him.

'Good. I'm looking forward to reading the character assassination of Kevin Douglas. Before you disappear, I went through the spice rack while you were getting the paper. You told me you'd checked the use-by dates.'

'I had.'

'I'll just say one word: oregano.'

'Well, I'm sorry if I missed one. Did you throw it out?'

'No, because I knew you'd want to see the evidence of your kitchen mismanagement.'

'You're very welcome to manage the kitchen yourself if you don't think I'm doing it adequately.'

'You do it adequately, I'm just inspiring you to do better. *You* run the kitchen, do the laundry and the cleaning, and *I* take care of any paperwork. That was the deal.'

'We could always swap roles.'

'I know what happened to the mouse, the bird and the sausage when they swapped roles – they all died. Brothers Grimm, you should read it.'

Susan made for the spice rack, mumbling, 'Orwell's *Animal Farm*.'

❖❖❖

Jessica and Jack came crashing down the stairs and caught Sean wheeling the water-filled pressure washer across the courtyard. 'Oh, dude,' said Jack. 'He ain't making you clean my paint off, is he?'

'No,' replied Sean. 'He's bringing some staff over from the shop to do the donkey work. I haven't seen your handywork yet.'

'You'll be proper impressed,' boasted Jack.

'How angry is he on a scale of one to ten?' asked Jessica.

'Outwardly about a two. Inwardly about a twelve ... His spleen's about to blow.'

Jessica grinned. 'We'll leave you to it. Catch you later.'

A short-winded Alan checked his watch and bade Sean a good afternoon as they met at the building's entrance. 'I'd offer to give you a hand, Aladdin,' he said. 'But frankly just coming *down* the stairs has knackered me today.'

'No worries. See you tomorrow morning at the nine-thirty meeting. And take care of yourself.'

The wheels on the pressure washer were no help when lugging the cumbersome machine up three long flights of stairs. Sean hoped there wouldn't be a next time but vowed, if there was, to transport the water tank separately.

The devastation before his eyes was total. The ploy to break into the shed and vandalise the contents had clearly evolved into a comprehensive wasting. It appeared that only the gargoyles had come through unscathed. Until his father arrived with the troops, his time would best be spent tidying up. The boxes had been crushed, so he'd need a few replacements, a broom and a dustpan from the store.

Walking to the store, Sean chewed over the eviction notices and the ensuing bedlam. The wretched notices were legal, but not necessary prior to a sale of Pendrick Court. The tenants had tried to negotiate the rescindment of the notices or, at the very least, an extension of the notice period, but his father had selfishly refused to compromise. You couldn't feel secure in your home when a landlord could evict you at short notice and without good reason. But his father had neither proposed, nor voted upon, the Bill that afforded landlords that power.

What option did the tenants have? When dialogue had been exhausted and no legal remedy existed, weren't they entitled to use any means at their disposal to obtain justice? But those means were questionably moral and now criminal. *Both* parties were probably immoral, yet only one party had acted illegally. Why then, in the battle of the lawful versus the lawless, did he, Sean, come down on the side of the lawless? Was it that the law was unjust or was it simply bias against the callous, mercenary man who had impregnated his mother to create his life?

The big question was: where would his father go from here? Would he acquiesce to the tenants' demands as a damage limitation exercise or would he hit back? Sean shuddered. Backing down was not his father's style.

He gathered boxes, broom and dustpan and returned to the roof.

❖❖❖

Two hours later, Kevin was in his shirt sleeves scrutinising the plastic sheds at a local garden centre. He'd chosen a padlock and chair, but was struggling to find a shed that justified its price.

Conscious that he wasn't in the best frame of mind

to go shopping, he took his time and tried to keep his irritability in check. He was still raw from the ravaging of his rooftop refuge. He was further incensed by his solicitor's enquiry as to how he would feel about receiving a conditional caution if he would agree to write a letter of apology to Edna Pembleton.

Those bastards threw dog shit at his windscreen, whipped up a media witch hunt, protested outside his home and business after a foiled attempt to burn them down, sent a lewd sex aid through the post, broke into his sanctuary and destroyed his property, and *he* was expected to apologise. There was more chance of a posthumously published work by Stephen Hawkins arguing that the Flat-Earthers were right all along than Kevin apologising to anybody.

His spirits were lifted fleetingly when a call from Sean announced that the rooftop was cleared and the paint removed. Kevin summoned a sales assistant and negotiated a fifteen per cent discount on a small shed that would take minutes to assemble and would suffice until Pendrick Court had been sold.

Sean agreed to accept delivery the following morning and to take the shed to the roof in readiness for his father's lunchtime arrival.

CHAPTER FORTY-SIX

SOON after six, a wilting Megan unlocked the door to Apartment 8. Not only had she been on her feet all day but the insulation provided by her mint-coloured tracksuit hadn't been necessary in today's elevated temperature. She plonked a canvas tote bag on the kitchen worktop and opened the fridge to take out a much-needed can of Coke.

She foraged through the fridge's contents increasingly manically as the Coke eluded her. Only when no item had been left unturned did she accept that her gluttonous and inconsiderate boyfriend had actually wolfed it all in her absence.

Before finally accepting a can of Sprite as a disappointing substitute, Megan checked the recycling bin for evidence. Sure enough, there lay four empty cans of Coke in the bin, two of them pinched in the middle. The leaflet from the council had asked residents not to crush their drink cans before recycling, as Jack well knew.

As Megan plucked two disfigured cans from the pile

to reshape them, she noticed what looked like lipstick on them. She rubbed her finger across the stain and smelled it, confirming her suspicions. Jack needed prompting to wash his hands and wear deodorant, so it was highly improbable that he was experimenting with cosmetics. No, these marks were made by a woman's lips, and there was only one woman whom Jack could lure to his apartment without the use of rohypnol. He'd been poking the Porky Princess.

❖❖❖

The industrious sun persisted at Pendrick Court, although it had long since withered in Phuket where midnight had already passed. Paul was leaning on his balcony's handrail and smoking a cigarette while he waited for Noi's video call.

It was ten days since the eviction notices were delivered. He had to know whether he was staying at Pendrick Court or needed somewhere else to live. Kevin had taken a severe and sustained shelling from the tenants' arsenal; if he was ever going to capitulate to enemy forces, now was the time. Paul would insist at tomorrow's meeting that Kevin was asked again to abandon the evictions and sell Pendrick Court with the tenants in situ.

Paul's business was thriving and his diary contained few gaps right up until the twenty-fifth of July. On top of a nine-hour day of appointments, he responded to emergencies in the evenings and at weekends. Nobody liked to turn away work, but he wasn't twenty years old. He was asking as much from his fifty-five-year-old body as could be expected.

He wanted to be on that flight to Phuket on the twenty-sixth of July. If Kevin was not going to relent, the search for a new home had to begin immediately. Paying advance rent and a deposit would not be a problem and he could move in as soon as it suited the landlord if he found the right place.

Noi was calling.

❖ ❖ ❖

Megan had been on her balcony texting news of Jack's two-timing to her friends, and feeling aggrieved with those who did not reply instantly to offer their support, when she saw Jessica leaving the building. She fled the apartment without even shutting the door behind her, ran down the stairs and across the court. She stopped Jessica with a screechy 'Oi!', just as the last few yards of her sprint were changing to a hands-on-hips stomp.

'Were you in my apartment today?' yelled Megan.

Jessica raised her eyebrows. 'Excuse me? There's no need to shout,' she said calmly.

'Cut the crap. Were you in my apartment with Jack?'

'We had a can of Coke on the balcony, while we looked—'

'Well, I don't want you in my apartment. Why don't

you find your own boyfriend and leave other people's alone?'

'Firstly, I was invited in. Secondly, I don't choose which men find me desirable.' Jessica's composure served to aggravate rather than diffuse the situation.

'Desirable! He's not blind.'

Jessica shook her head. 'Jealousy can be an ugly thing.'

'Rather like you in leggings, you fat tart.'

'I'm not actually overweight, I'm just blessed with an ample bosom. I've got it so I flaunt it.'

'Got it? You should be wearing dark colours and layers when you're that size, not spray-on clothes.'

'I'd rather have my curves than a visible rib cage and no tits. But if you're happy to look like a thirteen-year-old boy—' Jessica felt a sharp sting on the side of her face from Megan's hand. She resisted touching her cheek. 'That one was free. But try it again and I *will* deck you.'

'Oh really?' Megan stepped forward and flicked her hand towards Jessica's reddening cheek.

This time, the slap was blocked by Jessica's forearm. She swung back her other arm. With a powerful sweep and then a crack, her palm made contact with Megan's ear and sent her sprawling to the ground.

Dumbfounded, and cupping a pulsating ear, Megan's eyes filled with tears. She turned her head to hide her anguish and tried to stand. Initially she floundered, as though moving through thick mud, but then she managed to regain her balance. When she was certain she would not topple, she raced to her apartment, inky runnels of mascara coursing down her face. Jessica continued her journey to the pizzeria.

As she waited for Jack to finish work, Megan resumed her texting, updating friends about the battle with his lover. Had the friends seen Jessica leaving Pendrick Court, they would have been surprised at her ability to walk because, according to Megan, she had been tossed around the courtyard like laundry in a dryer.

CHAPTER FORTY-SEVEN
Saturday, 1st June

ALAN was simultaneously rereading yesterday's news-paper and eating a bowl of Rice Krispies when there was a strident knocking at his door. He wrapped his dressing gown over his middle, tied the belt and trudged in the direction of the racket. He opened the door to Edna eyeing him up and down like a drill sergeant. Further adjusting his dressing gown, he asked if she wanted to come in.

She marched through the doorway and into the kitchen. 'First time I've been in your apartment,' she said, surveying the room. 'Interesting how your kitchen looks out onto the court, yet Anah's has a view of the city.'

Alan offered her a seat at the table and excused his unfinished breakfast. 'So, what brings you to my humble abode so soon after the cracking of dawn?'

Edna stood and waved her left leg in Alan's direction. 'Vinegar! I've banged my shin and have no vinegar to put on the bruise. I'm hoping you'll have some to save me going to the shop before the meeting.'

Alan rose and stepped across to an overhead cupboard. 'Here we are. You're in luck. One bottle of white vinegar.' He placed it in front of Edna and sat down again. 'I never use it, so there's no need to return it. How did you hurt your leg?'

'Well, I like to know that in the event of a night-time power failure, I'd be able to get from my bed to the cupboard under the kitchen sink where I keep my flashlight. Last night I got out of bed and was feeling my way to the kitchen when I bumped into the coffee table.'

'Your blackout rehearsals sound dangerous. You're fortunate that you didn't break the skin. We've an hour and a quarter before the meeting begins. Would you care for a coffee?'

'That would be lovely, dear. I can tell you all about my near-death experience on Thursday and yesterday's visit from the police.'

Alan started to rise but Edna leapt up. 'I'll make the coffee while you listen and finish your cereal. You don't look too perky this morning.'

'I get a tinge of osteoarthritis for the first thirty minutes of the day. It soon wears off.'

❖ ❖ ❖

There had been no tears when Jack had arrived home the previous evening, just a noxious hour and a half of contention. Despite him swearing that there had been no physical contact between him and Jessica, Megan had condemned him to an undetermined stretch in the spare room for infidelity and mendacity.

Jack was resigned to his sentence; he even recognised that perhaps on this rare occasion he had merited his punishment, not because of what he had done but because of what he would have done given half a chance.

In the morning, he washed, dressed then waited in his cell until he heard Megan in the bathroom. At that point, he made a run for the door and escaped Apartment 8 without being seen. Soon after seven-thirty he was heading to work on his bike, relieved to have avoided a replay of the evening's accusations.

Having posted 'feeling sad' on each of her social media accounts, Megan decided she should wear something to work that would convey an air of melancholy yet show that she was willing to talk about the cause of her grief. Thankfully, her grey velour tracksuit had been laundered.

❖ ❖ ❖

Toby blitzed Madison with his high-pitched meowing and stared at her insistently. 'Shall I feed him?' she asked.

'If you don't mind,' replied Anah. 'He's started telling you he's hungry rather than me. I guess I'm no longer the woman in his life – I've been supplanted.'

Madison placed her hand on Anah's shoulder. 'If I weren't the younger model who's replacing you, I'd be here for you.'

'Just tossed aside like a paper cup.' Anah floated through the apartment opening curtains and blinds, while Madison pandered to the cat's insatiable appetite.

'What do you think will happen at the meeting?'

'I think our offensive is pretty much exhausted.' Anah looked vacantly out of the kitchen window. 'If we decide to call it a day, I've one last card up my sleeve. It's not an ace, but it's all I've got left to play.'

'I hope you're going to tell me what the card is.'

'If Kevin won't agree to sell the building with us in it, I'm going to offer to buy this apartment.'

'Obviously you wouldn't make the offer if you couldn't afford it. But why did you rent in the first place? Why didn't you buy somewhere when you moved from London?'

'I wasn't against the idea of buying. I was searching for a property to rent or buy that wasn't too far from your father. I stumbled across Pendrick Court and thought it was perfect.'

'Why did you want to be close to Dad?'

'If anything happens to me, your father would have inherited my estate. I thought it would be so much easier for him to go through my possessions if they were nearby.'

'Well, nobody could ever accuse you of being disorganised.'

'And there was always the chance that we'd speak again.'

'I would have come looking for you even if Dad had lived. I'm sure if I'd told him how much I liked you, and that I wanted you in my life, he'd have made contact.'

'Thank you for saying that, Madison.' Anah reached into a cupboard and pulled out two plates. 'My son must have been so proud to have you for a daughter.'

'As the end approached, we had many teary evenings when he'd open up. His words were awkward but nothing was left unsaid. He left me knowing he was proud of me, and I felt very loved.'

CHAPTER FORTY-EIGHT

SEAN moved his van into summer's golden light so Ishaan had room to set out the flimsy white chairs in the store, then he closed his eyes and tilted his face towards the skies.

'Hey, Blondie,' called Ishaan. 'You don't have enough melanin to be in the sun without sunscreen. You'll get melanoma.'

Words and warmth rippled over Sean's head and he let the rays brush his skin for a few seconds longer before joining Ishaan inside. 'Have you been reading Edna's medical encyclopaedia, *The Hypochondriac's Guide to the Galaxy*?' he asked.

'You don't think you can get melanoma from ultraviolet light?'

'Not after thirty seconds, no. I was converting cholesterol into vitamin D. You should do the same. I could hear your arteries crackling over breakfast.'

'Really? I'm surprised you could hear anything over the noise you make when you chew,' Ishaan retorted.

'I make that noise to drown out your revolting

hospital anecdotes. Nobody wants to hear what oozes from where when they're trying to eat.' Sean held out a can of Diet Mountain Dew to which Ishaan shook his head.

They waited at the entrance to the store. 'Would you look at that?' said Ishaan. 'Far left.' Alan was holding open the door to let Edna pass. 'Now the question is: did she go up to his apartment today or last night?'

'I hope you're joking.'

'Why? Older people have needs.'

'Stop! I don't want that image in my head.'

'Of course, she'd be on top,' Ishaan mused. 'That feisty firecracker would ride him like a pogo stick. Eyes right. Snow White's on her way over – and look, she's bringing Grumpy.'

'What, no commentary on *their* sex life?'

'Well, there's no need. It's obvious ... angry sex. I bet he's a biter.'

'You're depraved.'

'Check her for bite marks.'

Robert chose his seat carefully and Susan sat to his right. Sean welcomed them and then returned Alan's wave. He was still gliding slowly across the courtyard as if it were a glacier with Edna at his side.

'How're we doing?' Sean asked when Edna and Alan entered the store.

'Well, Alan's morning stiffness is dealt with but I've been left with substantial bruising,' Edna said.

Sean avoided eye contact with Ishaan and pulled out

a chair for her.

After Paul and Jessica had parked themselves in the circle of residents, Susan announced that they were only waiting for Anah and Madison because Megan and Jack were at work. Sean reclined, hands clasped behind his head and swung back to balance on two chair legs while Robert fiddled with his shiny red clipboard with fold-over cover.

Edna was so dazzled by Alan's reminiscences of the country pop music scene in the 1970s that she was unaware of the volume of her giggling. Although he didn't like to name drop, names were dropping faster than the price of Rolf Harris's artwork. He grappled with his chair, fighting to stand as a gesture of respect to Anah and Madison, when finally they appeared and took their seats.

Robert stood, cleared his throat and read from his notes. 'Our message to Kevin Douglas was explicit: cancel the eviction notices now and make the continuation of our tenancies a condition of sale, or suffer the consequences of our wrath.' His clipboard thwopped shut. 'Our threat has been carried out.'

'If he'd known what a punch we were going to pack, I suspect he would have cancelled the eviction notices,' said Alan.

Pleased as a blind pig that had found the feeding trough, Robert raised his hand in a gesture of thanks, taking credit for the consequences that had rained upon their landlord. 'While Alan's soaking and Edna's tumble onto the road were unfortunate and unplanned, their capture by numerous cell phones provided great momentum to our strike. Of course, our most powerful blow was the protest.'

Jessica clapped. 'The newspaper and social media campaigns, the rooftop raid, delivery of the butt plug, even Elizabeth spreading the word from the post office counter ... they all helped us to sock it to Kevin Douglas.'

'But,' said Paul, 'our actions weren't for revenge, they were supposed to force him into changing his mind. He doesn't know what we're planning to do next. Maybe now he's ready to withdraw the notices.'

Anah raised her hand. 'We need to speak to him again. Perhaps the offer of a truce, together with a statement to the newspaper from Edna and Alan explaining that his role in their misfortunes was a misunderstanding, would persuade him to revoke the notices. That is, if Edna and Alan agree.'

'I'll say whatever you want me to say,' Edna said. 'I just want to know I can stay in my apartment.'

'Me too,' Alan agreed. 'Anything to advance the cause. Do we ask Sean if he'll be our messenger again?'

Robert was quick to respond. 'Much as I appreciated Sean's assistance last week, I think you'll all agree that we're not just sending a message. No, this time we need to cut a deal. Kevin may have questions or conditions and an intermediary would delay the process.'

'I'm with Robert,' said Paul. 'Time is of the essence.'

Jessica nodded. 'Yes, we need to know if these evictions are going ahead and we need to know soon. If we are getting evicted, we've all got a lot to organise.'

Edna sprang from her chair and landed in the centre of the circle. Turning as she spoke, she addressed her neighbours. 'I've said I'll make a statement to the newspaper. I'm even happy to tell the police that my memory is now a lot clearer ... tell them that it wasn't Kevin's fault I fell into the road. But if he doesn't agree to our demands, I'm not happy to roll over and pack my bags. If he hasn't had enough, it's because we've not been hitting hard enough.' She resumed her seat.

'Before we discuss the possibility of any further action,' said Anah, 'we do need to establish whether it's necessary.'

'And to that end,' interrupted Robert, 'I suggest that I visit Kevin and see if we can now negotiate the withdrawal of these evictions. Does anybody have any objections?' Nobody replied. 'Then, when I've spoken to Kevin, I will contact each of you.'

Labouring to stand again, Alan silenced the tenants as his words resounded though the store. 'If we have concluded our business,' he began, 'I would like to set a date for a residents' party to be held in our courtyard. I propose the afternoon of Saturday, the twentieth of July. I sincerely hope we will be celebrating the continuation of our tenancy agreements, but if not we'll leave Pendrick Court with a bang.'

'I think that's a wonderful idea,' declared Susan.

'Let's put the date in our diaries. I have great confidence in Robert's ability to reach a settlement with Kevin.'

CHAPTER FORTY-NINE

WHILE the allies were filtering back to their respective apartments, Jessica sidled up to Madison to ask if she and Anah had time to share a pot of tea and a packet of Oreos. Anah declined the invitation because of her scheduled shopping trip but urged Madison to go. A morning with Jessica would be infinitely more agreeable than traipsing up and down the supermarket aisles.

Madison was quite content to spend an hour or so with a neighbour and followed Jessica up to Apartment 4. As they passed Apartment 3, she enquired whether Jessica had ever socialised with Paul.

'To be fair, I never had much to do with anybody at Pendrick Court until we received the eviction notices,' Jessica replied. 'Actually, that's a lie. I'd chatted with Sean a few times.'

'Sean seems like a decent bloke.'

'Yeah. He's a bit withdrawn, but if ever you need a hand with something he's your man. He's very easy on the eye, too.'

'I thought Paul was the quiet one.'

'Paul doesn't say much either. Not to worry – Alan talks enough for the three of them.' Jessica unlocked the door and led the way into her apartment.

'And Robert?'

'He's not really a people person. He speaks *at* you rather than *to* you. I actually feel quite sorry for his wife.'

'You seem to get on well with Jack.'

'Jack's harmless. It's good to be around people your own age and he's only a year younger than me.'

'And his girlfriend?'

'Megan and I aren't good friends. She thinks I'm trying to seduce Jack and steal him from her.'

Madison smiled.

❖❖❖

Having emptied his mail box on the way up to Apartment 7, Alan opened his post at the table. Perturbed, he lingered over his mother's bank statement. Twice a week, every week, there had been a cash debit of three hundred pounds. He blotted his brow with a clean handkerchief and opened the window as wide as possible. A semblance of a breeze edged into the kitchen.

If Mother had moved to Scotland, as his sister wanted, a local council would now be paying for her care irrespective of any savings. As it was, apart from a state pension and the attendance allowance, the care home fees were funded from his mother's capital – capital that should be inherited by her children.

If she had no capital, the council here would pay the fees. What sort of a system penalised you for owning your own property and saving hard? Alan wasn't embezzling money from his mother, he was ring-fencing it from the council. Technically, half of the ring-fenced money should go to his sister but she and her husband had more than enough.

Inheriting half his parents' property had been Alan's pension plan. If he didn't build a nest egg with his mother's money, he might be left with nothing. He now had almost £42,000 stashed under the sink in £20 notes.

Next year, the Bank of England was going to issue polymer £20 notes and withdraw the paper ones from circulation. He'd need a strategy or his security fund would be as much use as a marzipan football. Perhaps he'd split his hoard between a few different bank accounts.

He groaned and tried to recall if he'd put any wine in the fridge to chill.

❖❖❖

'Help yourself to another Oreo,' prompted Jessica, sliding the plate towards Madison.

'Thanks. So, how long have you lived here?'

'Just over two years. After my dad died, my brother

moved back to the family home. We lived together for the best part of a year until the house was sold, then I moved to Pendrick Court.'

'Sorry your dad died. I met Christopher at Thursday's protest. And your mum?'

'Mum died about ten years ago.'

'That's shitty.'

'I've had time to adapt, and Christopher is amazing. Have you got any brothers or sisters?'

'No. I think my parents were terrified they'd have another one like me. I was quite a handful.'

'Did you lose your mum too?'

'No, she's alive and complaining in Poole. She married a teacher who manages a high school down there. He was teaching with my dad when he started an affair with my mother.'

'Sounds like a horrible man.'

'He got what he deserved. He has to wake up to that sour-faced dragon every morning.'

'Sounds like you're not your mum's number one fan.'

'I can cope with a telephone call every few weeks. I think she's as relieved as I am that I'm not moving in with them.'

'Have you always been close to Anah?'

'We've only recently spent any real time together, but we're getting on really well. Last night she told me all about her move to England. She came in 1966—'

'The last time we won the World Cup.'

'Or between the decolonisation of Nigeria and the

civil war.' Madison washed down her Oreo with a swig of tea. 'She's a remarkable woman.'

'I like her. It will be such a shame if we all have to go our separate ways.'

'Do you think that's what will happen?'

'If Robert doesn't get anywhere with Kevin after everything we've done, it'll all be over. If Kevin won't budge now, nothing we do will change his mind.'

'And if it's all over, what will you do?' Madison asked.

'I'll just have to go online and see what's available for rent within walking distance of work.'

'The pizza place on Grove Road?'

'Yeah, Dino's Pizzeria. I love my job. Oh my God! I've just remembered. I've got an unopened tub of Ben & Jerry's Cookie-Dough Ice Cream in the freezer. Why are we eating Oreos, when there's ice cream within spitting distance?'

'Anah's bound to bring something back from the supermarket for lunch. I'd better not fill up on ice cream.'

'Then promise you'll come over one afternoon and help me eat it.'

CHAPTER FIFTY

'WELL?' snapped Robert, avoiding eye contact with Susan.

More than a little red-faced, Susan confessed that Chloe had secured the position in London and would be relocating as soon as accommodation had been organised.

'It didn't take half an hour for her to tell you that. No doubt you were colluding with her, fantasising about family reunions in London without me.' Robert sniggered. 'She'll ditch you like a used cotton bud the moment she makes some friends. She doesn't give a shit about you.'

'We didn't talk about me visiting them in London, but I'd like to very much. I was simply asking after my grandchildren's progress.'

'Well, at least you won't go bankrupt paying for your grandchildren's endless years at university.'

'Chloe's PhD got her the job in Baltimore. She left university debt free, and I've never regretted the bankruptcy for a second.'

'Of course you haven't. You came crawling to me. I picked up the pieces of your pitiful life.'

'Don't be so dramatic. You *invited* me to move in and I've paid my way ever since.'

'I put a roof over your head.'

'Halving your rent and acquiring an unpaid housekeeper.'

'You're an ungrateful bitch. It's not hard to see where your daughter gets it from. Where do you think you're going?'

'OUT! And I won't be here to serve you lunch.' Susan grabbed her purse and fled Apartment 1 to prevent an incandescent Robert from escalating the altercation.

Robert thundered to his bedroom, swearing like a pirate with a zipper-related penis injury, and threw open the wardrobe door. He grabbed a royal-blue lightweight blazer to wear as he went to pay Kevin Douglas an impromptu visit.

❖❖❖

Around eleven-thirty, the garden centre delivered Kevin's shed to Pendrick Court. The driver assured Sean that it could be assembled with a screwdriver; a drill would only be required when fixing it to the paving slabs. Disinclined as he was to assist with the assembly, Ishaan was conscripted into the working party and, together with Sean, humped the shed to the rooftop patio.

Sean decided they would put it together but leave the anchoring to their shop fitter the following week. The listless wind wouldn't have stirred confetti at a wedding, so there was no risk of mutilating an unsuspecting pedestrian three floors down. He informed his father of the shed's arrival and promised to call again when it had been erected.

❖ ❖ ❖

A reclining garden chair lay on the back seat of Kevin's Audi, which stood a few feet from his front door in the June haze. Robert opened a second button on his white shirt and pressed the doorbell under the video camera. A metallic 'hello' rattled from the speaker.

Lifting his heels off the ground to reach the microphone and articulating each word precisely, Robert announced, 'Mr Robert Page of Pendrick Court to see Mr Kevin Douglas.' An electric mechanism in the door clunked and Robert let himself in. Having mounted a vertiginous staircase, he knocked on the door at the summit.

Kevin opened the door, turned and walked towards the living room. Robert followed. At the end of the corridor, Kevin folded his arms and stood in a doorway, an enormous table laden with papers behind him. 'Why are you here?' he asked.

'I'm here on behalf of your tenants at Pendrick Court – except for your son. We're asking again if you will cancel our eviction notices.'

'Then I'm telling you again that I won't.'

'That's the wrong answer.'

'It's the only answer you're going to get, you cheeky bastard. Now piss off!'

'You're clearly enjoying the public humiliation that we're dishing out. Perhaps your masochistic tendencies are preventing you from seeing sense.'

Kevin exploded with a roar, grabbed the lapels of Robert's blazer and shoved him against the wall. 'Your pathetic little games stop now. Do you hear me?'

Robert's futile attempt to free himself from Kevin's grip did nothing but encourage Kevin to pin him with even greater fervour. 'I will not be manhandled!' he shouted. Kevin's bleached incisors and pocked skin were so close that he could smell the chicken pasty on his breath.

'You're a coward. You might impress the geriatrics and under-achievers at Pendrick Court but I can see right through you,' Kevin snarled.

'Yet the cowards, geriatrics and under-achievers are crushing you. We've seen to it that there's not a person in this great city who doesn't know what a scumbag you are.'

Detaching one hand from Robert's blazer, Kevin pulled back and propelled a fist into Robert's abdomen. The pain from the impact was immediately upstaged by Robert's distress at not being able to breathe. As his victim fought for air, Kevin hooked his striking arm around the back of his neck and leaned down so their cheeks were touching. 'One more stunt and I'm coming for you,' he whispered. 'And when I find you, I will pop your skull like a zit on my arse.' He hurled Robert, still gasping, to the floor.

Kevin fetched his e-cigarette from the kitchen and stood smoking it while Robert was recovering. The revival was taking much longer than Kevin had anticipated – so much so, he thought he might have to call down to Kelly for a bottle of e-liquid. However, after five minutes Robert managed to stand, his midriff bruised less than his pride.

'Mr Page,' said Kevin dispassionately. 'I'm glad we've had this meeting. It was good to finally bring the week's craziness to an end. I would just like to add that it would be in your best interest to persuade Edna Pembleton to speak to the police and clear up Thursday's silliness. Now you can piss off.'

Abased and ashen-faced, Robert arranged his shirt and blazer before leaving the building and emerging into the airless afternoon of the city. It was only as he set off for Pendrick Court that he realised his dishonour had been further compounded by the fact that, at some point during the mêlée, he had lightly soiled his underwear.

CHAPTER FIFTY-ONE

ANAH bent over to gather the shopping bags that littered the back seat of the taxi. Her load evenly distributed between two overburdened hands, she slammed the car door shut with her hip and noticed Susan entering the court.

As Susan drew closer, it was apparent that she had been crying. Anah's impulse to offer solace, and to satisfy her curiosity into the bargain, compelled her to invite her neighbour upstairs for coffee. Susan's initial resistance crushed, she unhooked some of Anah's bags and followed her up to Apartment 2.

Meanwhile, Toby's unfounded assumption that the approaching rustling indicated an imminent treat had him racing to the front door. When it opened, he was met with not one but two pairs of legs, around which he wove with the graceful rhythm of a slalom skier.

He loitered earnestly in the kitchen doorway until the shopping was unloaded and the prospect of any après-ski had faded like melting snow. After thirty seconds of manipulative meowing and pouting, a treat still wasn't forthcoming. He edged over to his feeding bowl, dramatically dismissed the contents and marched into the sitting room.

Susan sat, enjoying the nutty aroma of grinding coffee beans. 'I have to say, Anah, you've done an incredible job with this kitchen. It's stunning.'

'Thank you,' replied Anah. 'I refurbished the whole apartment last year. I thought I'd get all the expense and disruption over in one hit. It looks as though I shouldn't have bothered.'

'Hindsight is a wonderful thing.'

'It's only wonderful if it's coupled with the ability to travel back in time.' Anah smiled and poured hot water into the cafetière. 'Feel free to tell me to mind my own business, but you looked upset when we met in the courtyard.'

'It was just an argument with Robert. I don't want to burden you with my problems. You've got enough on your plate at the moment with the eviction, Madison's arrival and – and your son's death.'

'All my son's affairs are being dealt with by an executor and, to be honest, Madison is a godsend. Did you and Robert ever have children?' Susan froze, as though she'd just heard the chair crack beneath her. 'I'm sorry. Perhaps I shouldn't have asked—'

'No. I've just realised ... I feel such a fool. I've never introduced Robert as my brother. If *you* thought ... Well, everybody must think—'

'I jumped to conclusions and I dare say everybody else

did too. But there's no need for you to be embarrassed.' Toby reappeared in the doorway, scowled at Anah and let out a short, sharp squeak. 'He's telling me it's time for his exercise. I'll just take him downstairs and then I'll pour our coffee.'

❖ ❖ ❖

'Alan, it's Edna. I'm in my apartment ... unconscious. Please come quickly.' The call ended. Alan vanquished a flash of panic with a last mouthful of tepid Riesling and stood up like a volunteer gladiator in the arena.

Two-thirds of a bottle of wine on a near-empty stomach made the staircase a formidable opponent. Making full use of the handrails, he executed his descent with great fortitude. At the bottom, wheezing and slack muscled, he dredged up sufficient energy to cross the courtyard and climb the stairs.

As Edna opened her door, he said, 'I came as quickly as I could. I thought you'd fallen. You said you were unconscious.'

'I didn't mean unconscious in the sense of being out cold. I meant unconscious in the sense of being furious.'

'I'm not sure unconscious and furious are synonymous, but that doesn't matter now. May I sit down?'

'Yes, you look as though you're about to collapse.'

'Not at all. I'm remarkably fit for someone of my age.'

'I wish I could say the same, dear. You're very lucky.'

Alan sagged into the battered sofa. 'So what brought on your fury?'

Edna pointed at an advertisement in the local paper. 'Look, advice on homelessness. I gave them a call. It's good to be forewarned ... or is it forearmed?'

'Forewarned is forearmed.'

'Synonymous! Anyway, I spoke to a volunteer. They'd probably pay him, if he learned to stop mumbling. Did you want a cup of tea?'

'No, thanks. I'm keen to hear your story.'

'The council might have a responsibility to house me because of my old age. I told him I was eighty-three in September, but that doesn't guarantee they'll give me a place. Did you hear that? My mother and I were evacuated to some shit-ridden farm with no running water in 1939, and I might not be old enough.'

'At what age are you old?'

'That's just it. They can't put a figure on it.' Edna wagged her finger in Alan's face. 'I'll tell you for why. It's political correctness.'

'They don't want to be accused of ageism.'

'It's getting out of hand, dear. I go along with most of it. Your race doesn't tell me whether you're a wrong 'un.'

'An observation perfectly illustrated by Kevin Douglas.'

'Makes no difference to me, if you want to define your own gender.'

'I embrace them all.'

'I was baptised by a Methodist minister, but as far as I'm concerned you can worship a sun god if it brings you peace. But, Alan, when you're eighty-three, you're *old*.'

'A fact that nobody should dispute.'

Edna took a seat. 'How can calling somebody old be any more insulting than calling somebody young?'

'Perhaps they do have a figure but can't disclose it. Did the mumbler advise you to call the council?'

'He did. I told him a few of my ailments. Take some medical evidence with you, he said. If the council think I'd be a lot more vulnerable than an ordinary person, they won't expect me to sleep on the streets.'

'Edna, I'm sure that if our evictions go ahead there's not the slightest chance that the council will refuse to house you. But you must be prepared to accommodate their procedures.'

CHAPTER FIFTY-TWO

AFTER a lunch of Thai noodle salad and salmon with Anah and Madison, Susan returned to Apartment 1. Sean and Ishaan had defied the heat and accomplished their rooftop mission. Alan had faltered down a flight of stairs, shambled across a suffocating courtyard and ascended the stairs to Apartment 7 with the grace of a one-winged bumblebee.

Anah had finished her cigarette but stayed on the balcony to enjoy the afternoon sun. She could see Toby basking between the gargoyles. Jessica was standing on her balcony in sunglasses and a metallic string bikini, inflating a lilo. Below her, Paul was busying himself vacuuming out his van.

Anah knew Alan intended to ask her to coordinate the food for the residents' party the following month, and the task was stimulating her imagination. She was envisaging tables in the courtyard spread with colourful dishes from her kitchen when a black saloon pulled into the court and splintered her reverie.

The Audi ground to a halt outside the entrance to

Apartments 7 and 8. Kevin stepped out and removed a bag and a reclining chair before going into the building. He would not find Toby's luxurious sprawl a welcome sight, and Anah did not want to upset her landlord before broaching the subject of purchasing Apartment 2.

She glared at Toby, willing him to leap down onto Jack and Megan's balcony, but he continued to lounge in the sun's warmth. Tenants were expressly forbidden from accessing the rooftop but Anah had no choice: she needed to rescue Toby.

Without alerting Madison, she moved briskly down the stairs and across the court, pressed the trade button, entered the building and climbed the three flights of stairs. She scanned the patio. Toby lay next to a loathsome gargoyle with a paw hanging over the edge of the roof. The door to the shed was open and a noise came from within, but she couldn't see its source. Deftly and silently Anah made a beeline for Toby, who allowed himself to be swept up into her arms.

She turned towards the staircase only to see Kevin looking daggers at her from the shed doorway. 'Neither you nor that bastard cat is allowed up here,' he shouted. 'I don't sneak into your apartment without permission. Go – and don't let me catch you up here again.'

Locking horns with Kevin at this point did not seem judicious if Anah wanted to buy her apartment. 'My sincerest apologies. My behaviour is inappropriate. I'll try not to do it again.'

'Don't try, just make sure you don't.'

'Understood. I'll leave you in peace.'

Anah left the patio, hackles raised from having orders barked at her but congratulating herself on her restraint. Toby was oblivious to her annoyance, just grateful that she had fetched him. Getting onto the roof and back down again was getting more demanding as the years passed.

❖❖❖

'Referring to myself as an unpaid housekeeper does sound as though I begrudge what I do for you but I don't,' squirmed Susan. 'I was just retaliating. You made me angry.'

'You can't force an emotion on somebody. I didn't *make* you angry, you reacted angrily.' Robert sipped his tea complacently. 'But if it maintains a harmonious household, I'll happily take responsibility for your spiteful outburst and you can continue to play the long-suffering sibling.'

'So we can put this squabble behind us?'

'Of course. I am nothing if not magnanimous.'

'Thank you. I hate it when we quarrel. Talking of siblings, did you know that the other tenants think we're husband and wife?'

'Hell! They must think you're punching above your weight. I expect you're quite flattered.'

Susan paused and turned her ear towards the kitchen. 'You've turned on the washing machine. And changed your clothes.'

'I was sweating like a horse after walking to and from Kevin's apartment. I should never have worn my blazer.'

'You've spoken to Kevin?'

'Yes. I needed a shower and thought I'd save you a job by washing my clothes.'

'Thank you, that's very thoughtful. But what happened with Kevin?'

'Well,' said Robert, 'there's not much to report. He's obviously furious at the bad publicity.'

'But what did he say about cancelling the evictions?'

'After a long and heated negotiation, he said that if Edna got the police off his back he'd withdraw the notices.'

'That's fantastic. Oh, you are clever.'

'If Edna cooperates, we've no guarantee that he'll keep his end of the bargain. I don't trust him.'

'We've nothing to lose. When do you plan on speaking to her?'

'I was thinking that you might have more success with Edna than I would. She hasn't warmed to me, but I think you could connect with her.'

Susan blushed. 'That's just about the nicest thing you've ever said to me.'

'My language is too elevated for Edna and it reinforces her intellectual inferiority. She'll relate better to somebody on her own level.'

'Well, I felt valued for a few seconds.'

'She needs to tell the police that she was confused when she spoke to them, that she knew Kevin was no threat and she simply lost her balance in those stupid boots and fell into the road.'

Susan walked over to the patio doors. 'Kevin's car's here. He's obviously on the roof. I could go and speak to Edna now while you tell him that we're keeping our side of the deal.'

Robert shuffled uncomfortably. 'Let's wait and see what the police say to Edna. I'll need something concrete to take with me.'

'Okay. I'll pop over to Edna's apartment now.'

CHAPTER FIFTY-THREE

THE gunmetal eyes of the repositioned gargoyles were focused on the patio doors of Apartment 1. Kevin reclined at a comfortable forty-five-degrees angle, his jacket off and his shirt sleeves rolled up. He would never forgive the bastard who had sliced up his red-and-white striped deckchair, although he conceded that he wasn't missing it. Holding a less than fresh pork pie in his one hand, he dialled Sean's number with the other.

Sean grabbed a pen and paper and took the call on the balcony, leaving Ishaan to play Minecraft in the living room. Kevin confirmed that he'd have the shed secured to the patio on Monday and gave a list of the following week's deliveries to Pendrick Court.

Sean knew from experience that he didn't have his father's memory so he made notes. He winced at the news of another consignment of children's rucksacks embellished with video-game characters; he already had orders for more than seventy that needed to be packed that weekend.

Kevin had underestimated the day's heat; however,

he was going to persevere with the afternoon's vigil. The residents needed to know that the destruction of his bolthole had caused him no more than a minor inconvenience. 'We haven't got to worry about the antics of these bastard tenants any more,' he said.

'No?' Sean asked.

'No. I had a meeting with the ringleader, Robert from Apartment 1. He was told in no uncertain terms that their shit stops now. He's also going to see to it that Edna withdraws the statement she gave to the police.'

'Have you had any thoughts about warehouse space? I want to rent somewhere as close as possible.'

'Good idea because you won't be using the van to get to and from work.'

'What?'

'The van will be kept overnight in the warehouse. You'll have to get yourself a push bike.'

'I can't believe you! I'm going to spend my entire Sunday printing off address labels—'

'And your salary more than pays you to work any hours you're not sleeping.' Kevin ended the call and closed his eyes.

❖ ❖ ❖

Edna's sofa creaked as Susan shifted to get comfortable and gaped at the array of grimy mementos. Edna swept a pyramid of lotions and potions onto the floor to make enough room on the coffee table for Susan's mug.

What surrounded the hot tea could only be the spoils from a chemist shop looting.

Today was the first time Susan had been inside any of the other apartments at Pendrick Court. The elegance of Anah's residence contrasted sharply with the disorder of Edna's, yet both embodied a homeliness she hadn't known since Chloe had left for university. She was suddenly very aware of the emptiness of her present-day home life and her regret for not befriending her neighbours sooner.

Edna was thrilled with the opportunity to recount her capers at the hospital, with the police officers, and during the power-failure run through that had resulted in her bruised shin. Susan proved to be a most empathic audience, grimacing and laughing in just the right places to spur her on.

She thrust several grubby photo frames into Susan's hands as she took her newfound friend on a trip down memory lane, sharing tales of her late husband, their son, grandchildren and great-grandchildren. Only when she paused to draw breath and offer a second mug of tea, could Susan jump in and reveal the reason for the afternoon's visit.

Edna's pleasure was immediately replaced by irritated scepticism. 'Principles,' she stated, 'are the luxury of the well-to-do. I'd have no problem saying or doing anything that would secure my tenancy.'

'We have nothing to lose.'

'You're wrong, dear. If Kevin doesn't withdraw the

notices, not only will the evictions go ahead but he'll get off scot-free. I need a guarantee.'

'Kevin will never agree to put an arrangement in writing.'

'So,' continued Edna, 'he'll have to cancel the evictions before I speak to the police. I'm sorry, but Robin will have to renegotiate the deal.'

Susan thanked Edna for her time and left to break the news to Robert.

❖❖❖

In the Scottish Borders, many miles north of Pendrick Court, Linda was mesmerised by her mother's bank statement. Although she held joint power of attorney with Alan for their mother's affairs, she hadn't requested one for nearly three years. Together with the four-weekly nursing home fees, the account had been haemorrhaging hundreds of pounds a week via ATMs. Linda reluctantly crept to the conclusion that her brother was taking the cash for himself.

Guilt-ridden, she chastised herself for sidestepping her responsibilities but her self-loathing was dwarfed by the anger she was feeling towards Alan. She would have to call him, but not today. Her anger would simmer and boil over when he started to spout one of his cock-and-bull stories to justify the withdrawals.

The heat of Pendrick Court was not evident in the market town of Kelso, so Linda donned a cardigan before going into her back garden. With brooding eyes, she fixed her gaze across the slothful river. Her emotions were a mixture of fury and pity. What a wasted life Alan had had! On the back of his achievements at grammar school, he could have had a full scholarship to university, but he was wooed by the money he could earn in the print industry. Where did that get him? Years of drinking away his pay packet in the pub, and then redundancy.

It didn't take him long to drink his redundancy payment as well, then he limped towards retirement selling office supplies. He'd never had a partner and, despite his dazzling tales of his travels, he'd never been abroad. He was just a tragic man with a yarn to spin. Now, potless and pointless, he was syphoning off Mother's money. Bastard!

CHAPTER FIFTY-FOUR

IT was fast approaching six o'clock when Megan walked home after her shift. She checked her face in the bathroom mirror and cursed her decision to wear a velour tracksuit in the blistering heat. Thick layers of slap had prevented her face from sweating, and clogged pores always spawned a breakout of spots. She'd soon have a complexion like a gravel driveway.

In the kitchen, she grubbed around in the cutlery drawer until she found the gadgets. Within seconds, she had clicked open the circular security tag, folded the Calvin Klein polo shirt and placed it in a plastic bag.

Her friends were wrong: ditching Jack wasn't the only solution. Yes, of course she was worth more than this but she couldn't afford to live on her own, even with her stepfather paying the rent. In the absence of a better offer, Jack would have to do.

She would present him with the shirt and allow him to return from his exile in the spare room. Later, if he took a shower, she would instigate a love tussle beneath the sheets and refrain from criticising or dispensing instructions. Tonight her moans would be those of fulfilment, not exasperation.

Before she had time to change out of her tracksuit and scrape off her makeup, a gangling Jack guided his bike into Apartment 8. Megan smiled coyly and presented the shirt. Jack opened the bag, then held up the gift by its shoulders. 'I hope you like it,' said Megan. 'It wasn't from the sale rack.'

'Thanks. I didn't know Calvin Klein made clothes too. I've heard of his aftershave.'

'There's a lot of competition in the fragrance and perfume market,' replied Megan knowledgeably. 'He's diversifying into quality leisure wear and sports clothing.'

'Does this mean I'm forgiven?'

Megan re-stated Jack's wrongdoings before explaining the terms of his conditional discharge. Despite being guilty, she would punish him no further – provided communication with Jessica stopped immediately. Jack was no stranger to Megan's ultimatums, the terms of which he'd always agreed to and then swiftly ignored.

Their conciliatory embrace was interrupted by a text message on Jack's phone. Paul was asking if Jack could call round to his apartment the following morning. Megan pulled at his phone to check that the message was indeed from Paul and not the strumpet.

Clueless as to why Paul would want to see him, Jack replied that he'd be over at ten-thirty.

❖❖❖

'Are you okay up there?' called Sean from the courtyard.

Edna looked down. 'Not really, dear.'

'Can I help?'

'Yes, please. The door's unlocked. I'm on the balcony.'

Sean tapped on the door to Apartment 5 before he let himself in. 'What's the problem?'

Edna held up a stainless-steel nut feeder. 'I'm trying to attach this to the handrail. The man in the hardware store said it would go on easily. Fat lot he knows.'

Sean studied it for a few seconds then clipped it onto the rail. 'There we go. It was just a bit stiff.'

'Thank you, dear. The starlings will love that. Can I pour you a cup of tea for your trouble?'

'It wasn't any trouble and I'm not thirsty, thanks.'

'Is your friend waiting for you upstairs?'

'No. He left a while back. He'll be at the hospital by now.'

'Heavens above! What happened?'

Sean smiled. 'He's not there for treatment. He's a junior doctor.'

'A *doctor* only a few feet from my door and nobody told me? I shall have to catch him next time he's here. I could do with a second opinion on one or two matters.'

'He'd love that. Next time you see him, just come over. He's a whizz with urine samples. It's amazing what he can tell just by holding them up to the light.'

Awestruck, Edna assured Sean that she could manage a specimen in a glass bottle. 'Has Robert told you the good news?'

'I've not heard from Robert,' replied Sean.

'Well, we haven't got to worry about the evictions any more. Your father's withdrawing them in return for my revised statement to the police.'

'That does sound like good news. How sure are you that my dad will keep his word?'

'I'm not. That's why Robert's going back to your father to tell him to withdraw the notices before I speak to the police.'

'Let's hope Dad plays ball.'

❖❖❖

A pink and lavender sky made a captivating backcloth to the city's skyline. Pendrick Court was unwinding and preparing to close for the night.

While Susan took her bath, Robert fretted about Edna's refusal to speak to the police.

Madison was in her bedroom, lying on her stomach with her headphones on, listening to an album by Billie Eilish. Toby had joined her in an attempt to escape 'Un Ballo In Maschera', which Anah was enjoying in the sitting room rather more loudly than he would have liked.

A Byrds' album was poised on the record player, waiting for Paul to finish his video chat with Noi.

Jessica was absent from Pendrick Court. She was keeping Dino on his toes, shouting through pizza orders on Grove Road.

The medical encyclopaedia lay open on the kitchen table in Apartment 5, where Edna was engrossed in an article on deep-vein thrombosis.

Sean was upstairs in Apartment 6 printing address labels and wrapping rucksacks.

Alan was sitting in silence in his kitchen with Jim Beam for company.

On the floor above, Megan was painting her toe nails in the sitting room, wondering which would last longer: her planned bedroom frolics or Jack's shower.

CHAPTER FIFTY-FIVE
Sunday, 2nd June

ALAN reached for his alarm clock and drew it close to his face. How had he managed to sleep through until ten-thirty? He swung his legs off the bed and sat up.

Today was a bright new day and he was going to be positive. Perhaps Robert would text with news that they could stay at Pendrick Court. Perhaps the nursing home would call with news that his frail and distressed mother had freed up both a bed and his inheritance.

He would slice a banana onto his breakfast cereal and might even go for a stroll in the park. And today would be alcohol-free. But first he needed to pee. He manoeuvred himself into the en suite, placed the flat of one hand against the wall and began a battle of wills with an enlarged prostate as he waited to come on stream.

❖ ❖ ❖

Paul handed Jack a mug of coffee. 'I won't beat around the bush. I asked you over because I'm offering you a job.'

Jack almost injured himself containing his excitement. 'Thanks.'

'You'd be working with me four days a week. The fifth you'd have to go to college to get your plumbing and heating qualifications.'

'Okay,' nodded Jack.

'You'd need to learn to drive pretty sharpish, too. If I could call through the parts I needed and someone could pick them up, I'd save so much time. I'm turning work away.'

'I'm keen ... dead keen. But if we have to move—'

'Don't worry about that. I could pick you up and drop you off until we got you your own van.'

'And the money? I don't know how much driving lessons would be.'

'You'd be on minimum wage until you'd got your qualifications. Forty hours a week, including your day at college, and I'd pay for your driving lessons. When you're qualified, we'd sit down and talk money.'

'When were you thinking I'd start?'

'I get back from my holidays on the ninth of August. So I thought Monday, the twelfth of August. That would give us time to sort out any move and a college course for September. You'd need to give notice at the supermarket.'

'I'm a worker not an employee, so I don't have to give notice. If I told them I was leaving, they wouldn't give me any hours. I'd keep schtum.'

'Okay. And until you're qualified, we'd have to take

our holidays at the same time.'

'Do you want me to sign anything?'

'Not right now. You need to go away and think. Come back with any questions you have and then, if it's really what you want, I'll get a contract drawn up.'

'Can I come back tonight?'

'When you've done all the thinking you're gonna do, text me and we'll arrange for you to come over again.'

Jack finished his coffee and shook Paul's hand, calculating the number of weeks until the twelfth of August. He swung his arms as he loped back across the courtyard and almost started skipping.

❖❖❖

Alan had barely finished his breakfast when he answered the phone sounding unnaturally ebullient. Linda cut short her brother's waffle by telling him that she had their mother's bank statement in front of her. In the silent interlude that followed, all her worst fears were vindicated. 'We need to talk face to face,' she continued. 'I'm busy tomorrow, so I'll drive down Tuesday. I'll visit Mother late afternoon, check into a hotel and see you—'

'There's no need to check into—'

'Let me finish. I'll see you on Tuesday evening. As soon as I arrive, you will be signing a form to disclaim your appointment as Mother's attorney.'

'You can't just—'

'Whether I contact the Office of the Public Guardian and report your theft of Mother's money will depend on how our conversation goes. I'll call you half an hour before I'm due to arrive. Goodbye.'

The violence of the call shattered Alan's optimism and waves of dread rolled through him. He sought succour from a bottle of Jack Daniel's.

❖❖❖

The clatter of Jack exploding into Apartment 8 brought Megan into the kitchen to investigate. He danced around the table, laughing. Megan allowed the folly to persist for ten infuriating seconds before calling it to a halt. 'Why are you jumping around our kitchen like a drunken stripper?'

'Guess what just happened.'

'You traded your bike for some magic beans?'

'Nope. Paul's just gone and offered me a job. A proper full-time job with day release at college and prospects.'

'Why?'

'He didn't say. Perhaps he thought we worked well together on the roof.' Jack planted his hands on Megan's shoulders. 'He's going to pay for driving lessons and give me a company van. I'm going to learn a trade. Ten more miserable weeks and I'm out of retail for good.'

Megan slipped from his grasp, moved through to the sitting room and onto the balcony. Whilst a qualified plumber sounded more impressive than a customer assistant – it even had social media bragging potential – any kudos she enjoyed would be from riding on the back of his achievements.

Jack followed her out.

'What if you can't cope with the college course?' she asked. 'Paul might let you go and you'd end up jobless.'

'Paul knows I've got no experience in plumbing and heating, so I'll have to start with the basics.'

'What if you can't manage the basics?'

'Thanks!'

As Megan contemplated the horror of Jack's elevated status, Christopher walked into Pendrick Court wearing his dog collar. 'Look! There's a priest heading towards Paul's apartment,' she exclaimed.

'He's not going to Paul's apartment. He's going to see Jessica.'

'They're supposed to be celibate. I don't blame *him* though. She's probably been grooming him on the Internet. She'll soon cure him of any lustful desires. He'll never go near a woman after today.'

'He's not here for that. He's her brother. I met him at the protest.'

'Well,' scoffed Megan, 'if a priest isn't visiting her for sex, he can only be here for one other reason – exorcism.'

'You are pleased I've been given this opportunity, aren't you? It's a chance to make something of my life.'

'I could have made something of mine,' replied Megan

defensively. 'If it wasn't for the physical requirements, I could have been a model. Lots of people have said so.'

'You can still be a model, if that's what you want. Not all models are beautiful.'

'I was referring to my height.'

CHAPTER FIFTY-SIX

JESSICA wrapped her arms around her brother, squeezed him tightly then led him to the sofa. 'Now, I know you prefer not to eat cake and biscuits, so I've got some Braeburn apples or pickled onions.'

Christopher didn't try to conceal his amusement. 'Every time we meet, you give me a reason to love you even more.'

'What are you talking about?' she asked, walking into the kitchen.

'Only you would think to substitute pickled onions for a biscuit.'

'You could eat them after your coffee.'

'I thought I'd have tea. I wouldn't want to deny you the pleasure of delivering your "More tea, vicar?" line.'

Jessica tipped some ginger snaps onto a plate and popped teabags into two mugs. While the kettle was boiling, she joined Christopher on the sofa, putting one hand on his knee and leaving the other free to access the biscuits. 'Last night, I told Dino about our eviction notices and the protest outside Kevin's shop. He looked really concerned and offered me his spare room.'

'Does he live above the pizzeria?'

'No. There are offices above. He rents an apartment five minutes away.'

'And do you think the offer is genuine? I mean, with no strings attached.'

'He might be hoping for strings but he's not the sort of bloke who'd help himself. You'd have to make it quite clear that the strings were there for the plucking.'

Christopher helped himself to a ginger snap. 'If you want to keep your strings to yourself, moving in with Dino might not be a good idea. You don't want to give him false hope.'

'That's what I thought. I'll give it – or rather *him* – a lot of thought before I decide whether to take him up on his offer. Kettle's boiled.'

❖❖❖

Sunlight and a Dolly Parton ballad echoed around Apartment 1. Susan was ironing in the sitting room, contentedly placing each finished shirt on a plastic coat hanger and hanging them on the door handle.

Robert, markedly less content, was looking through the patio doors onto the courtyard, fluctuating between nail and cheek biting. How long would it be before Kevin discovered that Edna hadn't eliminated the threat of prosecution? When he did, it wouldn't be her upon whom his displeasure rained. Robert knew who'd be in the firing line.

With as much dispassion as he could gather, he cleared his throat and turned to Susan, who silenced the music. 'Kevin's not going to renegotiate our deal. I'm certain we've had his best offer. If Edna doesn't call off the police, the evictions will go ahead.'

Susan switched off her iron. 'I can see you're concerned. Perhaps we could steer Edna and Kevin towards a compromise.'

'That would literally be a renegotiation.'

'Bear with me. If, for example, Kevin were to cancel *some* of the evictions, leaving Edna's and some others in place, she would trust his intentions and Kevin would still hold the upper hand.'

'I know you're trying to help, but he will not make concessions.'

Susan was perplexed but didn't push the matter because Robert's rising impatience was so intense it was almost tangible.

'You have to convince Edna to speak to the police,' he said. 'And don't take no for an answer.'

❖❖❖

After a few soothing shots, Alan returned the Jack Daniel's to its cupboard. He needed to stay sober. In two days' time, Linda would be here. He would prepare the spare room; if he could coax her into having an alcoholic drink or two, she wouldn't drive back to the hotel. He could placate her, convince her that he was sorry. She was his sister so she would forgive him.

He should move the orange plastic box, whose biscuits for cheese he had replaced with stolen £20 notes. If Linda suspected that Mother's money was still in his apartment, nothing would stop her searching for it.

Sweating hard, he tried to think of an ingenious hiding place. Like the bursting of a bubble, a solution popped into his head. Clutching the work surface, he eased himself down onto his knees and opened the cupboard under the sink. He pulled out the orange box, dislodging bottles and cans, then he dug deeper and swept out the cleaning products. He found a reel of brown masking tape and scrambled upright. His eyes were stinging from the sweat which was running into them; his handkerchief wasn't going to cut it, so he swabbed his face with a tea towel.

Brushing the cupboard's contents to one side with his foot, he cleared a path to the kitchen table. He tore off a long piece of tape and wrapped it around the box, then he repeated the action, crossing over the first strip.

With the box and one smaller item in a carrier bag, Alan left his apartment and negotiated the stairs to the ground floor. The heat in the courtyard was intense. An inverted triangle of sweat appeared on the front of his shirt; circular patches the size of dart boards formed under his armpits.

He turned right, aiming for the entrance to Apartments 5 and 6, but after only a few steps he was struggling to breathe. He leaned against the building to absorb more oxygen. A minute or two later, he resumed his quest and reached for the intercom.

Confused as to why nobody understood the requirement to speak into the intercom, Edna pressed the entry button and gave permission to her unknown guest to come up.

Once inside Edna's apartment, Alan accepted her invitation to sit. She fetched him a glass of iced water, while he caught his breath. The refuge of the sofa and the cold liquid running down his throat were sufficient to resuscitate him.

He took the box from its bag and passed it to Edna. The contents, he explained, were cherished family photographs. His sister was visiting Tuesday evening and she was prone to nosing through his things so he didn't want her getting her hands on them.

Edna was happy to keep them away from his grasping sister.

Alan handed over the plastic bag and warned Edna not to walk about the apartment in the dark. She opened the bag and found a flashlight for her bedside table.

CHAPTER FIFTY-SEVEN

ANAH stood in the sitting-room doorway and smiled down on Madison and Toby who were lounging on the sofa. 'I'm just popping out to the shop. I'll be back in twenty minutes.'

Madison looked up and waved her phone. 'We'll see you soon. Toby and I are just catching up on the news. Apparently President Trump's arriving tomorrow for a three-day visit.'

'Then I'd better get baking when I return.'

'Any news from Robert?'

'No, not yet. Perhaps he can't get hold of Kevin. I did receive an email from your dad's executor Brian, though. He's updated your school with your new address and passed on my contact details.'

'I've been thinking about that. The funeral's a week tomorrow. I'm sure I'll be ready to go back to school on the Tuesday.'

'It's good to have a plan, but don't be hard on yourself if you're not quite ready.'

Anah descended the two flights of stairs. Before

she left the courtyard, she turned when she heard her name. Edna came belting towards her, spilling over with anxiety about Alan. 'He's putting on a brave face, but I'm really worried about him. He visited me this morning. I told him that Kevin had agreed to abandon the evictions in return for my revised statement to the police, but he didn't bat an eyelid. I think Kevin has ground him down to the point of no return.'

'Kevin is withdrawing the eviction notices?'

'As soon as we receive a letter cancelling them, I'll speak to the police. Alan looks terrible. I don't know what to do.'

'When I return from the shop, I'll go over and see if there's anything we can do for him.'

'Thank you so much, dear. That'll put my mind at rest.'

The sight of the black Audi drawing into the courtyard had Edna racing back to the safety of her apartment. Anah walked towards Kevin as he parked outside the entrance to Apartments 7 and 8. 'May I have a minute of your time, Mr Douglas?' she asked.

'If you're quick,' said Kevin,

'I understand that, with provisos, you've decided to scrap the eviction notices—'

'Absolute nonsense! The evictions are going ahead as planned.'

'I apologise for having my wires crossed. I have a proposition that I would ask you to consider. I would like to purchase my apartment—'

'Short answer, no. Long answer, no. And you've got a bastard nerve.' Ignoring Anah, he took a bunch of keys from his pocket and singled out the padlock key.

'I'm not asking for any special treatment. I would pay the market value.'

'On Wednesday I asked for your assistance to manage the witch hunt in the local paper. You sent me away with a flea in my ear.' He took a step closer to Anah and raised his voice. 'The following day, you demonstrated outside my home and business. I treated you with respect—'

'Before you take the moral high ground,' said Anah, matching his volume, 'let me remind you that you let me spend thousands on refurbishing an apartment from which you intended to evict me. You didn't do me the courtesy of speaking to me before I received the eviction notice through the post. *And* I overheard your conversation from my balcony in which you referred to me as Anal Annie. So don't talk to me about respect.'

'I have no recollection of referring to you—'

'It probably got lost in your homophobic and racist rant.'

'Racist! I never—'

'You referred to Ishaan as a Paki.'

'That wasn't directed at you. I've never minded your skin colour.'

'*MINDED*! My skin colour is not some social infraction for you to excuse.'

'I'm not debating semantics with a self-righteous

liberal Leftie. We'll have to agree to disagree and get on with our day.'

Anah glared with vampire eyes. 'I will get on with my day. But I do not agree to disagree, for fear of giving some credibility to your mindset.' With a disparaging flap of her shopping bag, she headed towards the archway.

❖ ❖ ❖

Ishaan swanned into Apartment 6, managed to step over a pile of rucksacks wrapped in brown paper and clambered onto the sofa.

'Mate, I've never seen you in shorts,' grinned Sean.

'You've never seen me when it's this hot.'

'Those legs wouldn't look out of place on a greyhound.'

'Thanks for boosting my self-confidence, Thunder Thighs.'

'What's that?' asked Sean pointing to the paperwork in Ishaan's hand.

'The particulars of some rental properties I picked up from an estate agent. For you.'

'Cheers. I'll look at them when I've got these packaged and loaded into the van.'

Ishaan put his feet up on the sofa. 'You told me that you moved in here because your dad didn't want you living under his roof. You never told me why. What did you do?'

'I was in my bedroom on a video call with Mum. He overheard us and he went apoplectic.'

'Because you were being deceitful?'

'I'm not sure. He'd always had a temper ... always shouted at me. But this time he completely lost it. He was literally screaming at me. He said he'd protected me for eighteen years and now I'd have to protect myself.'

'Protect yourself from what?'

'From her. He said she was dangerous, that her only interest in me was to torture him.'

'He must really hate her.'

'I didn't see hate in his face, I saw fear. While I was packing my things, he gave me an envelope with "6 Pendrick Court" written on it. Inside the envelope was the key.'

'Does your mum seem dangerous to you?'

'She's a little – eccentric. Anyway, help yourself to a drink. I must crack on packing these.'

CHAPTER FIFTY-EIGHT

ANAH'S usual preference was for heat over cold, but today she longed for a lungful of cool, invigorating air. Beads of sweat helped to cool her head as she ambled back to Pendrick Court with the milk, butter and chocolate in her shopping bag. She strayed slightly from a direct path to Alan's apartment in order to greet Christopher, who was in the process of leaving. They exchanged pleasantries before she walked around the Audi to get to the intercom.

Alan opened the entrance door remotely and stood holding open the door to his apartment. Moments later, he welcomed Anah into his home. A miasma of stale sweat and Jack Daniel's hung around him as he sat in his armchair, giving a strained smile to his guest.

Anah placed her bag on the floor and sat forward on the sofa. 'I'm not going to patronise you, Alan. I'm here because Edna is worried about you. She thinks you're struggling to cope with the stress of the evictions.'

'The last few weeks have been demanding, but nothing I can't handle.'

'Alan, as a concerned neighbour, and I hope as a friend, I'm telling you that you don't appear to be managing. I'm not judging you. I'm here to offer you some support, if it's wanted.'

'You're a good woman, Anah, but there's nothing you can do to help me.'

'Why don't you try me? I can be very resourceful.'

Anah's words prised off Alan's confident, jovial veneer to reveal the despondent insecurity beneath. 'I'm just predisposed to drawing the short straw. I look around at others' good fortune with jealousy and a sense of grief.'

'We can always find somebody better or worse off than ourselves, but finding them doesn't change our situation. We need to put our energy into making our own luck rather than comparing ourselves to others.'

'With all due respect, you're somebody that drew the long straw in life.'

Anah paused before responding. 'It hasn't always felt that way. When I fled my home, it was in the throes of a savage coup. I sought refuge in a country that didn't want me. I didn't feel particularly lucky.'

'Was it Britain that didn't want you?'

'Yes. And my son's death felt pretty unlucky too. Sorry, this shouldn't be about me. Let's focus on what I can do to help you move forward.'

'It's me who should be sorry. I'm being selfish and making ridiculous assumptions. And I'd completely forgotten that you'd just lost your son.'

'It's okay. Are you worried about finding a new home?'

'Edna said something about Kevin withdrawing the notices—'

'I believe Edna has misunderstood the situation. I'm afraid we are going to have to move out. But there's time enough to get organised. Perhaps you could speak to the housing team at the council. Or, if you prefer, I could bring my tablet and help you search for somewhere on the Internet.'

'I'm tied up for a couple of days but I will phone the council on Wednesday.'

'Excellent! I'll call and see how you get on. If you don't mind, I'd like to get this shopping into my fridge before it's spoiled in the heat.'

On her way home, Anah saw that Kevin's car hadn't moved during her social call to Alan; accordingly, Toby would have to suspend his time in the exercise yard and be confined in Apartment 2 until later in the day.

❖❖❖

For the second day in succession, Edna welcomed Susan into the living area of her apartment. The pair were stifled by the sweet, earthy redolence of a baking potato and the heat from the oven.

'Your visit's well-timed,' said Edna, handing a bulky black book to Susan. 'You'll be pleased to hear that I found a photograph album after you left yesterday. Do have a look while I make us some tea.'

Through deference rather than burning curiosity, Susan started leafing through the pages of the dusty album. 'You're a very photogenic family, Edna.'

'Sorry, I couldn't hear you above the whirring of the oven.' Edna leaned over and handed Susan a mug of tea.

'I said that you're all very photogenic.'

'Thank you. My late husband and I were, and so was our son eventually. He didn't blossom until the age of three. Before that he was quite unsightly.'

'I don't think he was.'

'You don't need to be polite, dear.' Edna lifted a plastic-wrapped vase from the coffee table. 'Let me take this out of your way. You don't want to sit there looking at a glass of my piddle.'

'You have your piddle in a vase?'

'It's waiting for Ishaan's next visit. Now, how did Robin get on with Kevin. Can we expect a letter cancelling the evictions?'

Lying to Edna was an agonising experience for Susan, but refusing to fall in with Robert's demands would be even more traumatic. His negotiations with Kevin had been such a triumph that she didn't want to be the person responsible for ruining his victory.

Kevin, Susan explained, was hurt by Edna's mistrust. Despite all the aggravation that the tenants had caused him, he had found it in his heart to quash the evictions. All he asked for was a goodwill gesture: clarification to the police of Thursday's misunderstanding. He was holding out an olive branch and if Edna wasn't prepared to take it, he would take his chances with the courts and the evictions would go ahead.

Edna sat motionless, save for toying with the vase. 'I appreciate all the effort your husband's gone to—'

'Robert's not my husband, Edna. He's my brother.'

'Your secret is safe with me, dear,' whispered Edna.

'There's no secret, Edna. It's not a romantic relationship, just a practical arrangement.'

'That's probably for the best. Do you believe Kevin will keep his word if I speak to the police?'

'Robert seems to think so and I trust his judgement.'

'Let me think on it overnight.'

'Thank you, Edna. It's a big decision, I know. Can I call around in the morning?'

'Yes. I'll be back from the chemist's by ten-thirty.'

CHAPTER FIFTY-NINE

WHITE noise from an oscillating fan was failing to choke the ticking of an art-deco mantel clock. Alan checked the time on his wristwatch and realised that he must have dozed off for at least thirty minutes. Still fuddled from the inroads he had made into the bottle of Jack Daniel's, he slooshed a further helping into his sticky tumbler.

It was four in the afternoon – too late to start preparing the spare room. He'd do that tomorrow. With a bit of luck, it might be cooler by then.

He hadn't eaten since breakfast so he tried to remember if there was anything in the freezer that would cook from frozen. There might be some breaded fish and some oven chips to line his stomach.

Linda's dreaded visit would be a humiliating one. How she would enjoy spitting accusations of criminality, reminding him of what a failure he'd always been and gloating.

If he failed to orchestrate her sympathy and she did contact the Office of the Public Guardian, embarrassment in front of her would be the least of his worries.

He would be exposed and disgraced before the world. No doubt the police would be involved, too.

Of course, he'd have to disclaim his appointment as their mother's attorney. That would mean no more withdrawals. But he wasn't going to return the money he'd already taken. He needed to convince her that he had spent it – but what would he say he'd spent it on?

Alan poured more Jack Daniel's. He'd stalled Anah until Wednesday, but he did need a housing plan. He didn't want to live in social housing. He wouldn't call the council; he'd say he couldn't get through because the line was permanently engaged. He'd take up Anah's offer to help him search for a place on the Internet. This time around, he'd be sure to rent ground-floor accommodation; stairs were far too taxing nowadays.

A gambling addiction! That would make clear where all the money had gone. That would explain why he had nothing to show for it. Alan's heart raced. There was hope. Linda would take pity on him, especially if he promised to seek help.

He held the bottle up to eye level then emptied the last measure into his glass. He drained the tumbler then staggered to the kitchen. He saw nothing inside the freezer that he wanted to eat. He moved to the window and looked out onto the empty courtyard.

He hadn't had a Chinese takeaway for an eternity and the restaurant was no more than a ten-minute walk. He imagined the crispy, greasy batter and the cloying Dayglo sauce of the sweet-and-sour pork balls and his mind was made up. He snatched his wallet.

Having locked the door, he grabbed the handrails at the top of the staircase and waited a moment for any signs that he'd need to pee within the hour. The bladder situation was promising, so he descended with calculated steps. At the bottom, giddiness and a shortage of breath forced him to sit on a stair. He was never going to make it to the restaurant and back. Perhaps he would telephone Jessica; she would know how to order a pizza and have it delivered to his door.

At seventy years old, he should have known that consuming an entire bottle of whisky in an afternoon in this heat was going to stop him fetching a takeaway. He admonished himself for being so foolhardy and retraced his steps. He gripped both handrails as tightly as he could and watched where he placed his feet. The journey up was more onerous than the journey down. He would sit at the kitchen table and call Jessica from there.

The heat and his physical inadequacies connived in impeding his ascent. Alan was now hyperconscious of his need to breathe. A tight, heavy chest compelled him to inhale before he'd finished exhaling.

Just two steps from the top, he struggled to lift his foot high enough to clear the stair. His legs buckled and his sweaty hands couldn't hold his weight. Like a felled oak, he tumbled backwards. His head bounced off a lino-covered stair with a lusty clunk and the stairs returned his body to the bottom.

CHAPTER SIXTY

'INSTEAD of fish and chips,' said Megan, 'why don't we have a hot dog and popcorn at the cinema?'

Without averting his eyes from the television screen, Jack asked what was showing. Megan had anticipated the question and was already tapping the screen on her phone. '*The Secret Life of Pets 2.*'

'What else?'

'Nothing we'd like.'

'You mean nothing *you'd* like. Let me see.' Megan handed over her phone. 'There you go. *Godzilla 2.*'

'I'll toss a coin.' She took a coin from her purse, flipped it, caught it, slapped it onto the back of her hand then pushed it in front of Jack's face. 'Tails. I win.'

'You didn't call.'

'Didn't have to. I always call tails. Get your trainers on.'

Sporting his new Calvin Klein polo shirt and a sullen pout, Jack followed Megan out of Apartment 8 and down the flight of stairs to the first floor. As she turned the corner and reached the top of the final staircase, she froze and gulped a mouthful of air.

'What are you doing?' snapped Jack. Her actions were explained when he looked down the stairs. 'Shit! Shall I call an ambulance?'

Megan didn't answer. She just stared at Alan, waiting for him to move.

'Right, I'm calling an ambulance,' Jack declared.

❖ ❖ ❖

'So Kevin won't sell the apartment to you?' asked Madison.

'No. He made that, and the fact that the evictions are going ahead, quite clear,' replied Anah. 'He's such a loathsome man.'

'If the new owners sell off the apartments individually, perhaps you can buy yours from them.'

'It's possible, but it does mean living in rented accommodation until that time comes.'

Madison jerked with a start as Toby leapt onto her lap and demanded some attention. 'This handsome moggy is not going to like being dragged away from his territory.'

'No. We'll have to keep him indoors for a few weeks until he's used to a new home. He might try and find his way back to Pendrick Court. I think that's my phone pinging.' Anah read the text message and walked over to the patio doors.

'What is it?' asked Madison.

'It's a text message from young Jack. He says Alan is

at the bottom of the stairs. He's called an ambulance. He and Megan are waiting in their apartment.'

'No mention of whether he's conscious or not?'

'No. There's little traffic on a Sunday, so an ambulance should be here soon. I think I ought to pop over and be with Edna when it arrives. She's been so worried about Alan.'

❖ ❖ ❖

The wind had forsaken Pendrick Court. Tarmac twinkled and red bricks baked in the scorching sun. Even the gargoyles faltered from their customary resilience and started to flag.

An ambulance crept around the courtyard and stopped outside the entrance to Apartments 7 and 8. Jack hit the entry button from upstairs and the crew entered the building.

Traffic noise succumbed to the warbling siren of a police car as Anah walked across to Edna's apartment. Edna hit her entry button and Anah climbed the stairs. Once seated next to Edna on the sofa, she presented Jack's text. Edna, instantly roused from summer's sluggish hex, braced herself to swoop in and bestow comfort upon an ailing Alan but was immobilised by Anah's revelation that the paramedics were already with him. She rushed to the balcony. 'There's a police car too.'

'If they take Alan to hospital, they'll want to know

his next of kin.'

'His mother's at the Bergamot Nursing Home. The poor dear's got dementia. He's got a sister, though. The nursing home is bound to have her details.'

'I should go down and wait for them to come out. Will you be alright?'

'I'll be fine. Just come back and let me know what they're saying.'

❖ ❖ ❖

Robert and Susan, Madison, Paul, Jessica, Edna, Sean and Ishaan were all standing on their respective balconies, awaiting some activity from the uniformed outsiders. A police officer was in Apartment 8 talking with Jack and Megan. Megan was uncommonly quiet and not a little unnerved.

Anah stood back as the paramedics brought Alan out of the building. His body was completely covered. A police officer approached her. 'Are you a neighbour?'

'Yes. I live in Apartment 2.' Anah was unable to take her eyes off the stretcher. 'I presume Alan's—'

'Unfortunately, Mr Marshall died before the paramedics arrived.'

Light-headed and shaking slightly, Anah managed to provide details of the mother's location and mention that there was a sister. She explained that she and Edna had seen Alan earlier that day, that he appeared to be anxious about his impending eviction and had been drinking alcohol. She mentioned that the landlord had been on the rooftop patio during her entire visit.

As the ambulance pulled out of Pendrick Court, Anah left a contact number with the officer and called Madison with the news. Then she climbed the stairs again to Apartment 5. From the sofa, Edna shouted instructions to enter. The old woman sat with her arms held out in front of her. 'I can raise both arms. Is my speech slurred?' she asked.

'Your speech sounds fine to me,' Anah said.

'And the side of my face hasn't drooped?'

'No.'

'It's not a mini-stroke then.'

'I'm afraid I've got some very bad news, Edna. Alan's accident was fatal.'

'It was no accident. Kevin *murdered* him.'

'Edna! That's a very—'

'I don't mean he threw him down the stairs, I mean he drove him to drink. Kevin Douglas has blood on his hands.'

Anah drew closer. 'But how are you? Would you like me to make you some tea?'

'No, dear. I'm fine. I do death very well. You should be with Madison.'

CHAPTER SIXTY-ONE

THE wind popped its head into the courtyard to let the residents know that rain was on its way. Nobody noticed. The police officers had spoken briefly and tactfully to each of them. Satisfied that nothing suspicious had been seen or heard, they drove to Kevin's apartment to speak to him too.

Susan was leaning against the kitchen sink, taking her mind off Alan's death by contemplating a weekend in London with her grandchildren and Chloe. Robert was sitting in silence, trying to convince himself that Alan fell by mischance and not at the hands of Kevin Douglas.

Upstairs, Madison and Anah were on a sofa – the former listening to music through wireless earbuds, while the latter, e-reader in hand, was losing herself in historical fiction.

Jessica had left for work. Ishaan had been cajoled into the mammoth task of rucksack packing.

Megan was awaiting reactions to her 'feeling stressed – found a dead man in my apartment' post. Jack was irritated. Before he had left to buy some fish and chips, Megan had said she couldn't possibly eat a thing after seeing what she'd seen. Now his supper was on the table, the greedy bitch was picking food off his plate.

Edna was standing at the open entrance door to Apartments 3 and 4. Paul came downstairs and handed her a can of red spray paint. 'Is this what you wanted?' he asked.

'That will do nicely. Thank you.'

'You're not going to scale the walls to the rooftop patio, are you?'

Edna frowned. 'I wouldn't spray our walls, dear. I have to look at them.'

❖ ❖ ❖

Kelly had arranged for one of her staff to collate the day's newspaper returns so she could comply with Kevin's demand to see him in his apartment.

'I told him yesterday to resolve the issue that Pembleton woman has caused,' Kevin said angrily. 'Yesterday! I texted him this evening to ask if the matter's been put to bed and he replied that it's in hand.'

'Perhaps Edna Pembleton isn't cooperating,' suggested Kelly.

'Perhaps Robert Page needs a kick up the arse – something to spur him on. And that's where you come in.'

'You want *me* to talk to him?'

'No. I'm going to help you break into his apartment and make a bastard mess.' Kelly's expression revealed her lack of enthusiasm for the idea. 'I'm not proposing root canal treatment without anaesthetic.'

'But you're asking me to do something illegal.'

Kevin lowered his voice in an attempt to speak softly. 'My dear wife and my only child have forsaken me. You are my only ally. I think of you as more than an employee, I think of you as a friend.' Kelly blushed. Kevin found a smile. 'I would never put you in danger. My plan is watertight.'

'Well, I do think you have been treated abysmally. Okay, I'll help.'

'Good. We'll leave here at nine tomorrow morning and lie in wait at Pendrick Court until the Pages leave their apartment. Come in an hour earlier to make sure you're on top of work before we leave.'

❖❖❖

Edna waylaid Ishaan on the landing. She put his apparent disinterest in her medical history and specimen down to the aftermath of Alan's death and let him leave the building. She'd catch him again when he was less distracted.

As the clock approached midnight, Edna completed her black ensemble with a black bucket hat, left Pendrick Court and stole into the city streets. Her eyes were tired – she'd normally be in bed at this time – but determination kept her moving.

She stopped fifteen minutes into her mission, opened her black handbag, took out a sheer black stocking and tried to pull it over her head. Deciding that it would be easier to remove her hat first, she tried again then replaced her hat.

She walked a little further until she reached Kevin's apartment. Taking out the can of red spray paint, she shook it violently and eyed her canvas: the wall next to the door to Kevin's apartment. She waited for a solitary car to glide past then, using a considerable amount of her strength, sprayed the word *MURDERER* in five-foot-high letters over the wall and door.

Heading back to Pendrick Court and her bed, she was content with her night's work. There'd be snowboarding in Jamaica before she called the police and helped that piece of shit wriggle out of an assault charge – not even if he withdrew the eviction notices.

As the soporific tapping of her black shoes echoed on the deserted pavement, Edna thought of Alan, his thunderous laugh and anecdotes of past adventures. She remembered their taxi ride to the protest, both dressed for a royal wedding, and the flashlight he'd brought her. She swallowed the lump in her throat. Perhaps she didn't do death as well as she'd thought.

CHAPTER SIXTY-TWO
Monday, 3rd June

KEVIN was standing on the pavement in front of his apartment, unleashing a cascade of inspired invective at the defacement on his wall and door, when Kelly appeared. 'It's the same bastard paint they used on my patio,' he said, pointing in the direction of the graffiti in case Kelly had missed the five-foot letters. 'I thought this bollocks was over. The police were here yesterday, asking if Alan's dead body was at the bottom of the stairs when I left Pendrick Court.'

'He was a *big* man,' Kelly chipped in. 'It's not as though you could have stepped over him without noticing.'

'Now I'm wondering if one of them deadbeat tenants has told the police that I'd murdered the pretentious slob.'

'Best we get this paint off then, before somebody takes a photograph and posts it on the Internet.'

'Especially as it was only last week that one of my simple-minded staff tried to drown him in extinguisher foam.'

'Yesterday evening you thought of me as a friend.

Today I'm simple-minded staff.'

'Friendship closes its eyes to put downs, Kelly. I'll call Sean and get him to bring over the power-washer. You get somebody out here to meet him who's got the sense to wash this crap off my building. We need to get over to Pendrick Court.' Kelly nodded. 'And bring a bucket, brush and some detergent. The police said that Alan has left you some blood to clear up in the entrance hall.'

❖ ❖ ❖

Before Kevin and Kelly arrived, Edna was in the courtyard returning the can of red paint to Paul. 'Are you going to tell me what you did with it?' he asked.

Edna glanced over each shoulder before replying. 'I sprayed the word *MURDERER* at the entrance to Kevin's apartment. In great big letters.'

'You're one gutsy lady,' smiled Paul.

'And I've already spoken to Terry, that crazed boy on a scooter from the newspaper. Told him that Alan had a fatal fall down the stairs while Kevin was in the building. Told him the police had interviewed him – Kevin, not Alan – and that somebody had sprayed *MURDERER* on Kevin's door.'

'Remind me never to get on the wrong side of you.'

'I told him the police were still considering charging Kevin with my murder. If it wasn't for Jack jumping in front of the bus, I wouldn't be here talking to you. And photos of my graffiti will soon be all over the whole wide web.'

The sun cast a shadow from Kevin's car. As it passed over Edna, her eyes followed the Audi which came to a stop outside Apartments 7 and 8. She exhaled a burst of air through her mouth, not unlike a snake's hiss, waved goodbye to Paul and scuttled off to purchase more medical supplies.

❖❖❖

Kevin's plan was a simple one: when the Pages left Pendrick Court, Kelly would use the landlord's key to enter their apartment and vandalise it. He would ensure that the Pages saw him leave, thus eliminating him as a suspect. When Kelly has finished, she would leave the door to the apartment open and walk back to the shop.

Somebody had covered the bloodstain at the foot of the stairs with sheets of newspaper. Kevin picked up the bucket and told Kelly he would fetch a trash bag for the paper and some water from the store. He walked across the courtyard towards the heavy wooden doors.

Meanwhile, Kelly took a pair of disposable gloves from a packet she'd brought with her. She got on her knees, breathed through her mouth and screwed up her face as she gathered up the sticky sheets. The reddish-brown smears on the staircase should come off the lino easily enough.

❖❖❖

'I was not *abandoned*,' shouted Susan. 'He died. If he hadn't been a passenger in that car that night, we'd have been married and raised Chloe together. I know you're annoyed about these evictions, but why do you keep taking it out on me?'

Robert spun her comment through the patio doors and into the overcast courtyard with a flick of his wrist. 'Good grief,' he sighed. 'Does your sense of victimhood know no bounds? You need to stop blaming other people for your misfortunes and realise that you alone are responsible for your happiness.'

'Changing the subject would make me happy. Let's go and collect your newspaper together before it rains.'

'We could have gone an hour ago if you hadn't been on the bloody phone to Chloe.'

Susan donned her burgundy anorak and Robert his royal-blue blazer. They set off in silence.

❖ ❖ ❖

Before they had even reached the archway, Kevin was repeating instructions to Kelly, whose eyes were flitting around the windows which overlooked the courtyard. When she was certain that nobody was looking, she hurried across the tarmac, pressed the trade button to Apartments 1 and 2 and entered the building.

Kevin jumped into his car and, just as the Pages had done, turned left out of Pendrick Court. Several feet from the archway, he pulled up and rolled down the front passenger window.

'Mr Page,' he shouted. Robert and Susan stopped in their tracks. 'I came over this morning to clean up after Alan's accident. Dreadful business. I've finished now and I'm on my way home.'

Robert was caught off balance by Kevin's cordial demeanour.

'I had hoped to catch you before I left, Mr Page,' the landlord continued. 'I wanted to thank you again for offering to help Edna explain Thursday's unfortunate mix-up to the police. I don't want to appear ungrateful, but we do need to hurry her along.' With that, he waved and drove off into the city.

Robert's brows knitted with cynicism.

Susan was relieved that the bad blood had stopped flowing.

CHAPTER SIXTY-THREE

THE Pages' apartment was ready for a photoshoot; not a thing was out of place; there was neither a crumb nor a speck of dust. Kelly wandered through the sterile rooms wearing a fresh pair of disposable gloves. It was Robert whom Mr Douglas wanted to spook, not the wife. Evidently, they kept separate bedrooms so identifying Robert's personal effects was easy.

Kelly's fear had evaporated. If she was caught, she would state that her employer had given her the key and forced her to carry out the deed. Seventy pence an hour above minimum wage didn't cover taking the rap for burglary, even to protect a good friend.

She searched the kitchen cupboards until she found some bleach, which she took to the bathroom. While she ferried armfuls of clothes from Robert's wardrobe, she ran a bath into which she dumped the clothing and emptied the container of bleach.

Shelving in Robert's bedroom housed hundreds of speedway magazines displayed in chronological order. She grabbed them by the handful and added them to the textile soup. One wall in the sitting room was dedicated to framed certificates and photographs that tracked Robert's lacklustre career in insurance. Kelly unhooked each one, placed it on the floor and stepped on it until the glass cracked.

Any mess she created in the kitchen would doubtless be down to the wife to clear up, so she decided against it. She decided she'd already done enough to anger and upset Robert. Now he would understand that trifling with Mr Douglas had its consequences.

From the patio doors, Kelly checked for potential witnesses to her escape. Nobody was in sight and the courtyard was clear so, as instructed, she left open the apartment door, fled the building and slipped unseen through the archway.

She was fizzing with exhilaration and confidence. Having helped out a friend and dispensed justice, Kelly walked back to the shop as though parading through the grounds of her own country seat.

❖❖❖

Madison looked on suspiciously as Anah placed chunks of raw tuna into a lime-juice marinade. Anah washed her hands and peered through the kitchen window, declaring that the rain would hold off long enough for Toby to get some exercise.

Madison went through to the sitting room, satisfied herself that the Audi had gone, gathered Toby in her arms and carried him to the ground floor. She wedged open the door with her foot for an approaching Robert and Susan as Toby bolted across the courtyard. Standing in the entrance hall, the three of them exchanged kind words about Alan and their sadness at his death.

Susan suggested that the residents' party should go ahead as planned on the twentieth of July in memory of Alan. Although they didn't quite share her excitement at the thought, Robert and Madison agreed that it would be an appropriate gesture.

Susan removed her anorak before the three mounted the stairs.

Toby snuggled down against a gargoyle and raised his eyes skywards, pinning his hopes on Anah's forecast being a reliable one.

❖ ❖ ❖

Megan's resentment had been fermenting since the previous morning. Ten more miserable weeks in retail was what he'd said. Who was he to look down his nose at retail? Working in a supermarket was plenty good enough until Paul had filled Jack's head with delusions of – of not being a total knob.

She continued swiping her phone screen, monitoring Jack and becoming increasingly aware of a new-found arrogance to his gait. She'd seen it all before; people tried to advance way beyond their abilities. *Look at me. Somebody's recognised my potential*. No, they haven't, they've found somebody that doesn't give them any shit.

'I'm sorry,' said Megan slamming down her phone. 'I can't sit back and watch you make a fool of yourself. I need you to text Paul and tell him you don't want the job.'

'Why?' asked Jack.

'You can thank him, but he's making a big mistake and I don't want us getting dragged into it.'

'I might not get a chance like this again.'

'It's a lovely dream, Jack, but that's all it is.'

'No! I'm going to work for Paul.'

Megan stood up, her expression sliding into outrage. 'I'm not *asking* you to text him, I'm *telling* you.'

'You can shout and stamp your feet all you want. I'm not throwing away this opportunity.'

'Well, you can move your things into the spare room and you can stay there until you've seen sense.'

Jack stared across the room at Megan. 'I will,' he said calmly. 'But I'm staying there until we have to move out and then we're going our separate ways.'

Megan shook her head in disbelief. 'Are you trying to break up with me?'

'I wasn't trying. We've broken up. We're not a couple any more. I—'

'*You* don't get to break up with *me*.'

'It too late. You've been dumped.' On his way to gather his clothes, Jack texted Paul asking when it would be convenient to meet up.

❖ ❖ ❖

'Where are you?' asked Kevin impatiently.

'I'm in a café, enjoying a biscuit with my coffee,' said Kelly, taking another sip of her white-chocolate mocha.

'Well, get back here, now. You're supposed to be working.'

'I've washed a dead man's blood off your hallway and stairs and vandalised somebody's home at your request. I think I've more than earned my money today.'

'I decide when—'

'I think of you as more than an employer, I think of you as a friend. And friendship closes its eyes to extended tea breaks, Mr Douglas. You'll see me, when you see me.' Kelly ended the call and nibbled on her shortbread finger.

CHAPTER SIXTY-FOUR

'YOU know I locked it. You were standing right next to me,' said Susan. Her tone was more assertive than usual and persuaded Robert to end his line of questioning. They stood outside the entrance to Apartment 1, looking at the gaping door. 'Somebody's broken in,' she whispered. 'They might still be inside. We should call the police.'

'And if there's nobody here and nothing's missing, we're going to look like a right pair of chumps.'

'I'd rather look like—'

'I can see I'm going to have to take charge of the situation.' Robert rolled up his newspaper and handed it to Susan. 'You take this. I'll stay here, ready to catch any fleeing intruders. You go in and flush them out.'

'Do you think the sight of a sixty-four-year-old woman waving a paper cudgel is really going to have burglars running for cover? I'm sending a text to Sean and Jack.'

'Good. There might be a few of them. I doubt that I can pin down more than one or two on my own.'

Sean texted back immediately saying he was in St Edmund's Street making a delivery and telling her to call the police.

Jack ran past a still-traumatised Megan, grabbed a milk pan from the kitchen, tore down the stairs and across the courtyard. Seconds later, he was panting on the first floor in front of Susan and Robert. He turned to Robert. 'Get ready to call the police if you hear me scrapping. Susan, I think you should go up to the second floor.'

With the saucepan raised, he crept stealthily into the apartment. Susan waited halfway up the staircase to Anah's apartment, while Robert braced himself for a rugby tackle. In little over a minute, Jack re-emerged. 'Somebody has been here but they're long gone. Sorry to say it, but you *have* been burgled.'

❖ ❖ ❖

A drizzle drifted half-heartedly across the road to Pendrick Court leaving a fine mist on Kevin's windscreen. He flicked the wiper switch to sweep the glass just the once. He was working himself up into a frenzy replaying Kelly's insolent words over and over, pausing only when the echo of Terry's request for a statement rang in his head. Terry had asked if he wanted to comment on Alan's death and the graffiti?

Both would get their comeuppance very soon: Kelly, when she was summarily dismissed, and Terry, when he was dumb enough to print Kevin's false, off-the-record comment that the police had already arrested one of the tenants for Alan's murder.

This morning should be about celebrating Robert's punishment, not about raging over a pair of cocksure cretins. Kevin allayed his fury by visualising the Pages' alarm. By the time he climbed out of the Audi, he was revelling in Robert's torment and desperate to catch a glimpse of his suffering.

As he climbed the stairs to the rooftop patio, a single charcoal cloud was coasting across the sky in the direction of the gargoyles and a drowsing Toby.

❖❖❖

Robert was sidling around the sitting room as Susan methodically opened drawers and cupboards. 'Well, nothing's missing,' she announced finally.

'And nothing of yours has been damaged. This was an unsubtle threat from Kevin Douglas.'

'But this morning he was so—'

'He was toying with us. We are his alibi. He gave a key to some of his boys.'

'Are we going to report the damage to the police?'

'There's no sign of a break in. The only other keyholder has an alibi and nothing's been taken. Other than give us a crime reference number for the insurance company, there's nothing the police will do.'

'Do you want to claim on our insurance?'

'They'll question whether we left the property unsecured. We need to weigh up the cost of the damage against the excess we'd have to pay and any increase in the premiums.'

Susan sat down. 'God knows how far that appalling man will go. Do you think he'll do more?'

'Not if you can persuade Edna to speak to the police. If you can't, I'll have to deal with Kevin. This cannot escalate.'

'Edna said I could call round after ten-thirty. If you're not going to call the police, we need to clear this mess up.'

'You go and speak to Edna. We won't involve the police or the insurance company. I'll empty the bathtub.'

❖ ❖ ❖

His spirits rallying, Kevin strode towards the edge of the roof to rearrange the gargoyles. Suddenly he stopped and took a deep angry breath. That black moggy was here again, despite him telling Anah that the area was out of bounds to her and her bastard cat. She probably encouraged the damned creature to claw its way up here just to rub her contempt in his face. Well, he would demonstrate conclusively that the condescending bitch had bitten off far more than her oversized mouth could chew.

Without waking the cat, Kevin eased silently

forwards until he towered over the lolling form. With hands like a lobster's pincers, he grabbed at Toby's belly and jerked the animal above his head. Toby's eyes raged with liquid fire and his body thrashed. Kevin, aiming at the courtyard below, launched the cat with all his might.

Toby slammed into the tarmac before Kevin could even begin to adjust the first gargoyle.

CHAPTER SIXTY-FIVE

ANAH opened the door to a distressed Susan, who stumbled to find her words as she declined the invitation to enter Apartment 2.

'What are you sorry for?' asked a confused Anah. 'Please come in, you're clearly upset.'

Susan refused to move from the doorway. 'I was on my way to see Edna. Oh Anah, I think your cat's fallen from the roof.'

Anah said nothing; she just ran.

Madison appeared from the sitting room and saw Susan rooted to the spot through the open door. When Susan told her what had happened, she grabbed Toby's blanket from his basket and sped after her grandmother.

Susan plodded down the stairs back to her own apartment to be met by Robert and the smell of chlorine. She explained why she hadn't made it as far as Apartment 5 and that she needed to sit for a few minutes. 'I wasn't sure it was Anah's cat so I went over to it. The poor thing was lying on its side. It looked as though blood was running from its mouth.' She shuddered. Her eyes met Robert's. 'Kevin was on the edge of the roof, fiddling with the statues.'

'Do you think he kicked the cat off the roof?' asked Robert.

'I do. And now I'm wondering if he pushed Alan down the stairs, too.'

❖ ❖ ❖

Sean pulled into the courtyard. Seeing Anah and Madison kneeling close to his father's car, he jumped out of the van and ran over to see if there was problem. He crouched down behind the pair. Anah was caressing the lifeless body in front of them. 'Shit!' he said. 'Do you want me to run you to the vet's?'

Without moving her eyes from Toby, Anah replied, 'Thank you, Sean. The only thing a vet could do now is arrange a cremation. I'll take him home and let him rest in his basket. I'll call a vet later.'

'I'm so sorry. Did you see what happened?'

'No – but he wouldn't have fallen. Somebody pushed, kicked or threw him off the roof.'

Sean stood up in silence. There were no tears on Anah's face, just a lid on a seething vat of poison within. 'If there's anything I can do, please shout,' he said before turning back towards his van.

Madison spread out the blanket and Anah gently lifted Toby onto the soft fleece and took him in her arms. Together, they slowly crossed the courtyard.

Susan delivered a consoling nod as she passed them in the ground-floor entrance hall then she continued into the courtyard where Jessica and Sean were talking furtively. Jessica beckoned for Susan to join them.

'What happened earlier? Did you disturb intruders?' asked Sean.

'Jack came racing across and checked out the apartment for us. Thankfully, the intruders had left.'

'Did they nick much?' asked Jessica.

'Not a thing. Whoever entered our apartment had been given a key. They just made an awful mess and damaged Robert's belongings.'

'Do you think my father gave them a key?'

'Absolutely!' said Susan. 'I also believe that he was responsible for the death of Anah's cat.'

Jessica screwed up her eyes to block out the horrible thought. Sean writhed with shame to think that his father would stoop so low.

'And I suggest he helped Alan down the stairs too!' Susan concluded.

Sean excused himself and made for the rooftop patio. He sprinted up three flights of stairs onto the overcast roof. He called out in the direction of the shed, from which Kevin emerged.

'I'm glad you're here, boy. You've saved me a phone call. Kelly's leaving, so I'll need you to—'

'Before you give me more work to do, I'm giving you my notice. Unless you want them sooner, I'll drop off the store and van keys next Monday night.'

'Unfortunately for you, your inheritance comes with the job. So stop being such a drama queen and—'

'Then get your solicitor to write you a new will. I'm done with you and your business.'

Kevin's self-assurance swiftly collapsed into an angry heap of agitation. 'I haven't got the patience for your histrionics. Go and whine to one of your friends about me. Get it out of your system and get back to work.'

'I'll see you next Monday with the keys.' As he turned and descended into the body of Pendrick Court, Sean heard the clank of his shackles falling away above the noise of his father's fading bluster.

❖ ❖ ❖

'How are you today?' Susan asked Edna as she entered Apartment 5.

'Well I've got arithmetic at the moment – an irregular heartbeat. But the good news is I don't need Imodium or senna. Everything is moving like clockwork.'

'I'm glad to hear your bowels are working, despite the arrhythmias. Did you see Anah and Madison earlier?'

'No. Have I missed something, dear?'

'Sadly, Anah's cat fell to its death while Kevin was on his patio.' Edna gasped and took a seat. 'And while Robert and I were out fetching a newspaper, somebody let themselves into our apartment and destroyed Robert's clothes, magazine collection, photos and certificates.'

'Well, it doesn't take a genie to work out who was responsible.'

'To be honest, I'm really scared for Robert's safety.'

'You should be. First Alan, then the cat. They say deaths come in threes. Robert's probably next.'

'It's comforting to know I've not misjudged the situation.'

'Never mind deporting migrants, we need to deport all the native scum. This country would be better off without the likes of Kevin Douglas.'

'Have you given any more thought to contacting the police about him?'

'I have, dear. I know it's not what you want to hear but I want him prosecuted. No punishment is too severe for that man.'

Susan nodded in resignation. 'Thank you for at least thinking about it. Moving out of Pendrick Court and far away from Kevin might be best for all of us.'

'I called the Bergamot Nursing Home this morning. They promised to pass on a message to Alan's sister. I've asked if she'll contact me regarding Alan's funeral.'

CHAPTER SIXTY-SIX

WHEN Paul returned home for a midday sandwich, he saw Sean's van through the open doors to the store. Seeing Kevin's Audi parked in a corner of the court, he wondered what you could do on a patio under a dull sky that threatened rain.

Jessica came bowling down two flights of stairs, keen to update him on the morning's break-in and the alleged killing of Toby. Paul listened through his hunger and incipient rage. 'That's at least a forty-foot drop,' he said. 'If he kicked it off the roof, he intended to kill it. He has a key to every apartment, too. Any of us could return to a burglarised home.'

Jessica lowered her voice. 'And there's speculation that Alan's death wasn't an accident either. Anah was the last person to see him alive. When she left, Kevin was still in the building.'

'Our efforts to stop the evictions have fizzled out and all we've got to show for them are a dead tenant, a dead cat and a vandalised apartment.'

'Let's hope he realises that he's won and stops the

reprisals.'

'If he continues with the violence, we'll have to play him at his own game. You'll have to excuse me, though – Jack's nipping over in twenty minutes and I need to eat something before he arrives.'

❖ ❖ ❖

Madison lay on her bed staring at the ceiling. She clasped her phone in her hand but was too distracted to look at it. Anah sat on the kitchen floor by Toby's basket, sobbing quietly so her grief didn't disturb her granddaughter. She would get up soon and have a cigarette on the balcony but, for the time being, she needed to be close to Toby.

❖ ❖ ❖

'Where are you going?' asked Megan. 'You said you weren't working today.'

'I'm off to see Paul,' replied Jack with a confidence that Megan found quite objectionable.

'You're really going ahead with this plumbing nonsense?'

'Yep! New career. New life.'

'I suppose you and the Pendrick Court Slapper have plans to move in together.'

'I'm not leaving you to move in with anybody. I'm leaving you because we don't actually like each other.'

'You won't find another girlfriend like me,' scoffed Megan.

'That's the plan.'

'I'm going to jump in the shower. I've got an afternoon shift starting at two. And listen carefully when I say that I don't want *her* over here drinking all our Coke again.'

Jack rolled his eyes, left Apartment 8 and made his way towards Apartment 3. En route, he raised his hand to acknowledge Ishaan who was on his way to see Sean.

❖ ❖ ❖

Precisely two weeks after posting eight eviction notices, Kevin was perched on the edge of the patio removing dust and cobwebs from the gargoyles with a paintbrush. From his vantage point, he stared into Robert's sitting room, hoping it wouldn't be too long before he witnessed some serious anguish.

The sound of footsteps on the stairs made him stand and turn. He pointed the paintbrush at the trespasser as though casting a spell with a wand. 'Residents are not permitted on the roof,' he bawled. 'Piss off!' His scowl was replaced by a supercilious grin. 'You want to take a swing at me? Is that why you're here?'

Blindsided by his opponent's agility, Kevin felt a sharp pain as the heel of a palm struck him on each upper arm. He stepped back to correct his balance, but he had run out of roof. His left leg shot into the void and the rest of his body followed. His descent was terminated with a sharp thud and a resounding pop.

CHAPTER SIXTY-SEVEN

ANAH had left Toby's body in his basket. Having watched Kevin's abrupt execution from her balcony, she now looked down upon his corpse. The court was empty and there were no faces at any of the windows.

She took her mobile phone from her pocket, dialled 999 and told the operator she needed an ambulance. She explained to a call handler that her landlord had been carrying out maintenance on the edge of the roof and she'd just seen him fall. An ambulance and police car were dispatched.

As quickly as she could, she sent a text message to the other residents: *Kevin has fallen from our roof*. Then she called Edna's landline and shouted the message three times because twice Edna had asked for clarification that it wasn't little Robin lying on the tarmac.

Sean and Ishaan came careening down the stairs into the courtyard. Ishaan squatted down to examine Kevin. Just as Paul and Jack appeared, he stood up and put a hand on Sean's shoulder. 'Your dad's not breathing and there's no pulse. You can see from the head injury—'

'He's dead,' said Sean.

Madison stepped forward and placed a lambswool throw featuring winsome pandas on a powder-blue background over Kevin. Around the skull, the powder blue morphed into an exquisite deep purple.

Susan and Robert thanked Anah for the text message. Jessica offered to fetch Edna a chair, which she declined. Last to arrive was Megan with wet hair and wearing a bathrobe. She took two surreptitious photos but decided that a selfie would be in poor taste.

The high-pitched wail of sirens cut through the residents who circled the lifeless form. After two gut-churning deaths at Pendrick Court within the last twenty-four hours, only Edna had been expecting a third.

❖❖❖

Following its dramatic entrance, the ambulance made an inconspicuous retreat leaving Kevin splayed on the ground. The first police officer who arrived detained the onlookers and started to place a barrier around the scene. Another officer took a swab of blood from Toby to crossmatch it with a bloodstain that lay a few feet from the body.

Paul and Megan gave their details and a brief statement and were released to go to work. The remaining residents were interviewed while photographs were being taken in the courtyard and on the roof. Only Anah claimed to have witnessed the accident, which she was able to describe in meticulous detail.

The comings and goings eventually ceased. Kevin was removed and the clouds dispersed. Pendrick Court was left frozen in the shimmering sun of an unpredictable June.

❖ ❖ ❖

A numb Sean stood on his balcony as he called each of the shop managers and asked them to pass on the news of his father's death to the staff. A call to his mother helped him compile a list of relatives to whom he needed to speak.

Ishaan took a cold can of drink onto the balcony, which Sean accepted with a smile. He wasn't thirsty but he could sense Ishaan's desire to help.

'I won't be hypocritical,' said Ishaan. 'He was a sorry excuse for a man and a sorrier excuse for a father. I've cancelled my shift tonight. I'll be here for you as long as you want company.'

'Cheers. There's so much filling my head at the moment. I've got to get a medical certificate and take it to the registrar's office. Then I'll need to see Dad's solicitor—'

'But you haven't got to do anything right now. You could just sit down and turn off your phone.'

Sean turned off his phone, opened his can and followed Ishaan inside.

❖ ❖ ❖

In Apartment 3, Jessica and Jack were sharing a tub of Ben & Jerry's Cookie Dough Ice Cream. 'If Sean is heir to Kevin's estate, I bet he'll cancel the eviction notices,' said Jessica, waving her spoon.

'I never thought about that. Shame Kevin didn't fall off the roof two weeks ago.'

'Wouldn't it be great if we could all stay? Especially since we've all got to know each other.'

'It would've been but I've got to move on. Megan and I need to separate.'

'Oh my God! Will Megan stay if you go?'

'It's possible she'll find another chump to shack up with. But I need to find a one-bedroom or even a studio apartment. I'm going to start work for Paul in August, like an apprenticeship.'

'That's great news. And you never know, Sean might move into his dad's apartment above the shop. Perhaps you could rent his place here.'

'It'd be handy living close to Paul. Even if Sean stays put, I can always ask him to give me a shout if a one-bedroom apartment becomes vacant.'

'Edna will outlive all of us, so I don't think she'll be going anywhere soon. Of course, I might get whisked away by a knight in shining armour. Are you up for a pizza?'

❖ ❖ ❖

Robert was jerking jubilantly about the sitting room like a marionette while Susan finished cleaning the bathroom. After a few minutes, she walked through carrying two filled black bags. 'There'll be room for one of these in our wheelie bin,' she said. 'We could ask Anah if we could put the other in hers.' She left the bags on the floor and sat down.

Robert wasn't listening. 'As long as Sean doesn't have to sell Pendrick Court, we won't have to leave. There'll be inheritance tax to pay on the apartments and his father's accommodation, but he'll get business relief on the shops.'

'Don't get ahead of yourself. You don't know what Kevin owns or who he's left it to.'

'I'm being positive. We've been through two hellish weeks and the nightmare could be over. You should be rejoicing that we might get to keep our home.'

'It has been a harrowing fortnight, but I have no fondness for this place. Living here has been joyless – frankly, it's been a miserable experience for me. Neither of us is happy in the other's company, which is why I've agreed to move to London—'

'I knew you and that bloody daughter of yours were plotting something.'

'When she called this morning, she asked if I'd consider becoming part of the household and taking care of the children so she and Mark could both work full time.'

'Well, that puts me in a bloody predicament. I'll be lumbered with the full rent and all the bills.'

'I'll pay my share here until the end of July... and I'll

be back for the party on the twentieth of July.'

'Looks like I'm going to have to leave Pendrick Court after all. Two weeks of hell for nothing! I've never met a more selfish woman in my life than you.'

❖ ❖ ❖

Edna was sitting on her shabby leather sofa, holding a sherry glass containing a measure of Southern Comfort. Alan had been quite specific: he didn't want his sister to have his photographs. But would he be happy for her to have them now he was gone? She sipped on the sweet, fruity liqueur, trying to second guess his wishes.

Her mind was made up: she would throw away the photos. She would put the orange plastic box in the wheelie bin immediately so the matter was closed. She padded through to her bedroom, reached up into her wardrobe to fetch the box and took it into the kitchen area. She'd like to see some photos of Alan in his younger years. She'd have a quick rummage through and then put them straight in the bin.

She sliced a sharp knife through the masking tape. When she opened the lid and looked inside, she jerked backwards. Then she began tentatively searching through the bags, terrified that some might not contain money.

She had come so close to handing over the stash to Alan's sister and to putting it in the bin. Divine intervention had caused her to open it. Surely, this was the Lord's way of saying, 'Treat yourself to a new bag, Edna. You deserve it.'

CHAPTER SIXTY-EIGHT

WHEN evening darkened and the interior of Apartment 2 took on a blue hue, Anah drew the curtains, pulled down the blinds and turned on the lights. Tonight there was no aroma of baking cakes from her oven and the sitting-room speakers sat in silence.

She had gathered all of Toby's toys, brushes and bowls and was placing them in a large carrier bag when Madison walked into the kitchen. Toby was still in his basket, completely swathed in his blanket. 'If you want, I can take Toby to the vet in the morning,' the girl offered.

Anah closed her eyes for a few seconds and nodded. 'Thank you. I think I'd rather say goodbye to him here. I'll call the vet in the morning to let him know you're coming.'

'I'll get a taxi there but I can easily walk back.' Madison took a packet of coffee beans from the cupboard and jiggled them in front of her grandmother. 'I'm an expert with the French press now. Can I tempt you with a cup of coffee?'

'Thank you. And I really ought to eat something, too. So should you. We haven't had anything since breakfast.'

'How about a thick slice of bread with butter and jam?'

'Yes, I could manage that. Would you like me to cut the bread?'

'It's okay. I'll cut it.'

'I'm going onto the balcony for a smoke. I'm afraid I'm not much company. My thoughts are preoccupied with what that man did to Toby.'

'Well, he'll never be able to hurt any of us again. He got what he deserved.'

Anah lashed out her hand and grabbed Madison's wrist. 'Don't forget that.' She shook Madison's arm. 'Don't ever doubt that Kevin's death was warranted.'

Madison smiled and reassured Anah by gently stroking her face. 'I won't forget. But there's still one thing bothering me. What made you bring my panda throw into the courtyard?'

'So that when you covered the body, everybody would assume *you'd* brought the throw down from our apartment. It would also explain why your DNA was all over Kevin's shoulders.'

'Did you see everything?'

'Yes. I saw a murderer fall from the roof.'

Madison opened the fridge. 'I haven't forgotten that you like your butter spread thinly.'

Anah walked through to the sitting room and

stepped carefully onto the balcony's decking. She slid the glass door behind her and, balancing an ashtray on the wooden handrail, lit a cigarette and held it between the very tips of her fingers.

CHAPTER SIXTY-NINE
Friday, 3rd January, 2020

(An email from Anah Agu to Susan Page)

Dear Susan,

Thank you for your newsy message and good wishes. It's lovely to hear that you've enjoyed the last six months so much with your daughter and her family in London.

I was sorry to read that your brother is refusing to respond to your calls and messages and hope that his obstinacy soon fades.

Several weeks after cancelling the evictions, Sean confirmed that Pendrick Court would remain in his name for the foreseeable future, which was a great relief to us all.

As expected, the Coroner's inquests concluded that both Alan and Kevin's deaths were accidents. Alan's sister from Scotland eventually organised a funeral in the city, which their mother and most of us were able to attend.

Paul and your brother have swapped apartments. Paul wanted more room and your brother wanted accommodation that was cheaper to rent and run. Paul tells me that he has a Thai girlfriend who is applying for a tourist visa to come and stay with him.

Jack and Megan have ended their relationship. Megan is now living with her mother and Jack swapped apartments with Jessica. Jack is working for Paul. Jessica has found herself a new partner, Dino, and they live together in Apartment 8. They work together too at Dino's Pizzeria on Grove Road.

Sean has been busy with solicitors and accountants finalising his father's estate and running the shops. He's moved into Alan's apartment, so Apartment 6 is now vacant. He works from his father's former apartment above the shop, returning home late at night and leaving early every morning. We occasionally see his doctor friend, Ishaan.

Sean cleared the ground floor of all the products he was advertising online, selling them wholesale to a couple of market traders. Now there are two chaps working in the store here Monday to Friday, taking deliveries and distributing to Sean's shops. Sean says that, in time, he'd like to convert the ground floor into apartments. He has already instructed a company to erect railings around the rooftop patio and those wretched gargoyles are going.

While Madison is at school, I keep myself busy with household chores. We chat over our evening meal and then Madison disappears into her room to do her homework. She sometimes meets up with friends in the city on a Saturday but she seems really focused on her schoolwork. She'll be sitting her GCSEs this summer.

Edna still lives in Apartment 5, although she's currently in Australia. Apparently she inherited some money and bought *herself a business-class ticket to Melbourne to visit her son. Before she left, she was having the time of her life buying outfits for her holiday.*

I will leave you with the wonderful news that at the state opening of Parliament last month, the Queen's Speech set out Boris Johnson's promise to abolish the use of no-fault evictions by removing Section 21 of the Housing Act 1988.

I hope 2020 will be a marvellous year for us all.

Kindest regards, Anah

CPSIA information can be obtained
at www.ICGtesting.com
Printed in the USA
BVHW031053300321
PP12054500001B/2

9 781914 083075